An Airman's Deadly Affair

An Airman's Deadly Affair

By

NICOLLE SCHIPPERS

iUniverse, Inc.
New York Bloomington

This is a work of fiction. All of the characters, names, incidents, organizations, and dialogue in this novel are either the products of the author's imagination or are used fictitiously.

iUniverse books may be ordered through booksellers or by contacting:

iUniverse
1663 Liberty Drive
Bloomington, IN 47403
www.iuniverse.com
1-800-Authors (1-800-288-4677)

ISBN: 978-1-4401-8820-6 (sc)
ISBN: 978-1-4401-8821-3 (ebook)
ISBN: 978-1-4401-8822-0 (dj)

Printed in the United States of America

iUniverse rev. date: 12/17/2009

Chapter 1

Sweat pools under the ski mask as a clock ticks above the door. 0145. Perfect! Right on time.

My eyes slowly adjust to the darkness in the large room, dimly lit at the further end. I lift my mask just enough so that I can wipe away the perspiration slowly making its way down the back of my neck. Not a single drop can fall. I have come too far and waited too long for this. There will be no evidence left behind.

Pulling the night vision goggles down over my eyes, I creep behind a large steel shelf, looming over me in the darkness. I adjust the goggles and turn them on. Suddenly, the room flares green in front of me and I get my bearings. I look around for her. I know you're in here!

Somewhere in front of me, I hear papers being shuffled, the faint sound echoing off the walls. There she is! It's been a while since she and I have been alone together. I force myself not to laugh as sheer ecstasy churns deep in the pit of my stomach. This is going to be too easy.

I make my way past the first two shelves and pause to stare at the rows of slick black M9 pistols, illuminating an eerie green in front of me. I caress the cool metal of the one closest to me. You will do just fine.

I'm so close now. I can almost smell her perfume through my ski mask. Chanel. God, how that smell used to set me on edge.

Now it makes me want to vomit. I don't want to look at her, not yet. It is ironic. There was a time I couldn't get enough of her. But that was before.

The gun slides out of the rack beautifully, not making a sound. I pull a suppressor off the next shelf and screw it on. Cradling the gun in my right hand, I reach to the top of the tall locked cabinets. I find the small key hidden on top as I bite back the disgust threatening to choke me. Who was the brains who thought it was a good idea to hide the key to the ammunition closet on top of it?

I am so goddamned tired of all this mediocrity. Don't they know how important it is to maintain order? To keep everything mission ready?

Sliding the key in the lock, I feel the tumblers release. Shit! The metal latch scrapes against the door. The hairs on the back of my neck rise as I stand perfectly still. She slowly glances around. The muscles in the back of my shoulders begin to ache as I wait.

Somewhere outside, a tree branch scrapes against the building. A strong October wind howls. Taking her outer jacket from the chair, she pulls it around her for warmth and goes back to what she is doing.

The flimsy metal door opens without a sound. I'd oiled the hinges earlier when I walked through here perfecting my plan. I find what I am looking for and load the gun. My pulse skyrockets as I edge down the aisle, patches of light starting to flicker through the shelves and flashing bright in my goggles. I pull the mask away from my mouth and take a deep breath of air. It's time.

When I turn off the goggles, the light from the small desk lamp spotlights my target and suddenly my heart lurches. God, she is beautiful with her long blond hair pulled back revealing her slender milky white neck and just a glimpse of her full red lips, parted slightly. She's not looking at me, but she doesn't have to. I remember those eyes. I'll never forget them.

The cold hard steel of the gun starts to slip through my shaking fingers. It's time to get on with it!

Sweat sticks to my eyelids, threatening to drip into my eyes and blind me. I rub my eyes through the mask. She props up the thick blue book she's reading and I see the cover "Psychology 101." How perfect! She's studying how to mess with people's heads. I think you're good enough at that already, bitch. You're a member of the strongest military in the free world and you've pissed it all away!

She writes something on the bright yellow notepad on the desk. You've only cared about yourself while your comrades are off fighting in Iraq and Afghanistan, fighting terrorism, protecting our country. You don't care who you step on or screw along the way, just so you make it to the top.

You're a disgrace to this Air Force, the uniform and to the proud men and women who wear it.

My hand shakes violently as I think of all you have done!

"Clang," Damn! I bite back the curse as the sound of the gun hitting the side of the shelf ricochets off the steel.

"Who's there?" Her head whips towards me, just as I step back in the shadows.

"I said, 'who's there?'" she says, rising, drawing the pistol strapped to her waist. Her voice is trembling.

Silence.

She hesitates, her eyes darting around the dark room and then she lowers her gun and turns back to the desk. I spring from my hiding place and point the barrel of my gun at the base of her neck and pull the trigger twice. She drops to the floor, her face hitting the hard concrete.

Raw emotion courses through me. I wish she'd seen me, seen the look of extreme satisfaction on my face as I pulled the trigger.

"Teresa, is that you?" someone calls. "Where are you?"

Shit! Who the hell is that? No one else was on duty tonight. My heart races. I don't have time. I retrace my steps and push the gun onto its shelf and silently race to the door. My hand on the door handle, I can't resist looking back and see a woman standing over the body.

I open the thick door and slide through, running into the darkness, the woman's screams echoing in my head. My foot hits a tree root and I stumble and fall, crashing against the ground. I pull off the goggles and mask and try to catch my breath.

Dammit! I was so close. I left behind a damn witness. I should have known that bitch would be there.

I stand and breathe in slowly. I must think. The air is cold, chilling the sweat on my neck and face. I wait, hidden in the darkness, my mind reeling over this unfortunate turn of events.

I look back at the armory, silhouetted in the moonlight. A smile creeps onto my face as I cover it with my mask. My little witness is soon going to regret she was in the wrong place at the wrong time. But as I turn to disappear into the night, my excitement returns. This may not be so unfortunate after all.

Chapter 2

"Don't sweat it, Captain." Major Lohrs whispered to her co-counsel as the members of the jury came into the courtroom. "Look at their eyes. You know that when they won't look at the defendant there is a reason; it means they don't believe him or his story."

Major Emma Lohrs stood at attention, keeping her face impassive as the members filed into their box. This was her twenty-first trial as a prosecutor, thirty-seventh if you counted the trials she'd done as defense counsel, and she knew the signs. They'd been able to separate the facts from the contrived story the defense put on.

Emma's hands clenched at her sides as the last member came to stand before his chair and looked straight at her. When the judge entered the chamber and instructed them to sit down, Emma complied and unconsciously smoothed her thick, brown hair which was pulled back in a bun before glancing at the charge sheet on the table in front of her.

The case for the prosecution was really pretty straight forward. The defendant, Airman First Class Derek Downs, was charged with possession, selling and ingesting illegal substances; to all of which he plead not guilty.

Although he had only been at Winburg Air Base in Germany for five months, it had, apparently, been long enough for Downs to get in trouble . . . . a lot of trouble. Downs' first mistake was to take a liking to the city of Amsterdam and its bright lights and nameless other possibilities many of which were illegal. Unfortunately, since it was only ninety minutes away, Downs wasn't the only airman tantalized by the virtual smorgasbord of drugs to be found there.

As she waited for the judge to begin, Emma thought about the many other airmen she had prosecuted over the last two and a half years who had also unfortunately been pulled into the dangerous excitement of Amsterdam. Emma knew the city's attraction was especially strong to the younger airmen who were away from home for the first time. The city always seemed to win out over the fear of what their parents, let alone the Air Force would do to them if they got caught. As a result, seventy percent of the cases tried at Winburg had some relation to drugs.

Emma had briefed about the dangers of the temptatious city to so many new airmen that she had the process down to a science. She could tell which ones were already lost as soon as they walked out the door; those who would succumb to the incredible temptation to buy whatever drug they could get their hands on. But it was the few airmen who dealt the drugs who really got to Emma. These losers would swarm in on the fresh new airmen whose first paychecks burned holes in their pockets and who were more than willing to hand over their hard earned money for a chance to partake in a "once in a lifetime experience."

It was obvious to Emma when she had listened to his attorney's argument to the jury, that Downs' was one of the many who had failed to head Emma's warning.

"Even though everyone told him it was okay because it was legal in Amsterdam," Downs' argued through his attorney, "he didn't succumb to the pressure. He got in with the wrong crowd, but that's Airman First Class Downs only crime. He is innocent."

Emma, in turn, had argued that it was Downs and not just this 'wrong crowd' who had bought and used ecstasy. And pretty soon, not only did he buy and use it himself, he also brought it onto the base and sold it to other airmen. What was hard for the Defense to overcome was the fact that, unfortunately for Downs, his 'wrong crowd' had already been under investigation and surveillance by the time he joined them.

With the high number of drug cases on base, the Air Force Office of Special Investigations, or OSI, had stepped up their surveillance of drug operations about one year ago. OSI is the Air Force's criminal investigative unit which focuses on crimes like drugs, theft, and murder committed by military members. For the drug cases, OSI had moles infiltrated around base, especially in the dorms. Once they gathered enough credible evidence to charge the perpetrators, they would make the arrest.

Downs's crowd consisted of Senior Airmen Carnes and Winters, who were caught red-handed smuggling several plastic bags containing X on base. After reading the OSI's report, Emma had to admit that they were getting clever. In order to avoid detection by the gate guards, they had hidden the bags in empty plastic deodorant bottles. Fortunately for the prosecution, as soon as they were arrested, the two spilled their guts about everyone and anyone they had sold to, gotten high with, or seen use X, including Downs who, after a raid of his room, was charged with wrongful possession, use, and distribution of ecstasy.

With all of the evidence against him, Emma was surprised that he had pled not guilty. Usually, when the defendant was presented with all of the evidence against him, he made a deal with the prosecution and the Base Commander to put a cap on the sentence instead of leaving it up to a judge or jury to decide his fate. But as it was his constitutional right to do, Downs had pled not guilty and the members were now back with their verdict.

"Lieutenant Colonel Nuygen, have the members reached a verdict?" Judge Colten asked the foreman.

"Yes, your honor, we have."

"And Lieutenant Colonel Nuygen have you written your verdict on the charge sheet beside each and every count?"

"We have, your honor."

"Very well then. Bailiff, please retrieve the charge sheet from Lieutenant Colonel Nuygen so that I can review it to make sure it's complete.

Judge Colten, having presided over hundreds of military trials, remained expressionless as she read the charge sheet.

After a few minutes, Judge Colten removed her glasses and looked up. "I find the charge sheet in order. Will the defendant and defense counsel please rise."

As Downs and his two attorneys stood to attention, Emma could feel the excitement and nervousness of her co-counsel, Captain John Mullen, who was sitting beside her.

Captain Mullen was fresh out of Judge Advocate General's school in Montgomery, Alabama. This was his first litigated trial. As a senior attorney in the office, Emma was used to being assigned young, inexperienced co-counsel and actually enjoyed teaching them the ins and outs of a trial.

"Airman First Class Derek Downs," Judge Colten read, "as to Charge I, wrongful use of ecstasy, you have been found guilty. As to Charge II, wrongful possession of ecstasy, you have been found . . . . guilty. And as to Charge III, wrongful distribution of ecstasy, you have been found ... guilty."

Downs trembled as he listened to the Judge.

"As you know," she continued, looking him straight in the eye, "this means you will now need to be sentenced. Defense Counsel, Major Lohrs and Captain Mullen, we will now adjourn to my chambers to discuss scheduling the sentencing hearing. Lieutenant Colonel Nuygen and members of the jury panel, I thank you for your service, but you are not dismissed from your duty in this trial. As the defendant has been found guilty, there will be a sentencing hearing during which you will determine his sentence. The bailiff will be contacting each of you this afternoon to let you know when the sentencing hearing has been scheduled. Your orders will reflect the dates of the sentencing hearing accordingly. Again, I thank you for your time and service. You are dismissed."

"All rise," the bailiff called out.

"Congratulations, Captain," Emma said, turning to shake her co-counsel's hand. "Great job."

John, flush from his first victory, returned her handshake enthusiastically. "Major, I cannot thank you enough for letting me be your co-counsel." His hazel eyes shone brightly behind his small wire glasses. "It was such an honor to work with you."

"Well, John, your work is not done yet," Emma replied. "In fact you have just begun. I am going to let you handle the sentencing hearing. This time I'll sit second chair and assist you."

The blood drained from his freckled face. "Really?" he stuttered. "You . . . um . . . you think I can handle it?"

"Absolutely John," she replied confidently. "But, after we meet with the Judge, I suggest you get started. I know Judge Colton likes to schedule sentencing hearings within days of the trial."

Emma chuckled as John fumbled with his papers and books. "Well, I had better go then," he told her, his Adam's apple bobbing. "Wow! Me in charge of the sentencing hearing!"

Emma watched John rush out of the courtroom and envied the younger lawyer's excitement for his first hearing. She thought of the three cases with fast approaching trial dates that were waiting for her back in her office and tried to muster up some enthusiasm, but couldn't. For the first time in her career, Emma wondered if she'd lost her passion for the courtroom.

Chapter 3

Emma finished the required post trial paperwork for the court reporter and left the courtroom. Gathering her things, she trudged up the two flights of stairs to her office. Reaching the top, she paused to take a breath. She knew she should appreciate the exercise the forty-two stairs gave her as she climbed up and down them during trials, but she didn't. Instead, she cursed under her breath as she rebalanced her thick black briefcase, bulging trial notebook and UCMJ in preparation for the final trek down the long hallway to her office and found herself joined by her favorite paralegal, Master Sergeant Maggie Prane.

Even at this late hour, Prane's uniform was as immaculate as though she just pressed it. A beautiful woman with jet black hair and flawless mahogany skin, Maggie was petite and exuberant with a surprisingly hearty laugh.

Emma loved it when Maggie was assigned to assist her with trials. Not only was she organized and well prepared, she made courts a lot more fun with her zany and very loud sense of humor.

"Oh, hey there, Maggie." Emma gasped. "I thought you'd gone home. In fact, why haven't you gone home, yet?"

"Just had to fax the verdict sheet over to the wing and squadron commanders," Maggie said, following Emma into her office. "Besides, it's 2330 and very dark outside. Who else is going to protect you from the airman out there pissed off at you for putting their suppliers in the slammer?"

"I just call it job security," Emma told her, smiling. "If it weren't for them, what would I do with my time? I wouldn't know what to do if I weren't in the courtroom 24/7."

"You and me, both Major. Of course I wouldn't mind if the job security included jobs that ended at 1700, instead of midnight." Maggie sighed. "Well, if you don't need anything else, I guess I had better get home."

Busy trying to find a place for her trial materials in her already crowded office, Emma shook her head. "Nope, go home, but get plenty of rest. Tomorrow, actually today," she sighed after glancing at her watch, "you'll have to walk Captain Mullen through his first sentencing hearing. I'm turning it over to him. I put a copy of the sentencing witnesses and recommendation sheets on his desk and here are copies for you. I'll sit with him at trial, but want you to work your magic and walk him through the pre-hearing stuff. That way I'll know I've left him in good hands."

Emma laughed at the dumfounded look on Maggie's face. "But please try to take it easy on him. We don't want to scare him right out of the Air Force like you did with Captain Pettyjohn."

A loud chortle escaped from Maggie. It was the sound Emma had come to love.

"Now Major," she smirked, putting her hands on her hips. "I know you're not suggesting that my brilliant and correct, I might add, 'suggestions' to Captain Pettyjohn about how to be more successful in the courtroom had anything to do with his deciding not to continue his career. Besides, I wasn't the only one with 'suggestions.'" She dramatically tapped her finger to her chin. "Although come to think of it, I may not have been the most subtle."

A mischievous grin spread on her lips. "Well anyhow, you and I both know that man was not meant for the courtroom. I'm sure he's perfectly happy in some small town somewhere, helping a wonderful elderly lady draw up her will!"

With that, Maggie strode out of Emma's office. "See ya later, Ma'am!" she called out from the hallway.

Although she would never say it, Emma couldn't have agreed with Maggie more. In fact, she also had been pretty forward with Captain Pettyjohn after he had co-chaired a few trials with her. Every time he "helped" her she ended up working harder due to the amount of damage control required. He just was not at all cut out for the courtroom.

Emma sank into her chair and assessed the room. Everywhere she looked were piles of work needing attention: records of trials to review; investigative reports to read; charge sheets to finalize; and of course the ever growing huge stack of mail spilling out of the in-basket on her desk that hadn't been touched for a week.

Closing her eyes, she willed the work to disappear. But much to her chagrin when she opened them, the stacks only seemed to have gotten higher. Well, at least it was technically Friday so she had the weekend to tackle them. Plus, she now had a bonus few hours since she didn't have to baby-sit Captain Mullen. Thank God for Maggie.

An overwhelming sensation weighed down on her as she took another look around her office and tried to think of when she was going to get everything done. She started to straighten the paperwork on her desk in an attempt to organize her workload for the next day, but quickly saw it was futile. Emma threw down her pen and stood up. Right now she needed sleep . . . desperately.

Minutes later, Emma drove out the front gate of the base and waved to the three lone Security Forces guards, young men who wore helmets and flack vests as they carried menacing semi-automatic weapons in their arms, lucky enough to have been assigned the late shift. Since the base was put on a heightened security level after the base commander had received information about possible terrorist activity, the guards had the ever important job of making sure no one got on base who wasn't supposed to be there. Emma watched them move about the gate in her rearview mirror as she drove away.

Although many people stationed here lived on base, Emma had chosen to live in the quaint village of Esch, with its three hundred residents about twenty minutes away and had quickly come to love it. Of course there was the difficulty presented by the fact that only a handful of residents could speak English and Emma's German was limited to a few words, mostly dealing with food or beer. But she had come to know and depend on a thirteen year old neighbor boy who loved to practice his English and soon became Emma's permanent date and translator at the frequent neighborhood gatherings – even though she was 19 years his senior.

The drive down narrow, winding roads, to her village took Emma through the heart of the Eiffel region of Germany, some of the most beautiful countryside she had ever seen. But tonight, peering out her window into the pitch blackness, so tired she could barely focus on the road shining white in her headlights, Emma only wanted to get home.

After pulling into her garage, Emma gathered her things and made her way upstairs to the main level. Her cute little brown brick house came complete with all tile floors and a huge fireplace in the living/dining room. Windows and French doors lined two entire sides of the house opening onto a huge wraparound deck complete with flower boxes filled with brightly colored geraniums. Two of these doors opened off Emma's bedroom to the deck.

Not even taking the time to brush her teeth, Emma slipped out of her clothes, and pulled on her flannel p.j.'s before pulling the pins from her hair and letting her thick mane cascade down her back. Since the military required all hair to be above the bottom of your collar, she pulled it back in a bun every day. Crawling into bed, she snuggled under the wonderfully warm down German comforter. Sleep came immediately.

Emma didn't know how long she had been asleep when she was awakened by the sound of her phone. She groaned when she saw it was only 3:30 a.m. but came instantly awake when Agent Dan Panchen from OSI informed her that she was needed back on base immediately.

Dan Panchen had worked with Emma on several of her trials. As an agent for the Office of Special Investigations, he was in charge of investigating criminal activities of military personnel. Once the agent gathered all of the evidence against a member, he or she would make the arrest and hand over the evidence to Emma's office which would then advise the member's commander as to whether or not to issue formal charges and initiate a trial.

"Surely whatever you need can wait for a few hours when I get into the office," Emma protested.

"I'm afraid not Major," Dan said wearily. "I can't say much over this unsecured line, but we have a situation here on base." He paused, during which Emma thought she heard someone else's voice in the background. "It's big, Major," he continued more urgently, "and the Security Forces' squadron commander has asked that you, as the lead prosecutor, get up here fast."

Emma could tell by the tone of his voice he was serious. It must be pretty important if she was being ordered to come back on base. But that didn't stop the irritation she felt from being awakened from her much needed sleep. Nor did it stop her from pressing Dan for more information.

"Come on, Dan," she said. "Give me something that will keep me awake while I drive all the way back to base."

"There's been a murder in the armory, Major," Dan said in a low tone. And then the line went dead.

Chapter 4

Forty minutes later Emma pulled her 1995 silver Honda Civic into the armory's parking lot. She had made record time considering she'd showered before getting dressed in a crisp, highly starched Battle Dress Uniform consisting of a camouflage cotton blouse with a black t-shirt worn under it and matching pants bloused over polished black boots, this being a more comfortable alternative to the poly-wool blue uniform she had worn earlier. The camouflage Gortex coat she had pulled on over her BDUs kept her warm against the cold, early fall morning. Although she only had a few hours of sleep, Emma was ready to meet the Security Forces' Commander.

When she arrived, at almost 0400, it was still very dark. A lone overhead light dimly lit the parking area where she stood, barely illuminating the three other cars parked next to hers. Two of them were unmarked and the third was a Security Forces' patrol car. No one else was outside.

Although she'd never been to one before, Emma thought the lack of activity was odd for a murder crime scene. As far as she knew, there hadn't been a murder on this base for about ten years when a car bomb had gone off in front of the wing commander's office building. The OSI had linked the incident to terrorists leading to extreme precautions regarding who could get on the base ever since. But no such precautions seemed to have been taken here.

Emma pulled her coat up over her chin, not sure if she was chilled by the wind that was swirling leaves around her feet, or by what she was about to see.

"Colonel Carlson, Chief Master Sergeant Peterson and the OSI agents are in the back, Ma'am," the Master Sergeant who held the door open for her said. "Just follow the path between these shelves and you'll see them."

It was cold inside the large dimly lit room and Emma turned the collar of her coat up against the chill as she followed the path created by rows of shelving units until she came to a space occupied by a metal desk and four men. There was a strange sweet odor in the air.

Although his back was to her, Emma recognized one of the men as Colonel Kent Carlson, the commander of the Security Forces Squadron. In his mid forties and standing about six feet tall, the Colonel was a very handsome man whose dark brown hair was peppered with gray.

Emma often saw him at the gym and was always impressed by his muscular physique. She wasn't the only one. During the two years Carlson had been stationed at Winburg, he had acquired quite a following of adoring females. Emma had the opportunity to work with the good looking hazel eyed commander often since he was the one who signed the charge sheets of Security Forces personnel who were brought to trial. At times, Emma found him to be quite full of himself and vocal about his opinions. But, for the most part, he was fair and seemed to take her advice into consideration when he made his decisions.

Standing next to Colonel Carlson was Chief Master Sergeant Mike Peterson who, at fifty, was completing his last assignment before retiring. Although he didn't have the movie star looks of his boss, the Chief was also considered fairly handsome with the thick neck and muscular barrel chest of a football player. He kept his graying blond hair cut short in the traditional high and tight military style.

The Chief was the First Sergeant for the Security Forces Squadron. A First Sergeant, or Shirt, performed a vital role as the go-to person in a squadron for any issues concerning its enlisted members and as an advisor to the commander. Acting as both a mentor and counselor, he prepared and guided his troops while, at the same time, keeping up troop morale. Among his numerous other tasks, the Shirt was responsible for ensuring that squadron discipline be equitably administered.

It was a tough job and this Chief was particularly protective of his squadron, so much so that, at times, Emma wondered if he told her the complete truth about his airmen, particularly since his stories, often so stilted they seemed rehearsed, always appeared to differ from the evidence.

Agent Dan Panchen, who had summoned her from her warm cozy bed, looked, as usual, as though he were about seventeen years old with his short, curly blond hair and freckled round cheeks. Emma enjoyed working with Dan whom she had grown to think of as kind of like the brother she never had. A geeky brother, that is. Dan was always cutting himself up, laughing at his own stupid jokes and coming up with goofy metaphors. Tonight, however, as he listened to Colonel Carlson, he was clearly in a very serious mood, as was the tall dark haired man standing next to him. Emma didn't recognize him, but judging from the freshly pressed gray suit he wore, he was also OSI.

When the men turned toward her, Emma was struck by Carlson's grim expression. It occurred to her that this murder must involve one of his troops.

"Thanks for getting here so fast, Major," Dan said, edging his way between the Colonel and Chief.

"I understand that we have a serious situation and that you requested my presence, Colonel," she said, addressing Carlson.

Carlson did nothing to mask his distress. "Major, I can tell you that in all of my eighteen years as a cop, I've never experienced a crime that's bothered me as much as this one."

Before Emma could respond, Chief Peterson interrupted. "Sir," he said, "don't you think we should walk the Major through what we know so these men can get on with their work? After that, we really need to prepare a briefing for the Wing Commander."

"What? Oh, right. Yes, yes, you're right." He turned away from Emma to Dan and the other agent. "Agent Panchen of course this is your office's show so why don't you quickly brief Major Lohrs."

"Yes, Sir," Dan replied. Since it was clear that Carlson was in no state to perform introductions, Dan proceeded to do so. "Major, first let me introduce Agent Eric Myers."

Emma was struck by Agent Myers' rugged good looks. When his grey eyes met hers, she felt a shock rip through her at the intensity she saw in them. It was, she found, difficult to concentrate on what Dan was saying, but she gathered that he was from the Major Command headquarters at Ramstein Air Base, here on another assignment.

"Major," Myers replied coolly, not acknowledging Emma's extended hand and turning to Carlson. "Do you really think it's a good idea to involve legal this early in an investigation, Sir?" he demanded impatiently. "What could she possibly do in the investigation besides get in the way?"

Emma became immediately defensive, but remained silent.

"Major Lohrs is a very experienced and highly professional attorney," the Colonel replied adamantly. "I have worked with her on several occasions and it is at my request that she's here. We have a very sensitive case on our hands and I want to make sure we are following the letter of the law. When we catch whoever murdered my airman, I want to be damned sure we have all our evidence locked airtight. If I have anything to say about it, whoever did this is going to go to jail for a very long time. You will let Major Lohrs have every access to this investigation and to your office. Do I make myself clear?"

Undeterred, Myers's eyes bore into Emma. "Yes Sir."

Emma ignored Myers. Despite the fact that he had acquiesced to the Colonel, she had a feeling Myers had already dismissed her as a possible asset to the investigation.

"All we know at this time," Dan said, "is that, according to the log book, Senior Airman Teresa Conklin, age twenty-four, reported to the armory for duty at 2155 last night, taking the place of an Airman First Class Newman who was actually scheduled for the 2200-0500 late shift, but called in sick."

He stepped aside, revealing a woman's body lying face down sprawled in a pool of blood, and Emma found herself suddenly fighting nausea. But she did not turn away. Instead she forced herself to look closely at the back of Teresa Conklin's neck which Dan was explaining had been penetrated at the base by two bullets. The strange sweet odor was, she realized, the smell of blood.

Throughout her career, both as a prosecutor and defense counsel, Emma had seen many unspeakable things, child pornography, rape, aggravated assault, molestation, many of which she saw through the eyes of the victims of these terrible crimes. But for the most part, the gruesome details came in the form of pictures. In sheer self defense, Emma had learned to distance herself from their graphic cruelty in order to examine them with a detached interest. Tonight, however, coming face to face with her first murder victim, she was gripped by raw emotion.

Fully aware that the three men were watching, Emma fought down another wave of queasiness. She refused to make Carlson regret his decision to involve her. But more importantly, she was determined not to give that incorrigible agent any reason why she should be taken off this investigation. Putting on her prosecutor's persona, she steeled herself to look at the victim.

"Don't get too close!" Myers barked as she moved closer to the body. "The last thing we need is you traipsing through the crime scene and tracking blood all over the armory."

"It appears that someone has already done that," Emma retorted, pointing to the bloody foot prints leading away from the body.

"The Chief was the first to receive the call," Dan continued, clearly intent on avoiding a confrontation. "He called the Colonel and us. He also called Master Sergeant Perkins, his back up First Shirt, who you met at the door. Colonel Carlson and the Chief have assured us the scene is untouched and what you see is exactly the way they saw it when they arrived."

Out of the corner of her eye, Emma saw the Chief glance at the Colonel.

"They also didn't turn on any lights," Dan continued. "So it was pretty dark in here when she was shot. As you can see, this little desk lamp doesn't give off much light."

Seeing a thick textbook open on the desk with a notebook beside it, Emma determined that Conklin had been studying during her shift. It was not uncommon for Airmen to use the Montgomery GI Bill to take college classes in hopes of getting their degrees while in the military.

Dan was squatting down now, aiming his flashlight under the desk. "There's a gun under here," he told them. "We believe it's Conklin's standard issue since armory guards are required to carry a loaded weapon while on duty and her gun belt is empty. Probably she pulled it on her attacker before he shot her."

The large room was silent, its thick concrete walls shielding them from the blowing wind outside. Emma shuddered to think about this young girl all alone in this ominous building late at night. She must have been so frightened.

Myers looked towards the front door. "We know the perp had to come in the front door," he said to no one in particular. "So if she knew someone had breached security and gained access into the building and drew her gun, how did it happen that she was shot in the back?"

"Our team did a preliminary sweep of the building and found no visible sign of forced entry," Dan explained.

"If there was no forced entry," Emma said, "it must mean that either she or someone else let the killer into the armory or he had a key. Was anyone else on duty with Senior Airman Conklin?"

"No," the Chief replied. "As you know, with the war going on, we're undermanned in the Security Forces Squadron. So we were forced to reduce guard duties."

Emma turned to Myers. "Agent, you assumed security was breached, but if no one else was on duty with her how can you know for a fact *she* didn't let the perp in?"

"Major, the Chief said there wasn't another cop on duty, but he didn't say Conklin was alone," Myers said, not trying to hide his annoyance.

Turning, he strode past the body towards the back of the building, only to suddenly stop and look at her over his shoulder. "Well," he said, "do you want to be a part of this investigation or not?"

Biting her tongue out of respect for the Colonel and Chief, Emma followed him, leaving the others behind with the body. And as she did so, she sized up the opposition. Myers was, she guessed, in his late thirties and she supposed most women would find him attractive. But in her book, personality counted for more than appearance and he certainly didn't have much of one.

There were two uniformed men standing on either side of a room that looked as though it was used for a break room. A young woman clad in baggy sweatpants and sweatshirt sat on the couch holding a tissue to her eyes.

One of the men was Technical Sergeant Garcia, a cop who had testified as a character witness for the defense in a one of Emma's trials. The other man, whom Emma didn't recognize, also wore the Tech Sergeant stripes on his sleeves. Disregarding them, Myers spoke directly to the young woman on the couch who stared up at him with sad green eyes. Sniffing, she pushed her chin length wavy hair back behind her ear.

"Senior Airman Kennedy," he said firmly, but with a gentleness Emma would not have guessed him capable of. "I'm going to have these men escort you down to the OSI office. You're our only witness to what happened to Senior Airman Conklin and we need to finish our interview with you there. Okay?"

Tears welled up in the young woman's eyes. "But I told you everything I know," she told him. "Please let me go home! I don't want to get into any trouble. Please just let me go back to my dorm. Oh God, Teresa!" Sobbing she buried her face into her hands.

Ignoring Myers' scowl, Emma sat down next to the grief-stricken woman. "Senior Airman Kennedy," she said softly as the other woman looked at her. "Agent Myers needs to take a recorded statement from you. It's really important for you to tell them everything you know. I promise you as soon as he's done, you can go back to your dorm room. Just hang in there a little longer."

"Aren't you a lawyer?" Kennedy asked nervously. "I think you briefed me when I first came here. Oh God, I'm in trouble, aren't I? That's why they brought you in here"

Myers nodded to Tech Sergeant Garcia. "Take her down to OSI. I've called ahead and Agent Manning is expecting you. Whatever happens, do *not* ask her any questions and do *not* let her out of your sight until you turn her over to Agent Manning. Understood?"

The two men each took an arm gently helping Kennedy to her feet. As they led her out of the room, Emma made a mental note of the fact that she was wearing only socks on her feet. When she heard her scream, "Teresa! Oh my God!" Emma realized that the poor girl had just been led past the body. This was, she thought, an ugly business.

"What the hell do you think you were doing?" Myers demanded angrily.

"I was just consoling a young woman who obviously was distressed," Emma told him.

"You shut her up is what you did," he went on. "She thought we brought in the lawyer to hang her out to dry for being in the armory unauthorized. Don't talk to one of my witnesses again without my permission first! Got it?"

This time it was Emma's turn to unleash her anger, lack of sleep fueling her fire. "Let's get something straight," she snapped, standing up. "Number one, I did not 'shut her up' as you so eloquently stated. I wanted to calm her down. How was I supposed to know she was in here without permission? Second, you have no authority over me whatsoever. I'm here because Colonel Carlson ordered me to be. I've prosecuted more cases than you've probably investigated. And there's another thing. I've torn agents like you apart on the stand and loved every minute of it. Don't think I wouldn't jump at the chance to do the same thing to you! Get this through your thick head, Myers! You're stuck with me and we'll be working together, possibly for a long time. So you'd better start treating me with a little respect. Got it?"

Clearly taken by surprise by her outburst, Myers continued to maintain his ground, but Emma could see the intensity in his eyes soften. "Kennedy is an off duty cop who was in the building when Conklin was shot," he explained reluctantly. "She wasn't supposed to be here, but thank God she was because she's the only one who can give us anything about what went on here."

Emma waited for him to continue. She had drawn the line in the sand and apparently won a small victory.

"From what she told us," he went on. "she is a friend of Conklin's who came here to keep Conklin company during her shift. Evidently they're taking the same classes and studying together. Now she's scared because the Chief's all up in arms about her being here against regulations. No friends are allowed in the armory during a guard's shift, even other cops."

Myers paused and Emma could see he was frustrated.

"As you can tell," he continued, "she's in shock over what happened to her friend. So I need to get her away from the scene to try to calm her down. I don't know how much I'll be able to get out of her right now, but I've got to find out what she knows."

"The footprints I saw by the body were hers, weren't they?" Emma asked him, but already knew the answer. "You took her shoes for testing and to prevent any spoliation of evidence," she surmised.

"Very intuitive, Major," Myers answered, somewhat condescendingly. "Maybe you won't botch this investigation up too much after all." And with that, he turned on his heel and left her.

Emma glared at his retreating back. As a woman officer in the military and a lawyer to boot, she had had more than her fair share of experience dealing with men who felt threatened by a woman in power.

Sitting back on the couch, Emma looked around the small room. The past week of stressful late hours in the courtroom, coupled with a lack of sleep had finally caught up with her and now the gravity of the situation in the other room threatened to weigh down on her like a ton of bricks. Her only option right now was to ignore Myers and start to establish her role in the investigation.

To learn exactly what that role was, Emma made her way back to Carlson and the Chief who were now standing by the door. Myers stood beside them his eyes on her as she approached. Ignoring him would be a pleasure Emma thought.

"Major, I am going to leave," Carlson said. "The Chief just made the call into 9-1-1 and I called General Brandt and explained the situation."

Brigadier General Tom Brandt was the one star in command of Winburg Air Base. Although he wasn't directly involved with every investigation, a murder on his base was a different story. Due to the seriousness of the crime, Emma knew General Brandt would need to be kept apprised of all the specifics.

"I'm scheduled to brief him and Lieutenant Colonel Franks at 0630 in the General's office," Carlson continued. "I told Lieutenant Colonel Franks I had asked you to come down here. He said he wants you to meet him in his office later this morning."

Lieutenant Colonel Franks was Emma's boss. As the head attorney on base, Franks, a kind and fair man, who was also incredibly sharp and knew his way around military law like no other, consulted the General on a daily basis. Since Emma truly enjoyed working for him, she was relieved he had been notified about the murder and her assignment to the investigation.

"The ambulance is on the way," Carlson was saying. "In the meantime, Emma, I want you to stay here and use your legal eye to make sure they don't miss anything in this investigation."

Carlson's words didn't give Emma a better understanding of her role and it appeared they had the same effect on Myers who was about to protest when Carlson held up his hand.

"I assure you that I have the utmost confidence in the Major's ability, Agent Myers. She won't get in your way. I then want her to help interview Senior Airman Kennedy. We need to know why that girl was in this armory and what she saw. She's more likely to talk to another female than you two, especially since she knows she's in trouble for being here in the first place."

"Yes, Sir," Myers said, although his stony face revealed how he felt about being told how to run his investigation, including who would be involved. "Come on, Dan, let's get back to the crime scene."

"Sir," Emma said as the others left and the Colonel turned toward the door, "you said that in all of your years as a cop, you hadn't been bothered by a crime as much as this one. With all due respect, Sir, I am not sure I understand. I was under the impression you'd been involved in murder cases before."

A shadow crossed his face and suddenly he looked as though he had aged ten years. "You're right, Emma," he said. "But they all involved civilians, drunken bar fights, jealous lovers that sort of thing."

Emma felt compassion for the weary man in front of her who had just lost one of his troops.

"You're going to have to stay strong on this one," he said. "I have my reasons why I want you to be involved in this case, but I can't share them right now. Confidentiality is of utmost importance. Don't share anything you learn with anyone but me and your boss. I cannot tell you how vitally important it is to keep the facts of this case confidential. If anything is leaked, careers could be ruined."

He paused and Emma could see that he was deliberating whether or not to say more.

"You asked why I'm bothered?" he asked grimly. "As you know the armory is one of the most secure buildings on the base. It houses all of the weapons used by my men and women to patrol and protect everyone and everything on base. You've already been told it doesn't look like the armory was broken into. And as you said, that means she either let someone in here or they had access to a key. Emma, only a select few people on base have a key, including myself, the Chief, and the armory supervisor. Then, of course, there's the one in the Wing Commander's office. Senior Airman Kennedy told us she didn't hear Senior Airman Conklin talk to anyone which we can assume means she didn't let anyone in. And since there's no sign of a forced entry, that could mean only one thing."

Carlson paused, peering over Emma's shoulder back into the darkness of the armory where Conklin's body lay..

"This was not a random act," he went on. "The person who did this had access to the base and the armory, which means the killer is one of us and is running around loose on my base."

Chapter 5

It was not until the heavy door slammed behind him that the full import of Carlson's words sank in. "One of us," he had said. She stared at the door, deep in thought and was startled when Myers said, "Don't think I'm going to let you run my investigation."

Emma took a deep breath and forced a smile on her face. "Why Agent Myers," she said innocently, turning towards him. "Surely, you don't think I would try to take over the investigation from someone as experienced and astute as you?"

"I wouldn't mess with the Major," Dan said, grinning. "I've had the pleasure of working on several cases with her and she's invariably provided us with some valuable insight. You never know. She could actually prove to be a real asset on this case. Besides, she's not easily intimidated, even by the likes of such an 'astute' agent as you."

Grateful for an ally, Emma made a mental note to thank Dan later for sticking up for her. Not that she needed it, mind you. But it was nice to know that at least someone on this damned investigation would be friendly.

The armory door opened and after having their badges checked by the Master Sergeant on guard, several more agents filed through it, carrying cameras and other equipment they quickly set up throughout the room. In a few short minutes, the Master Sergeant was relieved and OSI had taken over the area.

"So you have a lot of experience with murder scenes, huh?" Myers said dryly as Emma watched the room come live with activity.

"No," Emma replied swallowing her pride. "This would be my first, but I assumed your guys would have been here earlier." Turning her full attention to him, she said, "How many murders have you investigated before, Myers?"

"Actually I've only been involved with one other murder case," he admitted. "We had a confession from the perp within twenty-four hours and were able to wrap up the investigation about two weeks later. Somehow I doubt this one will go so easily."

Suddenly, the large overhead fluorescent lights flashed on, momentarily blinding them. When she could focus again, Emma saw that the room had changed proportions, and the shelves that seemed to loom over her were not so high.

"I'll give you this Major," Myers said his brooding eyes never leaving hers. "Although it's not unusual to keep a crime scene quiet until we can do a thorough investigation, I was surprised by the Colonel and Chief's delayed response in calling 911. Don't get me wrong. I'm glad they called us first so no one could mess up the scene, but Carlson's demand for the high level of confidentiality is puzzling. He made Dan and I wait before we could call in our team."

Emma agreed that the men's failure to follow standard procedures didn't fit with her knowledge of their usually by-the-book nature.

"At first I thought the Colonel didn't want to create a scare on base," Myers continued, frowning. "That's understandable. People are going to freak when they hear what happened. But there's something else going on. As soon as we arrived and took over, I could tell there was more to his secrecy than maintaining order on base. That man was literally shaking when we got here. The blood was completely drained from his face. Once, when he thought I was out of range, I heard him mumble 'Oh my God, this cannot be happening. How could he have let this happen? What am I going to do?' "

Although she agreed it was reasonable for a commander to be upset about the death of one of his airmen, Emma felt the Colonel's reaction was a bit out of character for a man who prided himself on maintaining decorum.

"There's something not right here," he went on as he watched his agents gather evidence. "There's also the fact that Carlson was really upset that Kennedy was in the armory. Yes, she shouldn't have been in here, but the Colonel was over the top. The Chief literally had to pull him away when he started yelling at her. It all just doesn't fit. In fact, my guess is that your Colonel is trying to protect someone."

"From what I've heard, Colonel Carlson has had a long and stellar career," Emma said. "Rumor is he's looking at retiring in the next few years. I have a hard time thinking he is protecting someone. There's no way he would mess up his distinguished career or his retirement. There must be another reason for his behavior."

"I guess that's for me," Myers paused, "I mean *us* to find out, now isn't it."

"God, I'd love to throw something at him," she angrily muttered under her breath, as he went to speak to one of the agents who was nearby and appeared to be inventorying the M9 pistols lining one of the shelves.

"Here, take these." Dan said, passing her a pair of thin latex gloves. "But maybe you should wait to throw them at him until later."

In spite of herself, Emma smiled. As usual, Dan's easy going manner lightened her mood.

Pulling on the gloves, Emma glanced around to determine where she should start first.

"Just because you have those on, doesn't mean you have permission to touch anything." Myers called out to her. "Dan, why don't you and the Major come with me? When it's light enough outside, we need guys to take pictures around the perimeter. But until then I want to take a better look around out there to make sure we didn't miss anything. Hank, throw me a couple of flashlights."

Zipping up her coat and pulling on her hat, Emma followed them. Outside the sun peeked over the horizon, painting the sky vibrant red and yellow. A fine covering of frost glistened over the grass. Although the forecast called for sun, it wouldn't shine bright enough to ward off the chilly temperature normal for mid October. The wind had died down a bit just barely stirring the leaves that had begun to fall.

Emma breathed in the fresh crisp autumn air, grateful to be out of the stifling armory with the sickly sweet smell of blood. She glanced at her watch: 0545. Soon it would be light and the base would be alive with activity. Her faithful old Civic still sat in the parking lot in front of her. On either side of the sidewalk, despite the colder weather, the grass was still green.

The positioning of the rising sun indicated that the armory door was on the east side of the building. The long beige building had no windows, just solid concrete defying anyone to try to enter unauthorized. Looking up, Emma spied the lone security light hanging over the door that had previously lit her way. Although it was getting light outside, the security light was still on.

"He'd unscrewed the light." Dan said beside her. "When we got here it wasn't on. The killer unscrewed it so she wouldn't see him enter the building. That's why we think he used a key. Why unscrew the light if she let him in? I'm going to get a list of everyone who has or had access to an armory key."

"He sure had this planned out, didn't he?"

"Looks like it," Myers cut in impatiently. "Come on you two."

Following him, Emma and Dan walked off the sidewalk to the side of the building. Turning on the flashlight Myers had shoved at her, Emma shone its light on the ground around her, careful not to step on anything that may be evidence.

On the south side of the building, a dense forest of pine trees and scrub oaks made it difficult to walk. Thick orange pine needles carpeted the ground. Emma stayed against the building on a small patch of grass that created a natural path between the building and forest.

"I don't see any footprints here," Dan said. "These damn needles make it impossible to see anything on the ground. Eric's hoping that maybe now that it's lighter we can see where the killer broke a branch or something during his escape."

But they could see that at least for now it was a lost cause. The trees were too dense and it was still too dark. Myers told Dan to have the agents, trained at tracking, comb the area when there was more light.

"He had such a great cover after he left." Emma marveled. "The trees are so thick I can hardly see through them, let alone under them. He could have been right here when you arrived and you would never have seen him."

They made their way back to the armory door and could hear the faint sound of sirens in the distance announcing the arrival of the ambulance. As she stood by the armory door, Emma thought about the poor girl inside that it had come to take away and wondered if they would be able to find her killer or whether his identity would forever be hidden by the dark, dense forest.

Chapter 6

Back inside, Emma let the warmth envelop her. Someone had turned up the heat. After the early morning chill outside, the heat was more than welcome, although it did nothing to allay her growing sense of foreboding. This was not going to be an easy case to solve.

Dan took out a small notebook from his jacket. "Don't forget to keep your gloves on," he cautioned Emma.

Emma surveyed her surroundings. To her right ten rows of black metal shelving units filled three quarters of the room, separated by a narrow walkway. To her left were neat rows of M9s and rifles, after which two open metal cabinet doors gaped, exposing their contents, stacks of small ammunition boxes and M9 magazines. There were no handles on the doors and a key hung in a lock on one of them.

M9 weapons, Emma knew from her training, were semiautomatic weapons designed exclusively for the U.S. Armed Forces, but were also used by other law enforcement agencies. They were first used as the military's standard weapon in 1985 and remained standard issue today.

Beyond the cabinets was the open space where paramedics stood over Conklin's body, preparing to put it in a thick black plastic bag which would then be loaded on a gurney. Emma could see Myers talking to them and wondered if he was warning them to keep what they saw under wraps until further notice. She knew the Colonel wouldn't be too happy if the two medics blabbed about the scene. The investigation could be ruined and evidence compromised if information got out prematurely.

Emma walked closer to the scene after Myers was called away by one of his agents.

With plastic booties over their black boots, the medics knelt down to the body, the one at her head trying to avoid stepping in any blood. As they lifted the body bag, Emma saw that the taller of the two looked ashen. Emma's heart went out to him as he struggled to put the body on the gurney. Was it, she wondered, the first time he, too, had seen a dead body?

From where she stood, Emma could see the once beautiful face of the woman lying in the bag. Emma quickly shook away the tears that threatened as the bag was slowly closed.

As the paramedics wheeled the body out of the armory, Emma thought about how good it would feel to stand across the courtroom from the person who had done this, to see him cuffed and hauled away to jail. This thought gave Emma a renewed sense of purpose.

As everyone else was concentrating on the main area of the armory, Emma thought she'd take a better look at the break room where she had first seen Kennedy.

Glad the body was now gone, Emma quickly made her way past the desk which was now surrounded by the brackish blood to the back of the armory. Emma walked back into the break room and looked around. Right next to a pop machine was a tan refrigerator that had seen better days, abutted by a narrow counter. Directly across from the doorway was the long lumpy brown couch on which Kennedy had been sitting and to the right of the doorway were a TV and VCR sitting on top of a small brown table. The TV had been left on and a news anchor bid everyone a good morning.

Emma perched on the couch wondering what Kennedy had been doing in the armory. She said she'd been studying but Emma didn't see any books lying around. Sliding to the far end of the lopsided couch, Emma peered over the side. There stuck between the couch and the wall was an open dark blue backpack. Pulling her latex gloves tight, Emma picked up the backpack and searched its contents. There were no textbooks but she did find a bag of licorice, a bottle of water, some pens and a notebook. Emma pulled the red spiral notebook out of the bag and opened it to the first page.

It was a letter.

Hey you,

I can't tell you how long I've wanted to tell you this. It's so hard for me to write. I've been thinking about you night and day. I can't get you out of my mind. Every time you are near, I go crazy. This is hard cuz I don't know if you feel the same way.

Emma flipped the page looking for more of the letter, but it was blank. To whom, she wondered, had Kennedy been writing. Emma put the notebook back in the backpack. A search of the rest of the room also turned up nothing so Emma decided to see what the others had found.

After telling the agent who was dusting the desk for fingerprints about the backpack and notebook, Emma joined Dan and Myers who were talking to a tall female agent. Myers had taken off his suit coat and tie, his collar open exposing the tan skin underneath.

"As you can imagine in an armory, we're finding a lot of prints," the agent was explaining. "We'll run them against anyone who has ever been in the armory or been issued a weapon in the last few months, but this is going to take awhile."

"Fine," Myers replied. "We need to follow procedures, but the odds of us finding a conclusive print out of hundreds is slim to none."

"That's assuming the killer didn't wear gloves," Emma said.

Myers looked at her, revealing nothing. "Right," he replied and nodded to the other agent to follow him.

"What is with him?" Emma demanded as she watched his retreating back.

"I think he's a little intimidated by you, my friend," Dan replied, winking. "Look, why don't you help me?" he added, scribbling some notes in a small black notebook. "I'm trying to walk through exactly what the perp did after he entered the building. So he unscrewed the outside light and entered the building with a key."

"How did Conklin not hear him open the door?" Emma interrupted.

"Good question. Tom!" Dan yelled up to the agent standing by the front door. "Open the armory door slowly and try to close it as quietly as possible."

Tom complied and to Emma's astonishment all she felt was a slight pressure change as the door opened and closed.

"The walls are so thick," Dan explained, "they seem to absorb any sound from the door. Also remember, Conklin was even further back in the armory than we are. She was back by the break room where Kennedy was watching TV. She wouldn't have heard anything.

"So," Dan went on. "The question is how did he get around once he was in here? As you saw, it was pretty dark. There's no way he could have seen his way through these shelves to the back where Conklin was. Even if he knew the armory like the back of his hand, these shelves are so tightly packed in here, surely he would have had to run into them."

Emma agreed. "He couldn't have used a flashlight or she would have seen it. Could he have used night vision goggles? Anyone can buy them on the internet now-a-days. I had a child molestation case once where the defendant used them to make his way into the seven year old victim's room."

Dan stopped writing and winced. "God, I bet you wanted to hang that bastard. Damn, I hate the cases that involve children. The sick bastards. But, you may be onto something there."

Over Dan's shoulder, Emma saw Myers come back down the narrow aisle, stopping in front of one of the shelves with M9s lined up.

"The Master Sergeant showed us where to find the inventory logs of all weapons housed on these shelves before he left," he called to Dan, squatting down. "But I'd say we already know he used one of the M9s in the armory. I noticed this one during my first walk through."

Even from where she stood, Emma could see what he meant. While the rest of the M9s on the shelf were neatly lined up, the gun Myers had pointed too was askew. A small round steel bar ran the width of the shelf. The barrels of the guns rested on top of it allowing the rest of gun to nestle against the front lip of the shelf. The barrel of the gun catching Myers' attention lay under the bar on its side and was longer than the rest.

"Looks like whoever put this gun away was in a hurry," Myers observed. "We now also know why Kennedy told us she didn't hear any shots. He used a suppressor."

Emma knew that some M9s had stock barrels that had been threaded to accommodate a suppressor or silencer, as Hollywood called it, which suppressed the sound of the shot going off from the weapon.

After ensuring the photographer had adequately captured the location of the weapon, Myers' carefully picked it up in his gloved hands.

"Guess he wasn't so clever after all," Myers said examining one side. "Looks like our perp is right-handed."

Seeing Emma's confusion, Dan explained. "One thing that makes a M9 unique is that it can be positioned for either right or left-handed shooters. As you can see, our perp positioned this one so he could shoot with his right hand."

Myers moved to the cabinets. "This is where they keep all of the ammunition for every weapon used by the cops," he said. "It just so happens that the key is kept hidden on top of one of the cabinets. Not the best security measure in the world, I know. The Chief told me only the armory guards and a handful of others know where the key to these cabinets is kept. But I'm sure it wouldn't be hard for anyone to discover this 'incredible' hiding place."

"When we got here all of the cabinets were locked except this one," he said. Taking a handkerchief from his back pocket, Myers ran it over the top hinge of the cabinet.

When he pulled it away, a brown stain soiled the white cloth.

"Look at this," he said. "It's grease. Dan, hand me a piece of paper."

Myers took the small paper Dan tore out of his notebook and ran it over the top hinge of the neighboring cabinet. When he showed them the paper, the only thing on it was dust.

"It's possible our perp was in here before and oiled the hinges so they wouldn't squeak," Myers surmised. "This guy knew what he was doing. He planned everything out in advance. I'm having the guys check all of the magazines and boxes of bullets in these cabinets, but I went through this one myself."

Pulling the ajar door back open to reveal its contents, Myers picked up one of the thin black magazines with his gloved hand and held it up to Dan and Emma.

"This one, which you'll notice is loaded, is missing two bullets," he said. "We won't know for certain until the ballistics report comes back, but my guess is they'll find the missing two bullets from this magazine in the back of Conklin's neck."

"That would make sense," Dan chimed in, "given Conklin's wounds." Dan turned to Emma. "Bullets discharged from an M9 typically don't pass through a body, but instead cause heavy internal bleeding and organ damage."

Myers nodded. "So the perp came down this aisle and grabbed an M9 off that shelf. He then walked down here, took the key from the top of the cabinet . . . one that he'd previously oiled and unlocked it. Once he got the door open, he got this magazine, loaded in his gun and went towards the desk where she was studying."

Myers walked back towards where Conklin's body once lay. Emma and Dan close behind.

"We know he must have been fairly close to her," Myers continued, "since an M9 has a maximum range of about 50 meters."

"Emma thought the guy used night vision goggles which would explain how he did all of this in the dark," Dan told him.

"Could be," Myers replied nonchalantly. "But why didn't she hear him? Every time you touch something in here the sound echoes in the room."

To illustrate his point, Myers tapped the side of the cabinet. The sound echoed through the high ceilings of the room.

"Maybe she did hear him." Emma said, pointing to the open text book and a notebook on the desk. "It looks like Conklin was studying before she was murdered. Look at this notebook. She was taking notes."

Myers picked up the textbook and read the front cover. "Psychology 101."

Emma nodded. "What got me when I first saw her was how she was lying. She couldn't have been sitting here when he came up on her or she would have been slumped over the desk. Instead she was face down in front of the desk almost like she was walking back to it. And there's the fact her gun was lying under the desk. Why would she have her gun out if she hadn't heard something that scared her?"

Turning toward the cabinets, Emma went on. "My guess is she was studying, heard the killer behind her, got up from the desk and walked toward the shelves and him. She must have been scared and pulled her gun."

"Okay Sherlock," Myers said to her. "Say you are right. She heard him. Why did she walk towards him and then turn her back to him? Remember, the bullet holes were in the *back* of her neck."

"I don't know Agent Myers," she replied, hands on hips, her eyes flashing. "Are you saying this isn't plausible?"

Emma didn't give Myers time for a comeback.

"All I *do* know is that I am coming off of a weeklong trial," she firmly informed him. "I've had no sleep, and there's a mountain of paperwork waiting for me back at my office that I need to sort through by the end of the day. To top it all off I get thrown in a murder investigation, and I'm not even sure why."

Choosing her next words carefully, Emma continued. "I also know, Agent Myers, that you are dangerously close to acting like a conceited, egotistical man who has no concept what it's like to work with an intelligent woman who actually can contribute to the investigation AND hold up her end."

Dan's eyes were wide as he nonchalantly looked away, grinning.

"So Agent Myers, if you have a problem," she said, lowering her voice. "No, strike that. If you have a legitimate problem with me, let's hear it now."

Myers stood silently his jaw clenched.

"Nothing?" Emma said, forging on. "Fine! Now, if we're done here I suggest we go talk to *our* witness."

Spinning on her heel, Emma calmly grabbed her Gortex coat and walked out of the armory. Once outside she took a deep breath, letting the clean, crisp morning air fill through her.

It was now 0730 and the base was alive. Cars hummed in the distance carrying people to work. A lone goose, flying overhead, greeted Emma with a honk. Emma watched its long wings flapping until it was a dot in the bright blue sky and then felt a hand on her shoulder.

"You okay?" Dan asked, helping her into her coat.

"Thanks," she said sheepishly. "Sorry about that. No, actually I am not sorry. I've got a job to do and if Myers doesn't like it, he needs to take it up with Colonel Carlson."

"I've worked with Myers on several cases," Dan said gently, "and trust me, I know he can be a pain in the ass. But he is good . . . really good and he does know his stuff. He's also actually a pretty decent guy outside of an investigation."

As she opened her car door, she looked at him and saw that he was grinning. "I must say, it sure was fun to see him dressed down a bit, though," he told her.

Emma laughed in spite of herself as she got in the driver's seat.

"Come think of it," he went on. "I believe that's the first time I've ever seen him at a loss for words. Remind me to always be on your side of any argument!" Still grinning, Dan shut her door.

Chapter 7

Emma drove across base to the OSI office which was located in one of several standard beige three story buildings standing, as if in formation, on the southwestern side of base, housing the Security Forces offices and Contracting. The legal office was located two streets to the north and the Wing Headquarters building was a couple streets to the south. A few pine trees stood solitary watch in front of the various buildings. A tall chain link fence complete with three strands of barbed wire on top ran behind the buildings separating the base from the outside world.

Actually, if you didn't know the area, it was quite hard to find your way around Winburg, or any Air Force Base, for that matter since every building looked alike. It was quite easy to spot a new person on base if for no other reason than their painfully slow driving. Their appearance, head down with one eye on the road and one eye on the base map, gave them away every time.

After learning the hard way, Emma now made a point to have someone show her around a new base before she actually tried to find it on her own. She was especially glad she did this at Winburg with its long flight line separating one part of the base from the other. Luckily, the legal office was somewhat in the middle of base, not far from the Base Exchange, Commissary, and gym. But unfortunately, due to the size of the base, none of the other squadrons or headquarters were within walking distance of the legal office, unless of course you didn't mind making the one plus mile trek. So when she needed a charge sheet signed or to talk to a witness, Emma got in her trusted old car to once again entering the endless sea of beige buildings with brown trim.

Emma parked her car in the only spot open in front of the OSI building. As she reached over to pick her briefcase up from the passenger seat, she caught a glimpse of herself in the rearview mirror. Large brown eyes wistfully stared back at her. Her lustrous brown hair gleamed in the sunlight streaming through the window. "Not bad for a couple hours of sleep," she complimented herself after she applied some lip gloss.

Before going inside, Emma dialed the legal office on her cell phone to check in and left a message for her boss who was in the meeting with the General. The grass glistened in the morning sun as it melted away any remaining traces of frost. Overhead birds flew in perfect formation in preparation for the cold German weather coming over the next few weeks.

Although the front door looked like every other one on base, it soon became obvious the rest of the OSI building was anything but ordinary. After walking down a short narrow hallway with no doors or windows, Emma came to a thick, locked steel door, above which a camera moved back and forth, watching her every move. A black phone hung on the wall to the left of the door.

There were no signs or any other clues indicating how a visitor could gain access to whatever lay behind the door, but through experience, Emma knew to lift the receiver and wait for someone to come on the line and after answering some questions buzz her in.

Once inside, Emma found herself in a small room which was empty except for a table on which sat a computer and log book. She was greeted by a woman who, wearing black wool pants and a grey turtleneck, introduced herself as Agent Champlain. She was, Emma knew, one of the newer agents at Winburg. She had worked on the Down's trial Emma just completed and although it was her first time testifying, under Emma's guidance she had done pretty well.

"Good job, with the Down's case this week," Emma said, adding Dan's name as the agent she was visiting to the log. "By the way, we got him. Looks like we'll start the sentencing hearing soon."

Champlain blushed as she took Emma's ID and scanning it into the computer. "Thanks, Major," she said. "I'm sure you could tell that I was kind of nervous. I really appreciate your prepping me for the stand."

"Not a problem," Emma replied reassuringly. "And you couldn't tell at all. Don't worry. You'll get used to being up there."

When Dan arrived, which he did shortly, he led Emma down a long hallway past the agents' offices. Large fluorescent lights flickered above them. Emma followed Dan past the offices to the other end of the hall and through another door, which opened up to a staircase.

Emma knew from her past visits that there were several conference rooms and evidence lockers on the second floor. There was also a narrow room filled with computers where the agents specializing in information technology spent countless hours trying to recreate hard drives in search of pornography, emails and other incriminating files that had been deleted.

"We're going down to the basement this time," Dan told her. "That's where the interrogation rooms are. Usually only agents have access to these rooms." He smiled at her over his shoulder. "You must be moving up in the world."

He was right, of course. It was quite probable that no other JAG had been here.

Dan punched in a code and Emma followed him through the door. Myers was seated on top of the middle of the table facing a long window flanked by two speakers and staring straight ahead. His white shirt sleeves were now rolled up to his elbows and a notepad rested on his long legs. Beyond the glass, Kennedy was sitting in a nearly identical room, the only thing separating them was a long window that Emma guessed to be a two way mirror.

It seemed like a few minutes before he acknowledged their presence. "She's ready for us," he said finally.

Myers slid off the table. "Right now we have ruled her out as the perp since she shoots left-handed. And since she is our only witness, she's our only shot at finding out about what happened.

"Dan, you stay in this room and make sure we get everything taped. As for you, Major, regardless of what you think my reasoning is, I'm going to lead this interview. It's not because I don't think you'll have good questions," he added matter-of-factly opening the door. "But we've got to follow the rules, and unless you've been made an agent in the last few hours, I'm the one who knows them. Carlson wants you here to make her more comfortable. So do it. But don't get in my way."

"Fine."

As she strode past him, Myers stopped her. "I mean it. One slip and you are out of here. I don't care what Carlson says."

Chapter 8

Jaime Kennedy peered up at them through tear laden lashes as they entered. Emma took a seat next to Myers across the table from their witness. Wearing the same clothes she had had on in the armory, Kennedy slumped in her chair, clutching a tissue.

Emma found herself empathetic to the young woman in front of her who was barely functioning after the loss of her good friend. Regardless of whether she had broken the rules by being in the armory, no one should have to witness their friend's murder. Emma made a mental note to make sure Kennedy got an appointment to talk with a professional.

The Air Force prided itself on its great team of mental health professionals, four of whom were stationed at Winburg. As a trial lawyer, Emma had many times called them as experts to testify on the topics of depression, drug addiction, and abuse. More often than not, when she wasn't putting them on the stand she was sending people their way for help.

Unfortunately, in Emma's line of work, she saw a lot of people who needed help, many of whom came to Emma thinking an attorney could solve their problems, when in fact they weren't dealing with a legal issue at all. When she felt it was necessary, Emma would gently persuade a witness or client to seek counseling. She had learned over the years to be very diplomatic when raising the subject of mental health because for many people the very words caused them to come unglued.

Somehow Emma sensed the woman in front of her now wouldn't need much persuasion. For the first time since she was assigned to this investigation, Emma understood why she was here. Jaime Kennedy needed compassion and understanding and Emma was the one who could give it to her.

"Senior Airman Kennedy," Myers began, "Major Lohrs and I need to ask you some more questions about what happened last night. I know it seems like you've already told us everything you know, but it is important we go over what you saw again."

Kennedy looked at Emma.

As if sensing her concern, Myers explained Emma's presence. "Major Lohrs, as you already know, is a lawyer from the legal office, but I assure you she is not here because you're in trouble. She's here to help me find out what happened last night."

The airman's hand began trembling. "I can't," she moaned.

Knowing she would hear about not following his lead later, Emma pushed back from the table, her chair scraping the hard concrete underneath. Myers eyes narrowed as she glided around the table and sat beside Jaime. Emma produced a clean tissue from her pocket.

"Thanks," Kennedy whispered. Although she'd felt it when she walked in the room, Emma was startled at the depth of pain she saw in the young woman's eyes.

"Jaime, look at me," Emma said gently.

Her red rimmed eyes met Emma's. For a brief moment, Emma thought she saw fear flash in their green depths, but just as quickly the sadness returned, leaving Emma unsure of what she saw.

"I know this is very hard for you," Emma said. "No one should have to see what you saw tonight. I can't imagine how you feel after what happened to your friend. But I do know this. You're the only person who can help catch whoever did this to Senior Airman Conklin. You're her only chance. If you don't help us and tell us everything you remember, we may not catch him."

Emma paused, searching the troubled woman's face, hoping to see some glimmer of understanding of the vital role she would play in catching her friend's killer.

"Don't let him get away with this," she went on. "I know you're worried about being in the armory, but that's not what's important right now. What is important is getting this guy. Talk to us. Help us. But more importantly, help your friend. We can't do it without you."

Jaime's eyes faltered and she looked away. The room was deathly silent. Even Emma found herself holding her breath in anticipation. If this girl didn't talk the investigation would be one huge uphill battle, not to mention what Myers was going to say since she took over his interview.

As if on cue, Myers took over. "Major Lohrs is right," he began.

Jaime stared at the silver fountain pen he was holding. "You're the only witness to what happened this morning," he coaxed her. "I promise you I could care less why you were in the armory. But it is your duty as an airman to help us find this guy and stop him from hurting someone else."

"Are you sure?" Jaime finally spoke, her hands shaking. "Sergeant Garcia told me I was in big trouble for being in the armory. He told me to watch what I say 'cuz you could use it against me."

Furious at Garcia for intimidating her witness, Emma chose her words carefully. "I promise that our sole focus . . . sole purpose of this interview is to understand everything you know about what happened to Teresa . . . not to use it against you. If there is any time when you feel like you're saying something incriminating against yourself, it is your right to stop the interview and ask to have Defense Counsel appointed to represent you. Okay?"

Jaime looked to Myers for confirmation. "I'm not treating you as a suspect so I'm not going to read you your rights," he assured her. "You're a witness . . . the *only* witness to this crime and we're going to treat you as such. So what do you say?"

"Okay," she replied, taking a deep shaky breath. "I'll try to answer your questions. It's just that I'm so tired."

"We understand," Emma said, patting her hand. "We have nothing but time. So if you need a break, just let us know."

Myers nodded to the mirror, indicating that Dan should start recording the interview. "Senior Airman Kennedy," he said, "before we start I need to tell you that this interview is being recorded."

"But I don't see any microphones," Jaime said warily.

Suddenly, she stared at the large mirror in across from her. "Oh, I get it," she exclaimed. "There's someone on the other side of that mirror isn't there? Is he taping me?"

"Yes," Myers replied. "But you don't need to worry about it. It's standard operating procedure that we tape all interviews. That way we can review what's been said later and follow up with additional questions if needed. Are you ready?"

He flipped his notebook open and Emma found herself slightly admiring Myers' technique. It was obvious to Emma he was quite comfortable in the interrogation room.

"I'm also going to take a few notes as we go along," Myers told her. "Okay. Now we're going to start by getting some preliminary information from you for purposes of the recording and then I'll ask you some more specific questions.

"First, we'll get the introduction out of the way. This is Agent Eric Myers from the Office of Special Investigations stationed at Ramstein Air Base in Germany," he said clearly. "I am interviewing Senior Airman Jaime Kennedy at the OSI at Winburg Air Base also in Germany. Today is Friday, October 17th, 2008; time is 0753. Also present is Major Emma Lohrs, Judge Advocate of the Legal office also here at Winburg Air Base, Germany."

Myers jotted a few more notes and then focused on Jaime again. "Senior Airman Kennedy, you are assigned to the Security Forces Squadron and stationed here at Winburg Air Base, is that correct? No, don't nod. You have to answer in order for the microphone to pick up what you are saying.

"Now, you're here as a witness to the murder of Senior Airman Teresa Conklin," he continued, "is that correct?"

He went on to elicit the fact that Airman Kennedy had been stationed at Winburg for two and a half years, and that she had known the murder victim for almost a year of that time.

Myers put down his pen. "Senior Airman Kennedy, we're now done with the preliminary questions. Now I want to talk to you about what happened this morning in the armory. Why don't you start at the beginning? When did you arrive at the armory?"

Jaime inhaled deeply. "Sometime after 2300 after I'd come back from the gym."

"Why were you in the armory?"

Again, Jaime's eyes flew to Emma, who nodded reassuringly. "I went there to study," she said. "Teresa and me are in the same Psych 101 class. We're both trying to get our degrees and so a lot of times we study together. We usually study at night after we workout and we were gonna study last night, but Teresa called me before dinner and told me someone got sick so she had to take their late shift for them. I was bummed because we have a test coming up and I really needed her help. She's so much smarter with this psych stuff than me."

She stopped as a spasm of grief hit her. Again, Emma's heart went out to the young girl and she resisted the urge to put her arm around her shaking shoulders. It was, she knew, unwise to risk a possible future accusation that she had somehow influenced Jaime's testimony.

"Anyway, she must have heard the panic in my voice because she told me that we could study in the armory. She told me to come over after the late shift change at 2200, after she issued the changing gate guards their weapons. I asked her if it would be okay. And, she said it would be because no one else would be there. Besides she told me I could help keep her awake during her shift."

"Let's back up a minute," Myers broke in. "I need to make sure I have all the details. Whose shift did Senior Airman Conklin cover?"

Jaime shrugged. "I don't know. I just know she told me she had gotten a call from the Chief asking her to take the shift, saying he'd cleared her shift change with Sergeant Dort who's her supervisor. He's in charge of making the schedule for the guards there."

"Okay. So you said you sent to the armory around 2300?"

"Yeah, I think that's right. I went to the chow hall about 1800 with some guys from the dorm. After I ate, I went back to my room and watched some TV while I ironed my BDUs for the next day-well today. Around 2000 I went to the gym and worked out for an hour to an hour and a half, came home, took a shower, watched some more TV and then after the late news, I got ready to go to the armory Teresa said the shift change was at 2200. So it must have been about 2300 when I went got to the armory. I didn't look at the clock when I got there."

Myers nodded. "Okay, so why don't you tell me what happened after you got there."

"I knocked on the door and Teresa let me in."

"Was there anyone else in the armory when you arrived?"

"No, just me and her."

"Was the outside light on when you knocked on the door?"

"Yeah."

"Did Senior Airman Conklin log you in?"

"No," Jaime answered nervously, her eyes lowered.

Emma watched Jaime fiddle with the tissue in her hands and sensed Jaime was becoming uneasy.

"Okay, what happened next?"

"We went back to the break room to study," Jaime said. "We must have studied for about an hour and a half, but then I was beat. I told Teresa I needed a break. So I turned on the TV 'cuz I thought it would help me wake up. I know it must have been sometime after midnight, because the late shows were just getting over. You know the reruns they show on Armed Forces Network?"

"Where was Senior Airman Conklin while you were watching TV?" Emma cut in.

"She wanted to keep studying so she went out to the desk in the other room. She was going for an A in this class, you know. She was really proud of her grades," she added softly.

Fearing another breakdown, Emma asked her if she needed a break, but Jaime shook her head. "No," she said. "I just want to get this over with."

"You said Teresa was studying in the other room?" Myers asked, taking over again.

"Yeah. She told me she couldn't study with the TV on so she went there."

"Then what happened?'

The young woman's face contorted with grief. "I don't know!" she wailed. "I must have fallen asleep. Because the next thing I know I hear something that woke me up, so I went to go see and there's Teresa lying on the floor."

Tears flooded out her eyes. "I remembered yelling her name," she sobbed. "But there was so much blood. I didn't know what to do. I didn't know what to do."

Emma glanced at Myers whose lips were pressed together, his dark eyes revealing nothing.

"But you called someone, right?" she asked quietly, hoping that Jaime wouldn't become hysterical. "To tell them what happened? Who did you call?"

"What? Oh, I called the first shirt."

Myers was clearly puzzled. "The Chief?"

Jaime's cheeks glistened with tears. "But I don't remember much after that," she told him, burying her face in her hands. "God, I can't believe she's dead. Please don't make me answer anything else!"

"I know this is hard for you," Emma said, throwing her reservations to the wind and putting her arm around the girl's shoulders. "But we have just a few more questions and then we're done, okay?"

Myers stared at the top of Kennedy's head as she continued to hide her face. "Senior Airman Kennedy," he said firmly, but not completely devoid of compassion, "like Major Lohrs said, this is really important. You said you heard something. What do you mean?"

The girl raised her head and stared at him. "I don't know," she said, pushing her wavy hair back behind her ears. "Like I said I was asleep, but I heard a loud bang or something. I'm not sure. I mean I was asleep but it was like something was shutting. You know, like when you close your locker? That sound. That's when I got off the couch and went to see what was going on."

"Did you see anyone?"

She shook her head. "No, all I saw was Teresa lying on the floor."

49

"Did you hear anything before you heard the sound like the locker closing?"

Emma saw the fear in Jaime's green eyes as she said that she was not sure.

"I thought I was dreaming, but I think I may have heard Teresa yell something. I'm just not sure. I was just out of it."

Myers paused as he captured her comments in his notebook. "Senior Airman Kennedy, do you know if Senior Airman Conklin had any enemies?"

"No!" Jaime blurted, her face becoming alive for the first time. "Everyone loved her!"

With her green eyes blazing, Jaime straightened in her chair and thrust her chin forward. "She was popular, good at her job, got very good grades," she declared defensively. "Teresa didn't do anything wrong!"

Jaime was much more aggressive now and Emma realized that they were seeing another side of her entirely. Emma wondered what Myers thought about their witness' sudden change in demeanor.

Undaunted, Myers pushed a little further. "I understand. But how well did you really know Conklin? What I am getting at is this: did you know her well enough to know whether someone had it out for her? To know if anyone had ever threatened her?"

Shaking her head adamantly, Jaime confronted him. "Look! I told you. Teresa and me were friends. I met her right when she came here. She was a great person who did everything by the book. I don't know why anyone would want to hurt her!"

Emma watched as the airman shred her tissue into pieces, her eyes darting between them. "She's hiding something," Emma surmised to herself. "Why else would she feel the need to have to defend Conklin?"

Across the table, Myers remained silent, his face continuing to reveal nothing.

"Are we done?" Jaime said, rising from her seat, a defiant look on her face. "I really don't think I can answer anymore questions. You said I could stop."

"That's fine." Myers answered coolly, meeting the young woman's glare. "We can call it quits for now if you want. But let's get one thing clear. I don't want you talking about this to anyone other than the Major or me. Do you understand? If I hear you've talked to anyone but the Major or me, I will personally see to it that you do get in trouble! Got it?

"I get it," Jaime retorted. "Now can I go?"

But Myers wasn't going to let her go that easily. He needed to make sure she understood who was in charge. "Just one more thing. Did anyone else know you were in the armory?"

"No," she said, pulling on her coat.

Knowing they'd get nothing further from her, and wanting not to antagonize her further, Emma pushed back from the table and stood up. "Jaime, you've been through a very traumatic situation," she told her. "I'm going to have one of the agents take you over to see Dr. Scarsdale, who is a psychologist over at the hospital. She is a personal friend of mine and can help you work through what you have experienced. I will call her now and tell her you're on your way over."

Emma momentarily wondered if the anxious airman would refuse, but instead Jaime just nodded.

"Yes, Ma'am."

"When you are done there, someone will be waiting for you to take you back to your dorm," Myers said, escorting Jaime to the door.

The young airman stopped and turned a look of disbelief on her face. "But. . ."

"Listen," Myers stopped her. "You can't be alone while whoever killed Airman Conklin is still out there."

It took Jaime a few minutes to register what he was saying, and when it did, her shoulders dropped as did her defiant attitude. Jaime nodded solemnly.

"Don't worry. We'll talk to the Chief and have him arrange for someone to be with you 24/7. In the meantime, Agent Panchen will take you to your doctor's appointment. Here. Take my business card. You can call me anytime."

Myers opened the door and Dan greeted them on the other side. "We'll be in touch," he told the airman. "Remember, don't talk to *anyone* about this. As I said Senior Airman Conklin's murderer is still running lose out there and it's imperative that he doesn't know what we know."

When they were gone, Myers turned towards Emma, his face hard. She could tell by the furrow of his dark brown eyebrows that something was bothering him.

"Did you see how she reacted when I asked if Conklin had any enemies? She's hiding something."

Emma agreed. "At first I thought she was scared about being in trouble because of being in the armory. She seemed so worried about what was going to happen to her. Overly worried, in my opinion for something for which she'll probably just get her hand slapped."

Putting his notebook back in his pocket, Myers shrugged. "She's a kid," he said. "She knows she did something wrong and so she's scared. But I don't think that's all that is bothering our airman. What I do know is that our star witness has a whole new set of problems that she should be more worried about."

Emma wasn't sure what Myers was talking about.

"What do you mean?" she asked.

Myers' strong jaw clenched. "There is one other person besides us who knows that Kennedy was in the armory at the time of the murder."

Emma tried to concentrate on what he was saying, but the intensity of his gaze distracted her, and she stepped back, bumping into the doorframe in the process. Myers didn't appear to notice her discomfort.

"It appears we now know why the killer, so meticulous in every other aspect of his crime, put away the gun so haphazardly. Our little witness there came out and scared him."

Emma shuddered at Myers next words.

"Now the question is . . .will he come after Jaime Kennedy next?"

Chapter 9

Back at the legal office, Emma began to tackle the mountainous pile of paperwork on her desk. She'd left Dan and Myers, who were on their way to get briefed by their team as to what they had found, to tie up some loose ends at her office. But as she tried to read a case report for an upcoming trial, she couldn't get her mind off of Jaime Kennedy and the thought that the killer could come after her next. It was all too surreal to her to think a brutal murderer was out there somewhere on base.

"Hey, there she is," someone exclaimed. "Didn't know if you were going to make it in today. Sleeping in after your big trial, huh?"

Emma looked up at Captain Kyle Fuller and smiled. A fellow JAG, Kyle specialized in contract law. Although technically his job description entailed prosecuting trials, Kyle took on as few of them as possible since he hated the courtroom. At twenty-nine, he was tall and lanky with blond hair that always seemed in need of a trim, bright blue eyes and a boyishly handsome smile.

Emma had known Kyle for about one and a half years. Always quick with a joke, Kyle was fun to be around. They fast became friends and often went to lunch together to hash out one of Emma's cases. They also liked to talk about Kyle's love life or lack thereof.

Kyle was the consummate bachelor who had very specific qualifications for a girlfriend. Emma and the other attorneys tried to set him up with several likely candidates, but Kyle always found something just not quite right with them. Maggie liked to tease Emma that Kyle had a crush on her.

"There's no way he's just going to lunch with you to talk about your trials," Maggie had once said. "You know as well as I do that man doesn't know a thing about the courtroom. No, Ma'am! You take my word, Major. That boy is smitten with you. Did I just say smitten? Man, I sound just like my mother!"

"Earth to Emma!" Kyle once again broke her away from her wandering mind.

"What? Oh, sleep. Yeah, I wish." Emma knew she couldn't reveal anything about the investigation yet. "I had to go to the OSI office this morning," she said, purposefully vague, "to get some information for one of my courts."

Kyle flashed her a charming smile. "You can't get enough of the courtroom drama, can you?"

"If you only knew," she replied dryly.

"So, are we still on for the crud tourney at the club tonight?" he asked. "I've been waiting all week for this." And then, apparently sensing her hesitation, "Oh no you don't. Don't tell me you can't make it. We need you."

The "Club" was the Officer's Club located on base across the street from the Security Forces and OSI buildings. A cross between a night club and a restaurant, it was the place where officers could go and hang out. It had become sort of a ritual to go to the Club on Friday nights after work to drink and play crud, a game developed long ago by Air Force pilots that was played on modified pool table in a specific room decorated with camouflage netting, sand bags, spent munitions and other memorabilia, a unique military tradition. It was a game Emma loved, one with only a passing resemblance to pool in that there was a cue ball, but only had one other colored ball.

Two teams of three to five players matched up against each other to determine the last man standing. Just like air to air combat, the object was to take down all of your opponents while protecting your own, respecting the pilot's flying mantra which was to stay on each other's wings at all costs and to never leave a man behind.

Although the game could get loud, it was for the most part a friendly rivalry and a great way to unwind after a long week. Of course it didn't hurt when Emma's team, "Team JAG," annihilated their opponent.

Tonight there was an unofficial crud tourney at the club. Kyle had already signed "Team JAG" up to compete. Emma surveyed the growing mound of paperwork on her desk skeptically.

"I'm planning on it." Emma replied tentatively not wanting to let Kyle down. "I'm hoping I don't have to do anything for this new case, but I'll let you know."

Kyle's eager face fell. "The case can wait," he said. "I need you. The team needs you. Besides, the first round's on me."

"I'll let you get back to it so you'll be ready and able to make it tonight." And then without giving her a chance to back out, Kyle disappeared out the door.

After the day and night she'd just had, Emma could really use a beer, something to relieve the tension the day had generated. However, she knew herself well enough to be sure that she had to make at least a dent in this pile first.

She had just begun to review the first trial brief when Barb, her boss's secretary, called her to say that Lieutenant Colonel Franks would like to see her in his office now.

Lieutenant Colonel James "Jim" Franks had been in the Air Force sixteen years. Originally from New Jersey, he had entered the Air Force right out of college, starting out in the Communications Squadron where he worked for three years before being accepted into law school.

Franks had been stationed at Winburg for almost three years and joked that his love for the schnitzel was the reason behind his ever expanding waistline. After almost failing his fitness test about two months ago, Franks implemented a new physical training program for the legal office staff. The plan required everyone to meet at 0530 at least three days a week to work out together in the gym. Although his intentions were good, Franks' early morning meetings often prevented him from joining his staff. As a result while the rest of them got fitter, Franks' stomach continued to expand.

But despite this setback, Franks was a terrific boss. Although he was only forty-five, Franks was a fatherly figure who truly cared about his people and always put them first. His warm and gentle smile always greeted Emma regardless of what issues or problems he was facing. It never ceased to amaze Emma how her boss never let his hectic schedule get to him. His open door policy remained constant and Emma knew she could always go to him to talk about a witness or trial strategy. She felt very lucky to have such a supportive boss.

Upon entering the small room which served as a waiting area for those wishing to speak with Franks, Emma said good morning to his secretary.

Barb jerked her thumb towards the boss's closed door behind her. "Well at least some of us are having a good morning."

"That good, huh? And it's still early in the morning."

Barb Brinkman had been the secretary for the Staff Judge Advocate, lead attorney at Winburg for twenty-two years. If you wanted to know anything about the legal office or the entire base for that matter, Barb was the lady to ask. There was not much that went on within the walls of the legal office to which Barb was not privy to.

The phone beeped on Barb's desk. "Go on in," she said, going back to her newspaper.

As soon as she walked in the door, Emma knew her normally congenial boss was in a bad mood. Sitting behind his large oak desk, he was frowning at a paper he held in his hands.

"First of all, thanks for taking the call last night and going to the armory," he said when she was seated on the black leather chair facing him. "I know you had just come from the Downs' trial and couldn't have gotten a lot of sleep."

"Not a problem, Sir."

"Well unfortunately, until this guy is caught there are going to be a lot of late nights." Franks said, rubbing the bridge of his nose under his glasses. "As you know I had a meeting with the General Brandt and Colonel Carlson this morning. The Colonel briefed us on what they know so far, which isn't much. As you can imagine the General is very concerned about the safety of his base and stressed the need for the utmost discretion in what we communicate about the case and to whom."

Emma knew it would be hard to keep something as major as a murder a secret on base the size of Winburg.

After quickly briefing him on what she knew, Franks asked her to have a detailed report on what she learned from Kennedy on his desk by the afternoon.

Putting the paper down on his desk, Franks' tired eyes searched hers and Emma wasn't sure what she was seeing in them.

"Emma," he said, "I want you to know that I think it is highly unusual for a JAG to be involved at this stage of a criminal investigation. Colonel Carlson made it clear he wants you involved to make sure all rules are followed and that nothing taints the evidence so we have a solid case against this guy once he is caught. I voiced my disagreement with Colonel Carlson's request to General Brandt and asked that you be pulled off the investigation."

Emma fought back the urge to argue why she should be involved in the case. She was already too deep into the case and didn't want to have to sit on the sidelines now.

"So, am I off the case, Sir?"

Franks frowned and shook his head. "No, but that doesn't mean I am not going to keep trying."

Suddenly he stood up and came around to her side of the desk sitting down in the chair next to hers. "Emma," he said putting his hand on her arm, "this could potentially be a very dangerous case and I don't want to see you or any other of my attorneys harmed in any way."

Emma was grateful for her boss' concern but felt he was being a little bit dramatic. She could take care of herself and she'd given him no reason to think otherwise.

"I want you to promise me that you will keep me apprised of everything you learn," he continued. "But I don't want anyone else in the office involved, okay?" Franks stood up, indicating their conversation was finished. "Be careful out there."

Emma promised she would and was about to leave when he put his hand on her shoulder. "Emma," he said gravely, "there are a lot of things that go on around this base that neither you nor I are privy to. You must remember that the person who did this could be *anyone* out there and right now he has the complete advantage."

"What do you mean?" she asked and felt his hand tighten on her shoulder.

"Just remember that the killer is waiting for us to make our move. Emma, I don't want you to be caught in the middle if we make the wrong one."

Chapter 10

Maggie Prane, wearing a somber expression, was waiting for Emma when she returned to her office.

"What is the maximum punishment for assault?" she asked.

"Six months," Emma told her. "Why? Do we have a new case coming in?"

"Nope," Maggie replied noncommittally following Emma into her office. "I just needed to know so I can prepare my husband for how long I will be gone after I strangle Captain Mullen."

For a moment distracted, Emma looked at her, puzzled. Only when Maggie grinned did she understand.

"Well," Emma said dramatically pulling back her sleeve to reveal her watch. "That has got to be a record. It's only 1000 and you're already to take him down, huh?"

"Yep," Maggie chuckled. "That kid needs to be sent back to JAG school. He has no clue how to prepare witnesses, or really do anything for that matter. By the way, we got word from the judge the hearing will be on Tuesday."

Emma knew Maggie well enough to know she need something and fought back the urge to sigh. The mound of paperwork surrounding her would just have to wait a little while longer. "What can I do to help?" she asked.

"Not much, I promise. Just a swift kick in the butt would do to get him going. I can take care of the rest."

"Okay, where is he?"

"He hasn't left his office since early this morning when I gave him a list of things that needed to be done before the hearing," Maggie said. "Oh and you can congratulate me. I think I have a new record. This time I didn't even have to say anything to him and he's already scared of me. Man, I'm good!" Obviously pleased with herself, Maggie left the room.

Emma found Mullen just where Maggie said he would be, hunched over his desk, working feverishly. "How's it going, John?"

Sweat beaded on his brow and upper lip, which was twitching either from nerves or from coffee. After spying four empty cups of coffee on his desk, Emma guessed the latter.

"What? Oh hey, Major." John said wiping his brow. "Is it hot in here or is it just me?

"You may want to lay off the coffee, John."

"Good point," he said, "maybe I'll switch to Mountain Dew."

"That's sure to help," Emma said dryly, but the irony apparently escaped John who was already lost in thought.

"Okay, John," Emma said, taking a seat in front of his desk. "What have we got for the sentencing hearing?"

"Six witnesses" John replied anxiously. "Four military and two civilian. There's also one letter of reprimand for failure to report to duty on time and his three EPRs."

"What do his EPRs look like?"

EPRs or enlisted performance reports were required each year on every enlisted airman. Filled out by his supervisor, they depict how he or she performs on the job and overall as a member of the military and become part of his permanent file. The prosecution is required to present the accused's EPRs in the sentencing hearing to give the judge or jury an opportunity to learn more about the accused's performance.

A brief scan of Downs' reports revealed little of a damaging nature. Downs was, apparently, an average worker who did just enough to get by.

"Master Sergeant Prane will help you get your documentary evidence together," Emma told the young lawyer. "Make sure you label everything and make copies for the jury and judge. Also be sure to give a copy to the Defense beforehand."

John bent over his notepad, feverishly writing down what she was saying.

"John," she finally said when he didn't stop writing. "John!"

He looked up sheepishly as she shoved a paper in front of him.

"Here are some standard questions I ask sentencing witnesses in drug cases," Emma explained. "Look these over and use them as a guideline. Think about what you want to get across to the jury. What do you want them to know about Derek Downs? What about him makes his crime more aggravating and egregious? Prepare your questions and run them by me before you prep your witnesses."

Emma paused briefly to see if John was absorbing what she was telling him.

"Also, don't forget to prep your witnesses," she went on after he nodded. "Remember that civilian witnesses need special attention since they've never been in military courtroom before. Master Sergeant Prane will help with the logistics of getting base passes and maps. Your job is to make sure they understand exactly what is going to happen in the courtroom, how they should act on a military installation; and so on. You don't want them to inadvertently offend your jury members."

"Got it! Anything else?"

"Yes. Go over the sentencing instructions and determine which ones you want to ask the judge to give to the members. Again, run this by me first. Read and re-read what is required of you by the UCMJ as a prosecutor. And then prepare your sentencing argument and go over it again and again. Once you're ready, you'll argue in front of me as your mock judge."

The blood drained from John's face. "You mean I need to do my whole sentencing argument in front of you?"

"Yes," Emma replied calmly. "Relax. I know it sounds daunting, but when I was a new JAG my mentor made me argue in front of her. As much as I hated it, it made me more relaxed in the courtroom. She figured if I could say it in front of her, my toughest critic, the jury would be a snap. And you know what? She was right."

Anxious to get back to her own work, Emma stood up. "You've got a lot to do between now and the hearing so I'll leave you to it."

Emma paused as she looked at the young captain whose face was so pale his freckles stood out vividly. Remembering her first days in the legal profession, Emma pushed her own anxieties from the morning away and felt empathy for him.

"It will be okay John," she promised him. "Once you get one or two of these under your belt, they'll seem a lot less formidable. And don't forget I will be right by your side during the hearing. Trust me, you'll do fine."

"I know," John replied, although Emma wasn't sure he believed it.

On her way back to her office, Emma remembered vividly how nervous she had been when she had stood in front of her first jury, most of them higher ranked than she. Their eyes had drilled into her as she had argued the words she'd practiced for hours, and when she finally sat down, she had been convinced that they had not believed a word she had just said. Of course, that was before she figured out how to read the jury members on what they were thinking or how they were reacting to the case.

Speaking of reactions, Emma's mind flew back to her boss and their meeting earlier. It surprised her that he told the General he wanted Emma off the case, especially since his only argument to her was that he wanted her to be safe. Franks had personally assigned her to tough cases before where she sat face to face with rapists, child molesters, and those who had pulled knives and guns on other airman and not once had Franks tried to pull her off.

Emma knew this case was different because she had been assigned to the initial investigation, but still something wasn't quite right. Emma couldn't shake the feeling that Franks was holding back something from her.

Chapter 11

Emma spent the rest of the morning trying to make a dent in the pile of papers on her desk. Dan had called earlier in the day letting her know he and Myers were going to interview some people over the phone, but that she didn't need to be there.

"Oh, so he's keeping me out of the investigation, huh?" she'd replied trying to keep her voice light, but inside angry about being left out.

"No, that's not it," Dan replied quickly. "He just wanted to get some preliminary interviews done and then bring you in for the major players. We'll call you later."

Emma had tried not to let it bother her as she diligently worked through the morning. She would have to have another word with Myers about keeping her out of the loop.

Emma was just getting ready to take a short break to eat the salad she bought for lunch when her phone rang. Myers didn't even bother to say hello.

"Major, what do you know about Tech Sergeant Robert Dort, the victim's supervisor?"

"Hello to you, too, Agent Myers. Dort? Not much. I've seen him around the base, and have talked to him a few times about some of his airmen. He seems to be pretty straight forward. Why?"

"Dan and I are looking at Conklin's personnel file and there is a Letter of Reprimand in it signed by Dort, dated February 7th of this year."

"No doubt you're aware of the fact that it's not at all unusual for an airman to have a LOR in their file."

"I understand that, Major," Myers shot back. "But since you're the *expert*, why don't you tell me if it's usual for an airman to receive a LOR for failure to follow written procedures in the armory she guards."

Undeterred by his dig, Emma calmly replied "Yes, you are right, Agent. This *is* my area of expertise. You want to be more specific?"

"Let me spell it out for you," he replied. "Like I said, Dort gave Conklin this LOR for failure to follow written procedures in the armory. So I called to ask him about this. Much to my surprise he says he specifically remembers giving this to her. He tells me it was for allowing an unauthorized person in the armory with her while she was on duty.

"Where this gets interesting," Myers continued, "is when he tells me that this wasn't the first time she'd broken the rules. Apparently, he'd previously ordered her to stop and she blatantly disregarded his order."

"Really." Lapsing into a prosecutorial mindset, Emma processed this information. "If this wasn't her first time, why just an LOR? If he had consulted the legal office, like he was supposed to, we would have recommended she be given an Article 15 because she was a repeat offender. Plus she disregarded a direct order."

An Article 15 was a form of nonjudicial punishment which a commander may offer to a member he or she has reason to believe committed a minor offense punishable under the UCMJ instead of formally charging them and taking them to trial. Article 15s were often used for repeat offenders of minor crimes since they afford limited punishment, which a LOR did not.

"I'm glad to see you're finally following me." His sarcasm cut through the phone line. "But get this, that's not even the most interesting part."

"Okay, you have my attention," she responded.

"After I strongly *urged* Dort to tell me everything as I pointed out it was his duty to do, he told me that actually he did push for an Article 15, but was shot down."

"Shot down? By whom?"

"The First Shirt. Seems your Chief told Dort that he'd talked it over with Carlson and your boss and they felt her offenses didn't warrant a 15. Dort made it very clear to me that he was not too happy with their decision. In fact, he pressed them for an explanation."

"Did they give him one?"

"Nope, basically the Chief just told him to shut up and do as he was told. And get this? When Dort asked for Conklin to be taken off armory duty he was again shot down and ordered to keep her on the schedule. Let me tell you, this didn't set well with Dort who assured me he takes his job of securing the armory very seriously. He let me know that after this incident, Dort didn't trust Conklin one bit. So he made sure to always put her on the day shift so he could keep his eye on her. He also tried to make sure she was always paired with another guard, so she wouldn't be alone."

"That's interesting," Emma broke in, "since no one else was on duty last night with her."

"I'm not finished. Dort was furious when he heard the Chief had asked Conklin to cover the shift last night. I asked him if the Chief made it a habit to mess with the armory schedule and he said no. Boy, was he pissed. Dort made sure I understood it was his and only his duty to assign guards to the shifts."

"I've known the Chief to be overprotective of his troops," Emma protested. "Maybe he found out at the last minute about that airman getting sick so he didn't have time to run it past Sergeant Dort."

"But even if you bought that," Myers persuaded, "why would he ask Conklin to cover when he knew her history of not following proper procedures and inviting guests to keep her company while she was on duty? Why not ask someone else?"

"You got me there. I guess that's a question only the Chief can answer."

"Well," Myers said seriously, "that's not the only question I have for your chief."

"Meaning?"

"Meaning," Myers replied, "I'd like to ask him how someone in his squadron gets a LOR, but it's not mentioned in her EPR. Something like this is required to be written in an airman's EPR, isn't it?"

"Well, you can't put the punishment in there," Emma explained. "So they couldn't have mentioned she got an LOR. But they could have mentioned the basis or action that lead to the LOR and in fact, many times we recommend they do put this in. So it's not in there?"

"Nope, not a word. In fact, she has fives across the board. Says here she 'is a stellar troop who exhibits all of the characteristics of a top level performer.' Yadda Yadda."

A "5" is the highest score you could get on your EPR and usually reserved for the truly stellar performers. The fact Conklin who obviously broke the rules had received 5's troubled Emma.

"What did Dort have to say for himself about giving a troop who has been disciplined straight 5's?" she asked.

"Humph," Myers snorted. "He told me, pretty rudely I may add, to go ask the Chief."

"Looks like the Chief does have a lot of explaining to do."

"Well, well. You are catching on, Major."

Before Emma had a chance to respond, Myers went on, his tone cool.

"We also talked to some of Conklin's dorm buddies and members of her squadron. Now mind you we didn't tell them why, I know the official word hasn't gone out yet about her death. But we needed to find out more about our victim. The point is that they all say pretty much the same thing, which is nothing. Looks like she kept to herself and didn't go out of her way to make friends. To the best of their knowledge, she was either working or gone. I asked if they knew where she went and some thought the gym since they'd seen her there. Others didn't know, figured she had a boyfriend or something. None of them were aware of anyone who hated her or had it out for her. Most of them did give me Kennedy's name as someone who hung out with Conklin a lot. They told me she'd probably know the most about Conklin."

"Sounds like Kennedy's not only your sole witness to what happened," she said slowly, trying to keep her voice calm although she still felt a slight sting from his earlier comment, "but she's also the only one who really knows your victim."

On the other end, Emma could hear Myers say something to someone else before answering her. "Yeah," he replied, "and we know how just much she loves to talk. I'm going to try to talk to Conklin's parents and some people back home this afternoon to see what they can give me."

The sting was suddenly stronger as she learned Myers intended on excluding her from these key interviews.

"Great!" Emma said sarcastically. "I'll expect a full briefing on what you learn from them, ASAP," she added, hanging up the phone.

"What a pig!" she muttered before attacking her salad with a fury that rightfully should have been reserved for him.

Chapter 12

Several hours later, Emma was just finishing up answering the last of her emails when Kyle popped his head into her office.

"Time to go kick some pilot butt!" he said enthusiastically. Although he still wore his BDUs which were now slightly wrinkled from the day's work, a waft of strong cologne signaled that he was ready to go to the Club.

Emma was amazed to see that it was six o'clock. She had been so busy she hadn't even noticed the sun had gone down, leaving it dark outside her window. There was still work left for her to do, but she didn't have the heart to refuse him.

"Okay," she said pushing the papers into new stacks hoping to make it look like she had accomplished more than she really had. "Let me turn off my computer and I'll meet you downstairs."

Eager to get going, Kyle was already heading back to his office "You're on!"

Emma rubbed her pounding forehead and heaved a sigh. Most of her afternoon was spent helping John go over witness questions and prepping a couple of them. Although she felt the time was well spent since, in the end, John seemed a little less nervous, she was now even more behind on her own work. Dan had called her an hour ago and told her they were at a standstill with the interviews until they got some call backs so there was nothing she needed to do right then in the case.

Throwing some paperwork into her beat up black leather briefcase, and admonishing herself to work on it over the weekend, she put on her coat, quickly checked her makeup in the small mirror she kept in her bottom her desk drawer, put on a new coat of lip gloss and slammed the drawer shut. After the week she just had, one that had been made even more complicated by Conklin's murder, Emma felt she more than deserved a break. It was, she thought, time to kick back with her friends and have some fun.

The Club was always hopping on Friday evenings and tonight was no exception. A sea of camouflage, blue and green met them when they walked into the bar. There was no hard fast rule on base as to which uniform a person had to wear. But by and large most people chose to wear the more comfortable BDUs.

The olive green jumpsuits were reserved for the pilots who stood out in the dense crowd. Over the years, a friendly rivalry had built between the pilots and the rest of the officers. The pilots liked to argue the only reason the rest of the officers were here was because of them.

"You wouldn't even have a job, if it weren't for those of us who actually know how to fly a plane," they'd tease. "Don't forget this is the *Air Force*."

So for the most part, the other officers, who by the way, far outnumbered the pilots, did the best they could to shut up their green suited friends by beating them at the crud table.

The bar in the club was relatively new and featured a long narrow room lined on one side by a mahogany bar and a giant popcorn machine that didn't stop popping until the wee hours of the night. Pictures of F15, 16s and A10s, all planes flown out of Winburg, flanked a wide doorway that opened to the crud room.

After leading her to a table near the back wall where the other attorneys were already sitting, Kyle excused himself and went to enter their names on the game sign-up board as "Team JAG."

Six of the eleven attorneys that made the legal office were seated at the long table. Captain Susan Sparks had been in the Air Force for five years. Currently, she held the unenviable job as Chief of Legal Assistance whose main responsibility was to make sure all of the attorneys helped clients during legal assistance hours.

Military members and their dependants were entitled to free legal advice on base. Most came with questions about wills, divorce, and child support. But others came with more tricky questions dealing with some obscure law in their home state. The lucky attorney who took on this sort of client was in for several hours of tedious research as a result. So needless to say, legal assistance wasn't exactly a favorite on most attorneys' lists.

But Susan was the perfect person for the job, primarily because, at six foot one, she towered over most of the people in the office making it very hard for anyone to say no to her. However, although formidable in size, once Emma had come to know her, she had discovered that the redhead was really a softy at heart, someone who loved helping people and didn't mind a bit being holed up in her office for hours with a client.

To Susan's left was Captain Marsha Sloan, one of only four attorneys in the office who were married. At first glance, she could easily have been mistaken for a librarian. Her mousy brown hair and thin wire rimmed glasses did nothing to distract from this stereotype.

Next to Marsha sat Captain Chase Saunders, the unofficial leader of the "Three Amigo" bachelors in the office.

Upon arriving at Winburg eighteen months ago, Chase had made it clear that he had sworn off women, or at least any committed relationship with a woman. The young captain with black wavy hair wanted, instead, to commit to having a good time all of the time. And this, he told to anyone who cared to listen, included finding the best beer in Germany, even if that meant making a trip to every little tavern in every little village in the country.

Determined not to take on this momentous task alone, Chase immediately solicited the other bachelors, Captain Greg Banks, the Claims Officer, and Kyle to help him in his conquest. So every weekend the three amigos searched for the perfect beer, with such diligence that often they didn't even make it out of their own village.

Emma's Deputy Chief of Military Justice and the Deputy Staff Judge Advocate rounded out the team.

The only missing attorneys included John, who was probably still back at the legal office prepping for his hearing, and Frank Simmons and Frau Hanna Bremmer, the only two civilian attorneys in the office.

Kyle returned with two beers. "Thanks, man," she said appreciatively. "I need this after the week I've had."

"Nothing like a good beer and an exciting game of crud to wash away the crap we deal with during the work week." Kyle held his glass up saluting the others.

He then gestured to a group of pilots at the next table. "Oh, and by the way, team "Top Gun" said they're going to crush us tonight so we might as well get another pitcher now since we won't be in the game that long."

"Don't worry, boys," Chase said loudly, again raising his glass. "The next round will be on you after we kick your ass! Make sure our pitcher is the good stuff. We don't want any cheap shit!"

"Don't worry Saunders," someone from the other team countered, "it won't be the beer that's cheap. Only the people drinking it!"

"Salut!" Someone in the room called out and everyone, including Emma cheered, and she felt the stress of the day slip away. This was, she thought, much better.

"Uh, oh," Kyle whispered. "Don't look now but our very own version of the Mod Squad just walked in the door." Emma followed Kyle's gaze and immediately took another drink of her beer.

"So much for relaxing," she muttered, eyes fixing on the frothy golden liquid in front of her.

"Holy crap!" Susan swore lustily. "That hunk with Agent Panchen can inspect me anytime. Wow! He's gorgeous!"

"It looks like you'll get your chance," Marsha added. "They're headed our way."

Before Emma could escape or warn Susan, Myers and Dan were standing beside the table.

"Well if my favorite attorneys aren't all here," Dan greeted them cheerfully. "Mind if we join you?"

Susan quickly moved her chair over making space between her and Emma. "Sure," she said, "you gentlemen can scoot your chairs in here"

Emma glared at Susan who was too busy staring dreamily up at Myers to notice.

"Everyone, this is Agent Eric Myers from OSI European Headquarters at Ramstein," Dan announced.

"Please call me Eric," Myers said after Dan had performed introductions. Emma was surprised that he actually acted friendly.

Dan sat down moving his chair in such a way that Emma was forced to sit beside Myers, so close, in fact, that his thighs brushed against hers.

"Major," Myers acknowledged her.

"So," Kyle said, clearly curious. "You two already know each other?"

"Yeah, I met him when I was over at OSI this morning," Emma said before Myers could open his mouth. She wasn't ready to reveal her role in the investigation yet. Plus she didn't want anyone to think she and Myers were in any way connected.

"I see." Kyle said in a way that told Emma that he was summing up Myers as potential competition which, given the fact that she despised the man, was at the very least ironic.

Everyone joined Myers and Dan in ordering another beer. While the others decided what they wanted to eat, Susan peppered Myers with questions about himself, ignoring Dan who was squeezed between them. For some reason, the fact that Myers was clearly doing his best to be charming, pissed Emma who did her best to focus on the conversation across the table.

After a few minutes of being unable to keep herself from eavesdropping, Emma decided to give up. Since when, she wondered, had he become a gentleman? It must be that he saved his demonic side for her exclusively. With Myers preoccupied with answering Susan's questions, Emma sized up "the enemy."

Myers had taken off his suit jacket and tie and unbuttoned his two top buttons of his shirt, and perhaps because of that, Emma was uncomfortably aware of the muscular masculinity of him.

Shit! She felt herself flush as he caught her looking at him, but, she refused to look away. There was no way he was going to think she was somehow bothered by him.

A grin slowly spread across his handsome face as he raised his glass to her. "I was just telling your coworkers how you were giving us your legal perspective on one of our cases. So tell us, Major, how are you *enjoying* your time working with us. It appears you've had a little time to study us."

His meaning not lost on her, Emma returned his salute. "Well Agent Myers, I haven't made up my mind yet. I'm still sizing up your operation."

"Here's hoping you have more time to size us up," he said, arching his dark brown eyebrows.

"So who's ready to play?" Kyle interrupted them. "You play crud, Eric?"

He shrugged. "I've played a couple of times."

"Good!" Susan reached across Dan and put her hand on Myers' muscular forearm. "We could use you on our team."

"We already have a full team," Emma protested, "and I'm sure Myers has something better to do tonight."

"No, Susan's right, Emma," Marsha chimed in. "I can't stay tonight. Jerry and the kids are waiting for me. We're going to Brussels tomorrow for the weekend. In fact, I'd better get going. I still have to pack." Getting up from the table, she held out her hand. "Nice meeting you, Eric. And since it looks like you'll be my replacement, make sure you don't embarrass me. Okay?"

"But what about you, Dan?" Emma asked desperate to keep Myers from ruining her evening. "Don't you want to play?"

"Sorry Major," he replied. "I've got to go, too. I came here for a quick one, but since Marsha's leaving, I'll walk her out. See ya, everyone. Good luck with the game."

As Marsha and Dan left the table, Emma leaned over to Myers and hissed, "Don't you have some witnesses to harass or something?"

"Nope, I think I'll stay here and just harass you," he replied, his eyes twinkling with amusement. "Besides, this has turned out to be much more fun that I expected."

Chapter 13

After helping herself to some popcorn from the bar, Emma reluctantly joined the others in the crud room which was now packed with players and fans. Emma playfully joked with several of the people she knew as she made her way to "Team JAG's" table. Susan, standing very close to, was pointing out their members of their opposing team. Tall as she was, Susan still had to look up at Myers who stood about an inch over her.

Seeing her friend brush against him every time she moved, Emma promised herself that she'd have a talk with her. It was important that Susan realize that Agent Myers was very far from being the sort of man she thought he was. Ignoring the two of them, Emma went to stand by Kyle and Chase who were getting ready to give their obligatory pep talk to pump up the team.

"Okay, guys," Chase announced. "You know the drill. We play swift, we play hard and we crush them. Play by the rules, but remember to stretch them if the situation calls for it. Eric, you said you've played so just follow our lead."

As the captain of the team, Chase went first, easily annihilating his first opponent by striking the colored ball into the pocket on his return strike. Emma nursed her beer and stood by the table waiting for her turn.

Players sprinted around the table, quickly switching out. "Mort!" the crowd called out when Susan's ball stopped before she could hit it.

"Damn!" she cried out, coming back to the table.

Greg was next. "Better get ready!" he yelled, running up to the table, positioning himself face to face with the pilot who opposed him and sliding the cue ball down the table where it missed its target by inches.

The pilot at the other end yawned. "Ready for what?" he demanded.

Biting his lip, Greg tried again. Finding the perfect spot for his ball, he let it go. Bouncing off the side of the table, it smacked into the colored ball, at which time Kyle raced to the table, switching places with Greg and fiercely protecting the precious colored ball. In part because of his height, he easily blocked the ball before the shorter Top Gun pilot could try to strike again.

"Mort!" The referee called out, indicating the ball was dead. The crowd went wild.

Myers was up. Suddenly wanting to see him fail at something, Emma silently cheered for the opposing team. However, Myers effortlessly rammed the colored ball on his first try. Team JAG roared as the ball came to a stop before the pilot could hit it. Much as she hated to admit it, Emma realized Agent Myers obviously knew his way around the crud table.

The game went on as, one by one, the players started to fall, their three lives exhausted. Emma was down to one life when the judge called for a break after one of the pilots bumped into a pitcher of beer spilling it all over the table and carpet. When the teams went back to their respective corners to wait out the clean up, Emma reached for a handful of popcorn only to see Myers appear by her side.

"Where's your girlfriend?" Emma retorted, immediately regretting the words as they came out of her mouth.

Myers raised his eyebrow. "You mean Susan? Why, Major, you better be careful. You almost sound like you are jealous."

"In your dreams," Emma muttered before quickly changing the subject. "So did you get a hold of Conklin's parents?"

"Yes, but they didn't give me a lot. She was a good daughter from a very small rural farming town in South Dakota. I talked to the dad as her mom was packing getting ready to come over here. There are two older brothers and one older sister. Brothers are now married and work on the farm with Dad. Sister is married off but didn't move too far away from home. Sounds like Conklin was quite a bit younger than her brothers and sisters. My guess is she was an 'oops'."

As she listened to him, Emma was unnerved to discover herself warming up to the man who so easily fit in with her friends.

Myers took a swig of his beer. "I asked him if Conklin had any problems in school or anyone who may not like her, but he said no. Seems to me he quickly changed the subject, but I could be wrong. It was hard to get a lot from him. He was clearly upset about his daughter's death. He's working with her squadron to get over here to bring the body back home. It looks like they'll be here either Monday or Tuesday. I'll try to talk to them in person when they are here to see if I can get anything more out of them."

"It must be really hard on them to lose their daughter this way." Emma mused. "If you want, I can come with you to interview them. Maybe I can get through to the mom. The whole woman- to-woman bit has worked for me in the past."

Emma couldn't read the expression on Myers's face, but Emma took his silence as resistance to her having a major role in the parents' interview.

Suddenly Kyle appeared at her side.

"Okay, Emma. You're up," he said, putting one arm around her. "No pressure, now. But it all comes down to your shot. Top Gun is on their last leg. They only have one player left and you need to take him down. You can do it. I know you can."

Emma felt a surge of adrenaline as she grabbed the ball off the table, and slammed it down. The room grew still as everyone held their breath for what could be the last round.

"Watch out boys," Susan taunted the opposing team, unaware Emma's aggression had nothing to do with the game. "This girl's all business."

Completely aware that all eyes were on her, Emma carefully positioned her ball. "Come on, baby!" she whispered.

She rolled the ball on the table and . . . missed!

"Crap!"

Cheers roared around her as the members of Top Gun slapped their man's back.

Kyle held up his hands to quite the exuberant pilots.

"Oh calm down!" he told them. "She's just getting warmed up!" And then, in a low voice to Emma, "Remember no pressure."

Determined not to fail in front of Myers, Emma leaned low over the table. Squinting against the overhead light, she placed her ball in the perfect spot, and for a brief second closed her eyes.

"Smack!"

"Woo-hoo!" Team JAG cried and, opening her eyes, she saw that her ball had hit the colored ball perfectly. Suddenly Myers came out of nowhere and pushed Emma to the side. His muscular frame guarded the ball. An equally muscular pilot grabbed the cue ball and faced Myers.

The two squared off as the pilot rolled the ball, trying to get it past Myers' large hands.

"Yes!" Excitement rushed through her as the colored ball stopped before the pilot could try again.

Emma threw her hands up in victory as her team surrounded her, hugging her and slapping her raised hand.

After the last teammate had congratulated her, Emma caught sight of Myers who was still standing by the table receiving his fair share of kudos. Their eyes met and held as he raised his hand to her in a salute. Resisting the urge to smile at him, Emma let herself be swept away by Chase as he led his team to the bar.

"As promised, next round's on Top Gun!" he shouted. "Sorry guys, you know the rules. You lose, you buy the booze!"

After everyone had finished reliving the game, some members of her team started to leave. Suddenly Emma felt a hand on her arm. "We need to talk about your role in this investigation," Myers said leading her away from the bar to a private corner of the room.

"There's nothing to talk about. You heard Carlson. Looks like you're stuck with me."

"Emma, you're a JAG. You're not trained to investigate a murder. I can't take any chances here. The murderer is still running around on this base."

"I have an idea, Agent Myers," Emma retorted, her eyes blazing. "Why don't you stop fighting me and actually let me show you what I can do. You're spending so much time trying to keep me out of the investigation that you *are* taking chances by not using me and what I can bring to this case."

Myers' dark eyes narrowed. "Okay, Major," he finally replied. "You want to play with the big boys? Fine. I hope you didn't have any plans this weekend, because you don't anymore. I have a meeting with the Chief at his office at 0800 tomorrow. Be there!"

And with that he left, leaving Emma wondering if she just won a victory or started a war.

Chapter 14

Knees aching, I crouched close to the hard cold building. She doesn't see me! My heart races excitedly as the bitch and her poor excuse for an escort walk within inches of where I remain hidden in the dark shadows.

The crisp night air sends shivers down my back.

She's so close! Wait. What's she doing? Shit, she'd stopped right in front of me.

I can see the beads of sweat on her forehead as she wipes it with the back of her sleeve. Her sweatshirt is stained dark around her neck and armpits from her workout. Ha! How could she ever think she could get that ugly body into shape?

She's talking to someone but I can't see them from my position. Her little escort yawns looking bored. God, I could reach out right now and touch her. The realization makes me almost dizzy. "Snap," I whisper ever so slightly imagining her neck breaking beneath my hands. A rush of adrenaline courses through me. Shit, the temptation is almost overwhelming.

But no, I must wait. I can't mess up again. I should have known she'd be there this morning! I can't believe I didn't think of it. I pinch the flesh between my fingers until my arm aches. The pain comforts me and clams my head.

Kennedy says goodbye to her friend and unlocks the door to her dorm room and she and the escort go inside. The lights come on and her silhouette mocks me through the thin beige curtain.

It's a pity really now that she talked to that cocky OSI agent and the lawyer. It might complicate the plan a bit, but I'll just have to deal with them, too.

Soon.

The sidewalk is bare as I move out from behind my cover. Slowly I walk past the dorm window. No evidence left behind!

Chapter 15

When she arrived at the Chief's office at exactly 0750 the next morning, Emma was pleased to have beaten Myers to the appointment, although when her alarm had gone off earlier, she hadn't been so happy. Usually Saturday's were reserved for exploring a new village or just peacefully enjoying the outdoors.

Now as she stood in the hallway of the Security Forces building, Emma knew today would be anything but peaceful.

Five minutes passed before she spotted Myers wearing a long sleeve black polo shirt and crisp khaki pants. For some reason, it irritated her that he looked as good in casual clothes as he did in a suit.

"Major," he said, leaning on the wall a few feet from her.

"Agent Myers."

Emma wasn't sure if it was the beer or the man beside her that made her head suddenly feel worse. All she was sure of was that she needed an aspirin.

They stood beside each other not saying a word until, about two minutes later Dan arrived. He too wore khaki pants that hung on his lanky frame.

"I just got done going through Conklin's dorm room for the second time." Dan told them, looking from one to the other as though he sensed the tension. "As I told you earlier, Myers, there wasn't much there: uniforms, pictures of family, textbooks. We did find a journal."

This news caught both of their attention. Emma could see that Dan was eager to impress Myers. And she guessed why. If he handled this case right, it could mean huge opportunities for him at the Major Command level.

"Based on her writing," he went on eagerly, "it appears that Conklin was in love with someone."

"Does it say who?" Myers asked.

"That's the curious part. She briefly mentions going to dinner, and dancing with this man, but never names him. It sounds like they didn't do anything in public. But she was definitely into him. Maybe we've got a lead."

"It's not totally out of the norm," Emma pointed out, "for a girl to leave out the name of her love interest in a journal. Particularly if she's afraid someone might read it."

Myers looked at her. "Speaking from experience, Major?"

Emma ignored him. "I definitely think you should check into this, but I just don't want you to get too worked up about it. It also wouldn't be unusual for a young woman to make her dates seem more romantic and secretive than they really are. I'm sure this is something your dates have to do, isn't that right, Agent Myers?"

Before he could answer, the Chief came out of his office exactly at 0800, dressed in jeans and loafers, a long sleeved blue oxford tight over his barrel chest. By the frown on his face it was obvious he was none too happy to see them.

"Good morning, Major, Agents Myers and Panchen," he greeted them hurriedly. "Please come in."

As he turned back, Dan stopped the other two. "I wanted you to know we also found a key of some sort. It looks like to me the same key I use to get into my lockbox at the bank, but I'm having the guys check into it."

Myers nodded approvingly. "Let me know when they find out."

The walls of the Chief's spacious office were covered with awards and plaques. The furniture consisted only of a desk and a standard black vinyl couch with two chairs facing it.

"Sorry about the civi's," he said when they were seated. "But my wife and I were scheduled to go to Luxemburg City this morning so we're heading out after this meeting. I wanted to get a head start on the traffic."

"Not a problem," Myers replied, clearly not really caring where the Chief was going as long as he gave them some answers. "This shouldn't take long."

Emma watched the Chief shift uncomfortably on the couch. Although she had met with him several times to talk about his airmen before, she had never seen him so uptight. He fussed with the buttons on his collar almost as if they were choking him.

"Thanks for meeting us, Chief," she said, trying to mitigate Agent Myers' abruptness. "We just have a couple of things we need to clear up about Senior Airman Conklin's death and then you'll be on your way."

Myers took charge. "First off," he said, "where were you at around 0230 early yesterday morning?"

"Are you treating me as a suspect?"

"Of course not," Dan said, "That's a standard question we have to ask everyone."

Emma watched the First Shirt clench his jaw and had to admire Myers' interviewing tactic of getting right to the point to see if his witness was hiding anything. And in this case, Emma thought, it appeared that clearly he was, and yet, with a smile plastered on his broad face, he swore that he had been in bed with his wife. When Myers continued to press him, he hesitated before saying that he got a call from Senior Airman Kennedy that night.

"She was hysterical," he said. "She told me that something had happened to Teresa Conklin in the armory. I could hardly understand her. She was crying kept saying over and over 'Oh God, Teresa!' I told her I'd be right there."

"Is that all she said to you? "Oh God Teresa!"

"Well, no actually. She screamed at me."

"What do you mean she screamed at you?"

"She asked me how I could have let this happen to her. I had no idea what she was raving about, so I put on my uniform and raced over to the armory."

"You live on base?" Myers asked.

"Yes. Over in base housing about ten minutes from the armory."

"But, why would Senior Airman Kennedy call you?" Emma asked. "Why wouldn't she dial 911?"

"I don't know," he quickly replied. "As I said, she was hysterical. I suppose she said that because I am her First Shirt and she felt comfortable calling me."

Myers scribbled something in his notepad. "Take us through what you did once you got to the armory," he said.

"Right, the armory" the Chief rubbed the perspiration off the bridge of his nose. "Well, first of all I had already called the Colonel and picked him up on my way down there."

"Colonel Carlson came with you?" Dan interrupted.

"Something had obviously happened to one of his troops in one of his facilities. Don't you think it was imperative he know about it?"

"Why don't you go on," Myers commanded ignoring his question.

"As I told you yesterday," the Chief replied, "when we got there, I pounded on the door and Senior Airman Kennedy let me in. She was still hysterical. She kept screaming, 'Oh God, she's dead!' I went over to the body and felt for a pulse. There was blood everywhere so I tried not to step in it. But I could see there were already tracks through the blood, where Senior Airman Kennedy had stepped when she found the body. I couldn't get a pulse so the Colonel told me to call you guys."

"You didn't call an ambulance at that time?"

The Chief dismissed Emma's question with a flip of his hand. "Major, did you really want those yahoos in there messing up the crime scene?"

"Why don't you just tell us what happened after you called our office?" Myers interrupted. His face was grim.

"The Colonel stayed up front while I took Senior Airman Kennedy back to the lounge to try to calm her down. She wouldn't stop crying. I made her take off her bloody shoes beforehand so she wouldn't track any more. About ten minutes later, you guys arrived."

"So you don't know what the Colonel was doing during this time?"

The Chief looked at Myers, his eyes hard. "No, Agent Myers, I do not. But I can tell you this. He was clearly upset about what had happened to one of his airman, in his armory. It really shook him up."

Emma wanted to explore something he had said about his earlier conversation with Jaime that had puzzled her.

"You said that when Senior Airman Kennedy called you at home, she yelled, 'Why did you let this happen to Teresa?' What do you think she meant by that?"

To Emma's surprise, his face turned bright red. "That girl has been a problem since day one," he blurted out. "She doesn't hold herself accountable for anyone or anything and blames everyone else for her problems. Who knows why she said that? But it doesn't surprise me. She shouldn't have been in the armory in the first place. It was against the rules. Who knows? Maybe she was trying to deflect the fact that she was going to be in trouble onto me? That girl's a mess and I intend to deal with her accordingly."

"Hold on, Chief," Myers said firmly. "I understand there is the issue of her being in the armory. But you have to hold off on any punishment."

The Shirt scowled, clearly not ready to take orders from an OSI agent. But before he could lash out, Myers went on, clearly in control. "She's our only witness to what happened and the only one who can help us find the killer. You will not issue any punishment at this time."

"Agent Myers is right," Emma agreed. "If you punish her now, we have no hope of finding out who the murderer is. But while we are talking about punishments, we know Conklin got into trouble before for having unauthorized visitors in the armory. We've looked through Senior Airman Conklin's file and it appears she only had an LOR for failure to follow written procedures. We talked to Tech Sergeant Dort who told us you had recommended the LOR instead of an Article 15. Do you remember the circumstances behind this?"

Not missing a beat, the Chief answered impatiently. "Major, I cannot remember every punishment my three hundred plus airmen have received. I barely remember the situation you are referring to."

Not satisfied with his answer, Emma pressed on. "Come on Chief. Why would you recommend a LOR instead of something harsher?"

"Now Major, you know the law better than I do," he answered defiantly. "I cannot in good conscience recommend an Article 15 for a first time offender. Wouldn't you agree?"

"That was her first offense?" Emma asked, catching Myers out of the corner of her eye, who didn't pause in his note writing. She was surprised he was letting her take the lead.

"Yes," the Chief said confidently. "She had never been in trouble before, so I felt a LOR was sufficient and that is what she was given." He glanced at his watch. "Are we done yet?"

"Just a couple of more questions, Chief," Dan said in a conciliatory voice. "Then you can go. What can you tell me about why Senior Airman Conklin was on duty that night? We talked to Sergeant Dort who told us you had called him and told him Conklin was taking over the shift of a sick airman. Is that right?"

The Chief turned his attention to Dan. "Yes. I had received a call earlier that evening from Airman Newman who was sick and needed someone to cover his shift," he explained. "He told me he couldn't get a hold of Sergeant Dort so he called me. I told him not to worry, that I would find someone to cover his shift. I thought Senior Airman Conklin could handle it. So I called and asked her. She told me she would and I called Dort to tell him about the change."

"So you weren't worried about Airman Conklin taking the late shift given the circumstances surrounding her LOR?" Myers asked.

"I already told you, Agent Myers," the Chief said impatiently. "That was the only time she had someone in the armory unauthorized. She was reprimanded and I needed someone to cover the shift."

"Colonel Carlson told us that only a few people have keys to the armory," Dan said. "Can you confirm who they are?"

"Certainly. Colonel Carlson, General Brandt's office, Tech Sergeant Dort, and me. Why do you ask?"

"We're just trying to figure out who had access to the armory that night," Myers said. Emma could see that he was carefully evaluating the Chief's reaction. "It appears there was no forcible entry, which means that whoever the killer was, he used a key. I am assuming your key has been with you at all times?"

The Chief's cheek twitched ever so slightly. "I assure you that the key I have now was with me on my key chain Thursday night and that it was there on Friday morning when I went to the armory. Now," he added standing up, "is there anything else you need? I really must be going."

As they rose, Emma had the feeling that they were being dismissed rather than the other way around. "That should be it for now," Myers replied. "Thanks Chief. We'll follow up with you with any other questions."

"So why do you suppose the Chief hid Conklin's past history of letting unauthorized visitors in the armory?" Dan asked as they walked out to the parking lot together.

Myers shook his head. "I don't know," he said. "But we're not having much luck with people being completely honest around here. Looks like we had better find out more about the Chief and see what he is hiding and more importantly . . .why."

Chapter 16

Later on that evening, Emma sat at her small oak kitchen table and contemplated the case as she ate a bowl of noodles and vegetables. After the interview with the Chief, Emma had come home and pulled out the much neglected work from her briefcase. Several hours later, she was quite pleased with herself when she put away her last record of trial. The afternoon had been quite warm for a German fall day and Emma hated to think she'd spent most of the day shut inside. But she was glad to be done.

As she took a drink of her beer, Emma looked out her large kitchen window and could see her German neighbors, the son and daughter-in-law of Emma's landlord, who just happened to live across the shared driveway, preparing for yet another family get together.

Most every Saturday night, one of her landlord's six children hosted the rest of the tribe for dinner. Emma marveled at the emphasis they put on family and loved it when she was invited to join. Outside, the sun was just setting, casting reddish gold rays onto the trees as people milled around. Emma saw Flourion, her thirteen year old interpreter, putting plates on the long picnic table on their lawn.

These get-togethers always promised lots of food and plenty of kids running around laughing and playing. And of course, there would be beer. Germans didn't need any excuse to drink their favorite beverage . . . just a love of it and did they love it. Emma knew that later in the night when the sun went down and the kids went inside, the homemade schnapps would come out and so would the songs.

The schnapps was made at a small distillery located down the street from her house. It supposedly came in many flavors, but to Emma it all smelled the same . . . like pure turpentine. Once, at her neighbors' insistence, Emma had tested it, only to have the bitter mash scorch her throat. If she thought the taste was bad, the wrath of the fiery liquid the next morning was even worse. A quick study, Emma swore off having anything to do with that particular German drink again and stuck to beer.

But she did enjoy the singing that the schnapps seemed to inspire. It didn't matter that no one could carry a tune. According to her landlord's philosophy, the louder the better. Amazingly it didn't even bother the neighbors who were often awakened at all hours of the morning. Some of them would even come across the street in their pajamas to join in the festivities.

It was a fun place to live and Emma knew she would really miss it when she had to leave. But tonight, she turned off her kitchen light and ate her makeshift meal in the dark. It had been a long week and Emma wasn't in the mood to join in, although it seemed kind of sneaky, tomorrow was her first day off in a while and she didn't want to spend it with a hangover.

Suddenly, Emma stopped with her fork in midair. She had been so caught up in everything else she had missed a simple question: How had the killer known that Conklin was on duty that night when it wasn't her scheduled shift? As far as she was aware, the only people to have known about Conklin's change in shift were Dort, Jaime, and the Chief.

The Chief. There was a man who had not only lied to them in his interview about Conklin letting unauthorized visitors in the armory, but also had been extremely uneasy. He also had access to the armory since he had a key. And why had Jaime accused him of 'letting the murder happen to Teresa?'

But then there was Jaime Kennedy, herself. Why, if she blamed the Chief, had she called him first instead of dialing 911? And she had definitely become agitated during her interview when they asked her if Teresa had had any enemies. Could she have done this? She obviously knew Conklin's shift change, but . . . Emma shook the thought from her mind. No, Jaime had clearly been traumatized by Conklin's death. There's no way Jaime could have pulled it off, unless of she was an award winning actress.

Emma's thoughts shifted to her boss. According to Dort, the Chief had told him that her boss agreed with the recommendation for Conklin to receive a LOR instead of an Article 15. Emma made a mental note to ask Franks about this Monday morning.

The phone rang, interrupting her thoughts. She looked at the clock and was surprised to see it was 2000.

"Emma, I need you to come back to base." Myers gruffly ordered.

Emma's heart sank. There went going to bed early. "What's going on?" she demanded.

"There has been a break in at the dorms. Whoever did it trashed Kennedy's room."

Chapter 17

Myers met Emma in front of Jaime's dorm room, a four story stucco building with the doors to the rooms facing the outside of the building.

Jaime's room was on the ground floor towards the west end. Her door was open and random flashes of light lit up the dark night as an OSI agent took pictures inside. Security lights hung above them about every fifty feet. But despite their bright light, the dark shadows created by the tall evergreen trees lining it, eerily loomed around the sidewalk.

Emma buttoned her navy wool coat around her as the wind rustled through the trees, chilling her. Underneath, she wore a pair of black running pants and baggy yellow sweatshirt. Her long hair was pulled back in a ponytail.

Myers, on the other hand, did not appear to be bothered by the cold, even though his black hair was wet as though he just stepped out of the shower and he was wearing nothing more than a pair of black Nike nylon sweat pants with white tennis shoes and a navy blue Air Force sweatshirt.

"Kennedy and her appointed escort, a female Airman First Class, were coming back from the gym when they noticed the door to Kennedy's room was ajar."

"Airman First Class?" Emma couldn't believe a female airman of lower rank than Jaime had been assigned to protect and escort their star witness. Myers ran a hand though his wet hair and Emma watched as it immediately curled at the nape of his neck.

"I know," he said grimly. "It really pissed me off when I found out Chief Peterson assigned an airman to protect Kennedy. I've already taken care of it. I've ordered one of our trained junior agents not to let Kennedy out of her sight. We're also going to move Kennedy to another dorm room and I have arranged for my agent to have the dorm room next to hers so she can keep an eye on her at all times."

Myers paused as the OSI photographer came out to inform them that he was finished. "I'll give that young escort credit, though," he continued on after the agent left, "when she saw the door was unlocked, she refused to let Kennedy go in and instead dragged her upstairs to the TV room where they called us."

Through the window right next to the door, Emma could see Jaime sitting on the bed her face in her hands.

"As you can imagine Kennedy is a basket case," Myers said, leading the way into the room. The place looked like a tornado had gone through it. Clothes were strewn everywhere, and papers were scattered all over the floor covering Kennedy's personal belongings. A fine layer of white powder lay on top of everything, including the dark gray carpet and her bed. It looked, Emma thought, as if a bag of powdered sugar had exploded in there.

"The guys dusted for prints." Myers explained.

Emma's heart went out to the young Airman whose life had literally been torn apart. Jaime, who was wearing the same sweatshirt as before, looked at them and it was obvious she had been crying. Her face was caked with dried tears and she looked about the room as though trying to grasp what was happening.

Myers knelt down in front of her. "I know this is hard," he said softly, "but I need you to go through your stuff as best you can and see if anything is missing." Jaime numbly nodded as she looked around the room trying to gauge where to start.

Emma watched as Jaime slowly made her way around the tiny dorm room, poking at her things with her foot as she went. Puffs of white powder stirred in the air as she picked through her things.

The only furniture in the room were a bed, small desk with chair and a tall brown dresser with a small TV on top.

After about ten minutes of rifling through the mess, Jaime sat down at her desk and looked about her, dazed. Although no longer crying, she was clearly worn out and emotionally exhausted. Emma was glad she wouldn't have to stay in this dorm room. She was sure to feel more secure in her new room with a more competent escort.

Suddenly, Jaime slipped off her chair and started searching for something under her desk on her hands and knees, only to emerge a few seconds later wearing a sad smile and holding a large pink photo album. Falling back into her chair, she flipped through the pages until she came to a blank page at the end of the book. Tears began rolling down her cheeks again.

"What is it, Jamie?" Emma asked kneeling beside her.

"He took my picture," Jaime sobbed. "The one of me and Teresa. It was the only one I had and he took it." Clutching the book to her chest, she began rocking back and forth.

"Is there anything else missing?"

"No!" she moaned, "but it doesn't matter. That was the most important thing I had. It was my only picture of the two of us together."

And with that, she threw down the album and stormed out of the room. Myers nodded to an attractive woman hovering by the door, who promptly disappeared after the distraught airman.

"Don't worry," Myers told Emma reassuringly. "Agent Sanchez knows what she's doing. She'll follow Kennedy and make sure she's okay."

"You think the killer did this?" Emma asked surveying the war strewn room.

Myers shrugged. "Right now, it looks like it. But why would he only take a picture? If he wanted to take out our only witness, why not stay until she came back and finish the job?"

Despite the heat in the tiny room, Emma shivered. "I don't know," she said, "but you had better find him before he does come back and finish the job."

Chapter 18

Because of her hectic work week schedule, Emma rarely got the pleasure of sleeping in. So Emma really looked forward to Sunday mornings when she could relax and the world seemed a lot quieter, especially in Germany.

The Germans in her village took Sunday very seriously. It was a day for church and family and nothing else. In fact, there was a quiet ordinance all day on Sundays which meant no mowing the lawn, washing you car or making any loud noise that would disturb the neighbors. Even their world famous get-togethers were toned down on Sunday. Emma's landlord and his family still got together for dinner after church, but they stayed inside, indulging in nothing stronger than tea and coffee.

She'd gotten home about midnight after they finished up with the dorm room and interviewing several of the dorm residents to ask if they saw anything, which none of them had.

When she'd finally crawled into bed, Emma couldn't get to sleep. Instead she pulled the comforter around her neck and listened to the sounds of the night. Emma had never had a problem living alone before and in fact, usually loved the symphony of noises coming from outside; but, the night's events had really shaken her up. Only after checking the locks on all of the windows and doors, was she finally able to drift off to a much needed sleep.

So today, while the rest of the world was at church, Emma buried herself under her white down comforter and stayed in bed until ten o'clock. When she finally forced herself to get up, Emma skipped her normal routine of showering and instead opted to go see if she could find something to eat in the kitchen, only to come up empty. Because of the interview with the Chief yesterday, she had not been able to go grocery shopping.

So she opted for the one piece of bread left in the drawer. Popping it in the toaster, she boiled some water for a cup of tea, and took her breakfast, meager as it was, out on the deck where the warm sun warded off just enough of the chill.

Everywhere she looked, there were vibrant colors from the clumps of geraniums to the russet of the oak leaves and the mums that overflowed the pots on the doorsteps.

After breakfast, Emma decided that, since it was much too beautiful a day to be cooped up indoors, she would go for a bike ride. Although running was her exercise of choice, Emma loved any form of exercise which helped to keep her weight at a trim 128 pounds. She had just washed her face and changed into a pair of dark blue jeans and a red sweater when the phone rang.

Annoyed at having her tranquil morning interrupted, Emma almost didn't answer it. But fearing it could be her mother who often called Emma on the weekends to check up on her, she obediently picked up the phone and then immediately regretted it.

"Good morning, Emma," Myers said in his familiar baritone. "When do you want to come in and discuss the case?"

Although she resisted the urge to hang up on him, Emma didn't mince words. "Now Agent Myers, I was sure a guy like you would be in church this morning, repenting."

"Sounds like someone didn't get enough sleep." Myers chuckled. "I'm hurt you would think I'm a sinner who needs saving."

"Well, you know what they say: it's never too late for redemption. So please go in peace or better yet leave me in peace. Sundays are my day to unwind. I'm sure there is someone there on base that you can harass."

"Actually there's not." Myers answered. "Dan is with his family, and most of the witnesses aren't home or at least not answering their phones."

"Smart people," Emma retorted. "Wish I hadn't answered mine."

"So what do you say?" Myers urged, apparently immune to an insult. "Want to come up here?"

Refusing to lose her only day off to a man who would give her anything but peace, Emma stood her ground. "Sorry Myers. I have a date with my bike and I'm going on a long ride to enjoy this beautiful day. I'll see you . . . "

"Great!" Myers cut in before Emma could finish. "I love to ride. You have a bike I can borrow? Where can I meet you?"

"Hold on a minute!" Emma stopped him. "I seem to have missed the part where you were invited."

"Oh come on Major," he cajoled her. "Riding is so much better when you are with someone else. Come on. I promise I won't talk about the case. Besides, I actually can be quite a charming guy."

"Can be and are charming are two completely different things," she fired back.

"Okay, I understand. I just thought you wanted me to brief you about the investigation. If you don't want me to run things by you, then . . . "

"Okay," she interrupted him, rolling her eyes, "meet me at my house. I have a spare bike and there is a bike trail right here that goes for miles."

Emma then grudgingly gave him directions to her house.

"Great!" Emma could hear the enthusiasm in his voice. She was surprised that he seemed excited to spend the day with her. "See you in about twenty minutes."

"Okay," Emma told him, not bothering to sound more enthusiastic than she felt.

Catching her mother stare back at her from the picture on the table beside the phone, Emma held her hands in the air and exclaimed. "Okay, okay, Mom. I promise I will make it to church. But did it have to be today where I would be punished for my sins?"

Chapter 19

Twenty five minutes later, a sleek black BMW convertible pulled into her driveway. Emma watched from inside her garage where she was oiling her bike chain, as Myers unfolded his long legs from the tiny sports car.

Emma let out a whistle. "Nice wheels, Agent. I didn't know they paid you guys so well," she said as she wiped her hands on an old rag and walked around it examining the black leather interior of the two-seater.

"She is a beaut, isn't she?" Myers replied proudly, leaning against the hood with his arms folded across his chest.

Emma couldn't decide if the car was made for the owner or the other way around. Either way, they looked good together. Myers was wearing a dark pair of Levi's with a black sweater that fit snugly across his chest. Small aviator sunglasses hid his eyes, but Emma knew all too well how piercing his grey eyes were behind the glasses. Emma went into the garage and got her bike. She wasn't about to waste any of this beautiful day on small talk with this man.

Wheeling it out of the garage she pointed behind her at the spare bike. "That one's yours," she said. "Let's go."

"You want to wait up?" he huffed as he scrambled to get on his bike and catch up. "Not that I mind the view."

Emma immediately squeezed her brakes and slowed down until he caught up with her. "So do you make it a habit to crash other people's plans?" she demanded.

"Nope. Only yours," he assured her, grinning.

Not wanting to encourage any more talk, Emma continued pedaling and soon found herself begin to relax. A slight breeze blew her long hair back from her face. Whenever she wasn't in uniform, Emma liked literally being able to let her hair down. She got tired of having to put it up all of the time, the long heavy tresses pinned tightly to her scalp.

The bike path was made of asphalt and took them through fields of alfalfa, wheat and occasionally sunflowers, their fragrances filling the air. Scattered along the path were benches and picnic tables for the weary traveler to take a rest or grab a bite to eat.

Although she pointed out a few things like the centuries old vineyard she'd been to several times, for the most part they rode in silence for the next hour. Emma was grateful Myers didn't feel the need to talk and pleased when she saw him enjoying the scenery as much as she did.

Emma's favorite part of the ride was when the path ran along side the majestic Mosel River for several miles, with its breathtaking views of both the river and the vineyards that lined the hills. When they rounded the corner and got their first glimpse of the river, Emma heard Myers suck in his breath.

"Incredible."

"I never get tired of coming here," she told him pleased with his response. "I think it must be one of the most beautiful places on earth."

She led him to the water's edge where she got off her bike and parked it next to a picnic table facing the river. Pulling out two bottles of water from the bag strapped to her bike, Emma threw one bottle to Myers and sat down, stretching her legs out on the long bench and lifting her face up to the sun.

In front of them, the river's water ran lazily downstream. She closed her eyes, and then, uncomfortably aware that he was watching her, opened them and turned towards him using her hand to shield them from the sun.

"I think I like you away from the 'JAG world,' Major," he said when her eyes met his.

"It's nice to see there is actually a woman beneath those awful baggy BDUs. I must say, I was beginning to wonder. You always look like such a hard ass and so serious with your hair pulled back. You should wear your hair down more often. It makes you look," he paused searching for the right words, " . . . a little less hard ass."

Turning away, Myers took a drink of his water, but not before Emma saw that he was smiling.

"Is that your idea of a compliment?" Emma asked while again raising her face to the sun. "Although as far as being a hard ass," she added lazily. "you do have a way of bringing out the best in a girl."

She heard him chuckle. "So how did you come to be a JAG anyway?"

Emma pondered her answer. "Well, the JAG decision was easy. It was the lawyer part that I'm not really sure of."

"Okay now you have my attention," Myers teased.

"What I mean is," she smiled back at him, "I'm not sure why I became a lawyer. No one in my family was a lawyer. No one tried to convince me to be a lawyer. I just have always wanted to be one since I was in about second grade."

"So what made becoming a JAG an easy decision?"

"Well," she explained, "that came out of law school, which I discovered wasn't all I had dreamed it would be."

Emma told Myers of how it was law school where she came face to face with some people she had avoided throughout her life, people with political agendas: wannabe politicians who would do anything to get to the top of the class rank, including ripping pages out of library books pertaining to the weekly assignments, or Emma's favorite, hide the books altogether so no one could complete their homework. It was the first time in her life that she wondered whether she had made a mistake about being so determined to enter that particular profession.

"So," Emma went on, "when I talked to the recruiters during my second year, I knew that I didn't want to be an associate, stuck in a basement for years surrounded by mounds of research material, while the senior associates and partners got to chair all of the trials. The Air Force was my way of getting straight into the courtroom."

Myers raised his eyebrow inquisitively. "So don't tell me that all it took to sway an independent and determined person like you was a couple recruiting speeches."

Laughing, Emma explained. "First of all, thank you for finally realizing that about me – the independent and determined part, that is. Second, I did have another fairly significant influence on my decision to become a JAG . . . my uncle."

Emma's uncle had been an officer in the Air Force for as long as she could remember. He was a fighter pilot and Emma couldn't help but beam every time he let her come with him out to the flight line to see his plane. He had always been a huge influence on Emma and helped her understand how the values of the Air Force were so closely align with hers.

Once in uniform, Emma quickly came to understand her uncle's passion for the Air Force. As an officer, Emma adapted to a different mindset, one of respect towards others and the country she was so privileged to serve. The word 'respect,' one spoken haphazardly in the civilian sector, took on a new meaning for Emma who was amazed at how this new concept changed her life. Emma was proud to serve with her fellow men and women in blue, many of whom became life long friends.

"I must admit," Myers said, his gray eyes on her, "you've inspired me."

"Right," she quickly replied. "Okay, enough about me."

Myers reached over the table and placed a hand on her arm. "No really," he said softly, "we need more people like you who have drive and dedication."

Pleased by his compliment, but very aware of his hand on her, Emma gently pulled her arm away and gazed at the river. "Thanks."

For the next few minutes he remained silent and not daring to look at him, she listened to the birds overhead and the clink of chains as other bicyclists rode past them on their trek down the path.

After a while, Emma gained the courage and looked over at Myers who now had his eyes closed. She took a minute to unabashedly gape at him. As much as she hated to admit it, he was a very handsome man.

A five o'clock shadow hugged his strong jaw. Emma envied the incredibly long dark lashes that right now hid his probing dark gray eyes. His hair was tussled from the ride and Emma resisted the urge to lean over and run her fingers through its thick black waves. But what fascinated her most was that, for once, he looked at peace.

When, suddenly he opened his eyes and looked straight into hers, she could feel herself flush.

Embarrassed, she looked away. "You think we're going to catch this guy?" she asked, hoping he couldn't see her red face.

Myers sat up and shrugged. "We have no choice. He's out there running around base and we have no idea of his motive or why Conklin. In fact, we don't know anything about him. Tomorrow, I'm going to talk to everyone who has any connection with Conklin or the armory.

"There has to be someone out there who knows something. I find it hard to believe that no one but Kennedy seems to know anything about her. There's no way you can tell me a young woman who is stationed in Europe stays to herself all of the time studying. And I don't buy the schoolmarm her parents are making her out to be either."

Emma thought about her own education and how hard she had studied in law school and the long hours spent at the library. She wasn't ready to admit it to Myers, but Emma hadn't had much of a social life then either.

"And where's the boyfriend?" he went on, leaning his elbows on the table and staring at the river. "She's a smart, very attractive twenty-four year old woman. Where is this love of her life she talks about in her journal? Why hasn't he come forward? Good God, his girlfriend just got killed so where is he? It just doesn't add up."

Emma watched a lone duck trying to catch the crickets that were jumping on the edge of the river. Finally victorious, the duck waddled further down river to find more lunch.

"Good question," Emma replied, turning to face him. "We do know they went out, but according to what Dan read in Teresa's journal it was always in secret. So what does that mean? Why were they hiding their romance? If there really was one. Was he married? Was he an officer?"

"Or both," Myers interrupted.

Emma drew her breath in slowly. "Or both," she repeated.

It was an important point. In the military, adultery was still a crime, but fraternization was also a crime. It is against the UCMJ and therefore against the law for an officer to date an enlisted member. Depending on the circumstances, the punishment for the enlisted member could be severe. For an officer, the punishment was much the same although most commanders held an officer to a higher standard because of their commanding status and their position of authority over enlisted members.

"One of the things that puzzles me is how the killer knew that Teresa was on duty that night." Emma said. "I mean, she wasn't on the schedule and didn't agree to take the shift until the last minute. How did he know she would be there?"

"Good question. The only people who for sure knew she was working were: Dort, the Chief and Kennedy. We can ask them tomorrow when we talk to them."

"We? So you are now going to include me on the interviews?" Emma asked, still slightly bristling from having been left out of Friday's interviews.

"Why not?" Myers replied nonchalantly. "You haven't screwed up things so far."

"Thanks!'" she said, laughing and throwing her empty water bottle at him.

"Good shot," he said rubbing his shoulder. "Remind me not to tick you off in the future."

"It will be good for you to be on your best behavior around me. But somehow, I doubt you won't tick me off again."

"Ha!"

"So enough about the case," Emma went on, anxious not to let the case cast a shadow over this gorgeous day. "Tell me something about yourself, Agent Eric Myers."

"Practicing your interviewing skills on me?" he said good naturedly. "Well, there's not much to tell."

"Somehow I really doubt that."

"All right. You win, but don't say I didn't warn you." He took another sip of his water, his dark hair glinting in the sun.

"I was born at Offuit Air Force Base, in Omaha. And basically grew up in the Air Force. My dad was an officer in Security Forces. He is a great guy, worked hard but always managed to find the time to be there at my football and baseball games."

Myers smiled as he looked out over the water. "I idolized my dad and everything he stood for. He was a great cop and officer and I wanted to be just like him.

Emma watched Myers as he talked about his dad with obvious admiration. The influence his dad had on Myers' career sounded very similar to the influence Emma's uncle had on hers.

"I've lived all over the world since we moved around every three to four years. Let's see, we lived all over the U.S., Europe and Asia. I loved every minute of it. I loved traveling. I loved moving to new places. I loved the Air Force –the whole bit. My mom stayed at home with my younger brother, Troy, and me. I think what made moving so easy for me was because my mom loved the Air Force, too. She made the most of every place we lived. My parents finally retired about five years ago in Arizona where they now play golf every day."

"Where's your brother?" Emma asked.

"He's back in the Midwest, living in a suburb of Minneapolis with his wife and three kids," Myers answered, frowning. "Troy didn't take to moving around as much as I did and he really wanted to settle in one place to raise his kids. He also wanted a more stable career and so now is an accountant for a big accounting firm in Minneapolis."

She searched Myers' face. "You sound like you two are close."

Myers shook his head. "I'm pretty lucky. I love his kids and his wife. They're great. I just don't get to see them very often. What about you? You have any brothers or sisters?"

"Nope," Emma replied. "Just me and my parents."

Myers raised his eyebrow and smirked. "Only child, huh? Now that explains a lot."

Before she had a chance to throw something else at him, Myers changed the subject. "So tell me, Ms. Attorney. What do you do when you're not raking some poor schmuck over the coals?"

Emma thought about his question. She hadn't had much free time in the last several years due to her enormous court load.

"I like to travel," she said finally.

"Really? Well you're certainly in the perfect place for it. What are some of your favorite places?"

"I've only taken a few side trips here and there," she admitted, thinking of her "Places I've Got to See" list, many of which hadn't been checked off yet. "I'm waiting for my schedule to open up a bit so I can take some big trips, but unfortunately that doesn't look like it's going to happen any time soon. But I think the place I most want to see is Prague. There's something about that city that fascinates me."

"You're right," he said warmly. "You do have to visit it. Prague is one of the most beautiful cities in the world."

"You've been?"

"Yes. Several times. I can walk for hours in that city and always seem to find something I somehow missed before. Every cobblestone street seems to end at the river where beautiful bridges arch over it. Tiny parks hidden in out of the way places, vendors pedaling their homemade wares add to the charm."

Emma was startled by the longing in his voice as he talked about the place that had clearly affected him deeply.

Maybe he was human after all. Or at the very least, she now knew they had something in common.

She couldn't believe this was the same man who blatantly exercised his authority over her just one day ago.

"You need to go," he said softly. "Really, you do. Just let me know and I can set you up with some of the most fantastic restaurants and places to stay. You'll never regret it."

Emma knew that he was right. Ever since she was a little girl, her parents had stressed the importance of seeing the world. And here she was, in the heart of Europe and hadn't taken the time to do just that. After this investigation, she was definitely going to take some time off . . . to see Prague.

Myers got up from the table. "Come on," he said. "Enough talk. Why don't you show me more of this beautiful countryside? That is, unless I've already worn the poor only child out."

"Ha!" Emma said, hopping on her bike and striding towards her bike. "We've just started. Try and keep up, will you?"

The two rode their bikes along the river for several more miles. Every once in a while, Emma, catching sight of Myers out of the corner of her eye, was again struck at how different he was out here than back on base. Emma didn't think it would be too hard to get used to this man beside her.

When the trail finally parted from the river, they began to climb through the steep vine covered hills. Emma had ridden this path many times and it had taken her several months before she had the strength to master the entire hill without getting off for a break. The path had several switch backs that wound up the hill and it was about a one mile ride to the top.

Coming around the second switchback, Emma's legs started to burn and her knees throbbed. Despite the fall chill in the air, tiny beads of sweat rolled down face. Her only comfort was the fact she was sure that, behind her, Myers must also be struggling.

As she peddled around the curve, Emma looked back, expecting him to be stopping to rest, only to find that he was right behind her. Increasing her speed with an effort, she reached the top of the hill before him.

Pulling over to the side of the path, she stopped her bike to give her legs a rest. Straddling her bike, she put her hands on the back of head and took a few deep breaths. Myers followed suit which, she found, pleased her. But she did have to give him kudos for keeping up with her. Her assessment of him working out earlier must have been right.

"Not bad," she said wiping her brow with the back of her hand.

"Thanks," he puffed. "That's quite the hill. You sure know how to show a guy a good time."

"I only save this hill for the special ones," Emma assured him, "those who crash my Sundays."

About an hour later they pulled into her driveway. Surprisingly, it had been a very relaxing day and Emma actually was glad Myers joined her.

Stiffly crawling off her bike, Emma closed her eyes and stretched her arms towards the sun. She sighed. Maybe she had gotten to Myers. Maybe he had seen today that she really wasn't so bad after all and they could work as a team.

Emma heard him come up next to her as she continued to stretch her back and legs.

"Thanks for letting me come along," he said in a low voice.

"No problem," Emma told him, wheeling her bike into the garage. "You weren't so bad to have around after all. "Better be careful, though," she added smiling mischievously. "You wouldn't want the word to get around that you aren't such a badass after all."

"Me? A badass?" He replied feigning shock. "Now you truly *have* hurt my feelings."

Emma rested her bike on its kickstand and held out her hand. "I promise to keep it our little secret. Deal?"

"Deal." he finally replied taking her offered hand.

Shock waves rocked straight through her as Myers' hand grasped hers. Instinctively she stepped back, her hand still held firmly in his.

"I think I might just like making deals with you," he said huskily. Their eyes met and held.

Emma quickly pulled her hand away and brushed away her hair back from her face. What was she doing? She couldn't afford to have feelings, *any* kind of feelings, for Myers.

"Well," she said folding her arms over her chest. "I guess I'll see you tomorrow."

"Yep, tomorrow," he said slowly, as though reluctant to bring the conversation to an end. "I'll call you when we set up the interview times."

Emma didn't realize she had been holding her breath until the black sports car was out of sight and she slowly exhaled willing her heart to stop pounding in her chest. They had to catch this guy soon, she told herself, if for no other reason than that she didn't know how long she would be able to handle working so closely with Myers. Any other time, she may have actually considered something more than a professional relationship, but now, given the gravity of their assignment, that was entirely impossible.

Closing the garage door, she went inside, telling herself that she might as well accept the fact that it was the wrong time and wrong place to have any feelings for Agent Myers.

Chapter 20

I watched her carry her tray of food and put it down on a table. Her face is sullen as she plops into her seat, and pushes her stringy hair behind her ear. God, it looks like she hasn't taken a shower in days.

Poor thing. If I didn't know any better I'd think something was bothering her.

Beside her is the attractive young woman who has been her constant companion the entire day. I was furious when I found my little airman escort had been let go. What the hell were they thinking assigning another damned woman as an escort! Didn't they know that would only add to their problems?

Still, this new one is a red haired beauty all right. God, does that woman have a set of tits on her! I could get used to watching her tight ass as she walks past me, her eyes scanning the crowd, ever watchful. What a pity she had to be dragged into this.

Dammit! If one more kid slams his tray down on that conveyor belt behind me, I'm going to shove it up his ass. Half eaten meatloaf and mashed potatoes covered in gravy cover the plate on the tray. Christ! How can they eat that shit?

I move closer to my target. Poor little bitch! Look at her picking at her food. Her little friend is gone and now she's stuck with someone a thousand times better looking than she is. I almost regret having to put her out of her misery. This is much more fun for me and a lot slower and more painful for her.

A group of airmen barge noisily into the large room, making my ears ring. Damn! I can't stay in this shit hole any longer. Sooner or later, someone's going to notice me watching her.

I'm at the door now. And here she comes, the red head close behind her.

It's time. That bitch had been around too long. Turns out she either doesn't know I was in the armory that night or she's too scared to tell them. But I know so far those goddamned OSI agents don't have anything on me.

Hell! I'm not taking any chances. That stupid girl could spill her guts at any time. No, she deserves to die, just like her precious little friend. This time there would be no witnesses.

I step outside into the shadows as the door behind me opens. My body shakes in excitement as she and her escort walk in front of me, their breath clouding in the frigid air. She looks around nervously.

Don't worry. I'll let you know exactly who shot your little friend ... right before I snap your friggin' neck.

Chapter 21

The next morning at 0630, Emma had just put down her briefcase and turned on her computer on when Barb came bursting into her office.

"Lieutenant Colonel Franks wants to see you in his office right away," she said. "General Brandt has requested you and Colonel Franks meet him in his office at 0700 to brief him on what is happening with this case."

"Good morning to you too, Barb," Emma said calmly although inwardly she felt her blood pressure rise.

It was rare for Barb to be frazzled by anything, but this morning's meeting clearly had her in a state which must mean the boss was beside himself.

"Please tell Lieutenant Colonel Franks I'll be there shortly," Emma said and then, picking up the phone, "I need to get a hold of Agents Panchen and Myers to let them know about the briefing."

Myers picked up his cell phone on the first ring. "So you were summoned, too, huh?" he said.

Emma cradled the receiver between her shoulder and her ear as she sent an email to Maggie, letting her know she would be gone most of the day and asking her to assist Captain Mullen. "So how are you going to break it to him that we have no leads yet?"

"Thanks for leaving that up to me," Myers replied sardonically. "*We* are just going to brief him on the facts as we know them and let him know that we're still in the process of interviewing everyone, some for the second time."

"All right, but be ready. General Brandt likes to move fast and he's not a patient man. We'll probably come out of there two inches shorter than when we went in."

If Franks had been stressed on Friday, he was almost in a state of complete panic this morning.

"Please tell me we have something to report to the General," he said anxiously, as soon as she stepped foot in his office.

"Yes, Sir. We do have information," she answered, choosing her words carefully. "As you know, there are many people to interview and OSI has several of them lined up today."

"Good. I want you to clear your schedule and be there for all of the interviews. I'm pulling you from all courts until this investigation is done."

Emma was surprised at his change of heart about her involvement in the case. "Yes, Sir," she said crisply. "I'll need to talk to the defense and judge about the Downs' sentencing hearing that is to start tomorrow. John is handling it but I can ask the judge for a change of counsel to replace me. I think it would be a good idea to have Chase or Greg sit second chair to coach John since this is his first sentencing hearing."

Franks nodded. "Fine. Do it. I want your full focus on this investigation. The General wants answers and he wants them now."

"Here is my brief that I finished last night detailing what we have learned so far," she said and waited for him to scan it before going on to say, "You need to know there are several issues surrounding Chief Peterson that will need to be addressed."

"The Chief?" Franks said, startled.

"Yes, Sir. I've detailed inconsistencies in his statement and the facts as we know them. But I wanted you to be aware that something is just not making sense. It appears the Chief has not been entirely truthful with us. Agent Myers will be addressing our concerns with the General, but I wanted to let you know since he is now a suspect."

"Thank you," Franks said, dismissing her. "Go back to your office and prepare for the General's meeting. I'll meet you in fifteen minutes and we'll drive over in my car."

Emma went back to her office, anxiously debating how best to tell the Wing Commander that one of his highest ranking enlisted airman was a suspect in the murder of one of his own troops. Something told her this wasn't going to be a good day.

Chapter 22

When they arrived at the Wing Headquarters building ten minutes early, Franks disappeared in search of a cup of coffee leaving Emma in the General's waiting room, guarded by Captain Lori Angeles, the General's executive officer, who sat at a desk right outside the General's door. Across from hers was an empty desk which was usually occupied by the General's civilian secretary, Fran.

The executive officer was a rotating position on base to help the General with varying tasks. Personally appointed by the General, the chosen officer customarily fulfilled the position for about one year, and was in charge of managing the General's day to day activities, including everything from keeping his appointments to helping with dignitary visits. But her main job was serving as liaison between the General and anyone needing his attention, after which she would go back to her originally assigned career field and squadron.

Although many young officers found themselves floundering in the face of the enormous responsibilities imposed by the job, Lori Angeles had thrived. With her beautiful olive skin and almond shaped eyes, she was the consummate organizer who kept every one on task, including the General. Although having only been in the position a few months, Angeles had her job down to a science and soon the General's office had been running like a well oiled machine. When you needed to know about what was going on around base, Angeles was the person to go to.

Emma met Angeles a year earlier at the hospital where she worked as a medical administrator. The two became fast friends.

"Good morning Lori."

"Hey, Major." Lori nodded at the closed door behind her and whispered. "I hope you are ready for this brief, because the General is in quite a mood today. Of course, he has been in a bad mood every since this whole thing happened. Are you close to catching this guy?"

Emma shook her head. "I wish."

"Gives me the creeps," Lori said, rubbing her arms. "I can't believe we have a killer running lose around base. I have someone walk me to my car now after work. I'm not going to take any chances.

"I can't blame you," Emma responded, "but I'm sure we'll catch the guy soon."

"All of the commanders are up in arms about this one," Lori told her. "Although I must say you guys have done a pretty good job of keeping everything hush, hush. The word is that not many people on base know what has happened. The General has been very clear that it is business as normal as far as everyone else is concerned. They're getting ready to brief the masses today, but the General wants everyone to have their stories straight. He doesn't want widespread panic on his base. Man, headquarters is sure on his back about this. They call here about every hour."

Lori leaned forward. "One thing you might find interesting. Colonel Carlson has been in and out of here a lot lately."

"But that doesn't surprise me," Emma said, confused. "It was his airman who was killed."

"You're not following me," Lori quietly insisted. "What you might find interesting," Lori continued after Emma had sat down in the chair beside her desk, "is that Carlson was meeting a lot with the General *before* the murder, too. I must say each time the Colonel left madder than before."

Emma knew her friend was taking liberties in telling her this information. As an exec, Lori would be privy to things she would not be able to share with anyone. The news must be pretty important if Lori was willing to reveal it.

"I just want you to know that something's going on there," Lori continued earnestly. "You know I can't say anything that goes on with the General, but all is not right with Colonel Carlson. And then there's this . . . ."

She broke off abruptly as Myers and Dan walked in the door. "Thanks, Lori," Emma said in a low voice. "Incidentally, I forgot to ask you. Does the General have a key to the armory?"

"It's in there," Lori said, pointing to a file cabinet in the corner. "Why?"

"Do you know if it was missing or did the General use it recently?"

"The General doesn't use any of these keys," Lori told her. "They're just back up. It's been locked in here the whole time."

"Who else besides you has access to this cabinet?" Emma asked her, aware that Myers and Dan were watching them from across the room.

"No one. If they want this key, they have to go through me and no one has asked me for it."

At that moment, Franks walked into the room and almost simultaneously, the General emerged from his office and, after telling Lori to hold his calls, motioned them inside.

Emma had been in the General's office two times before today, both to give updates on major courts-martial. It was a large office with several bookshelves lining one wall. Numerous plaques, awards and gifts from various foreign and domestic dignitaries adorned the shelves and wall space above them. The huge picture window behind the General's massive dark oak desk allowed him to see most of the base he commands, including the flight line where his heart still lay.

General Tom Brandt had trained at the Air Force Academy to be a fighter pilot. For years he had flown high above them before receiving his first star and accepting the wing commander position which now mainly kept him confined to his desk. Although his schedule didn't allow him to fly as much anymore, the General would forever be a pilot at heart and still wore his flight suit whenever possible.

Tom Brandt looked like a commander. About six feet tall, lean, with thick black hair peppered with gray, he had a presence about him which commanded people to stand up and follow his lead.

Although the General was known for having a fairly even keel, his temper could be whipped into a fury. Luckily, Emma had only heard about his temper, but never seen it and hoped today wasn't the day she would get to.

"Good morning, everyone," General Brandt said. "Agent Myers, I appreciate your assistance on this matter and have relayed my appreciation to headquarters and your superiors. All of you, please be seated. I know it's early and I appreciate you coming on such short notice. But I know you are aware of how serious this is and how much we need to get some closure on this case. The Group Commanders and I were able to keep this thing pretty much under wraps over the weekend and it appears not much information got out."

Emma heard the concern in the General's voice.

"Lieutenant Colonel Franks and I notified the local German authorities on Friday about our situation," the General continued. "They're on alert for any suspects out in the community, and have assured us they will help in any way possible. They also assured me they will use the utmost discretion in revealing any information about this case. As you know, I didn't want to tell people about the murder right before everyone left for the weekend for fear we'd create wide spread panic on base."

Emma looked at her boss and saw his eyes were downcast and his lips pursed. She guessed him having to tell the Germans about the murder had not been too pleasant.

"I was notified early this morning by one of my commanders that the rumors are starting to come out that something has happened," he went on, sitting forward in his chair and clasping his hands in front of him. "Before any more rumors start flying, I'm going to have the Commanders give statements at mandatory commanders' calls for each of their squadrons at 1000 today. So what do you have for me so we can prepare what we are going to say to the troops?"

Emma glanced at Myers wondering if he would take the lead as she proposed last night. He didn't disappoint her.

"Sir," he said, "we're still in the process of interviewing everyone even remotely involved in this case, but here is what we know so far. We are fairly certain this was an inside job. You see there's no evidence of a break-in," Myers explained. "The armory door wasn't tampered with so it is more than likely the suspect used a key, one more piece of evidence to indicate that our suspect is one of our own. We got the ballistics report back and the bullets found in Senior Airman Conklin were from a M9 magazine which was stored in a locked cabinet in the armory. We have also confirmed the bullets were fired out of a M9 weapon also stored in the armory."

Emma watched the General's face harden at Myers' news.

Myers leaned his elbows on the table and looked intensely at the Commander. "Our man knew what he was doing, Sir," he said gravely. "He let himself into the armory and took one of the weapons off the shelves. He knew where the key to the ammunition cabinet was kept and used it to unlock the cabinet, pulled out a magazine, loaded his gun and shot Senior Airman Conklin two times in the back of the head."

Emma shuddered as she remembered Teresa lying in a pool of her own blood.

"From what we can tell," Myers told them. "Teresa Conklin was studying at a desk before she was killed. But she must have heard something because it appears she got up from the desk and unholstered her weapon. We aren't sure what happened then, but at some point the killer got right behind her and shot her twice in the back of the head. We found her gun under the desk."

"What about the witness that was in the armory that night?" Brandt asked his lips pursed tightly. "Surely she heard or knows something."

"Regrettably, Senior Airman Kennedy was asleep on the couch in the back of the armory and says she didn't hear anything until after Conklin was shot," Myers told him. "Our suspect used a suppressor so Kennedy didn't hear the shots. She thinks she may have heard something slam, but she isn't sure. Airmen Kennedy and Conklin were good friends and had been studying for a test.

We're hoping to get more out of her but she's still pretty shook up about the whole thing."

"I can imagine."

"Sir, we do have another pressing issue," Myers went on. "I'm not sure if you're aware, but Senior Airman Kennedy's dorm room was broken into and ransacked on Saturday night. The good news is Airman Kennedy was in the gym at the time. And as near as she can tell the only thing stolen was a picture of her and Senior Airman Conklin."

"Good God!" The General sat back and rubbed the back of his neck. "We have her fully protected, right? I mean that girl is not to go anywhere without an escort."

Emma spoke up. "Well, that is another thing we wanted to talk to you about, Sir. Senior Airman Kennedy did have an escort that night . . . a female Airman First Class."

Outraged, the General slapped his hand on the table. "Who authorized this?" he demanded.

"Chief Peterson asked for the airman to escort Airman Kennedy, Sir." Myers replied.

General exchanged looks with Franks. "I see. I hope you have gotten Senior Airman Kennedy a more experienced escort, Agent Myers?"

"Yes, Sir. I have assigned one of our trained OSI agents to be with Airman Kennedy 24/7."

"Who do you think broke into her room?"

"It's not clear at this point." Myers answered. "That's why we're so concerned for her safety. It may have been the suspect. It looks like he was surprised by Senior Airman Kennedy in the armory that night. If he knows there was a witness, there is a high chance he will come after her."

"I think it appears he already did by breaking into her room," the General interrupted gravely.

Myers took a deep breath. "Sir, may I have permission to be frank with you?"

"Absolutely."

"We are finding it hard to investigate. As I said, we think this is an inside job, so we need everyone, especially the Security Forces

Squadron, to be frank with us. If he was familiar with the armory, it would stand to reason he is in that squadron. The problem is, Sir, we're running into a lot of roadblocks."

"Please explain."

"Well, Sir. People are not telling us the whole story. Take Chief Peterson for example. When we talked to him, it appears he lied to us about Senior Airman Conklin's prior disciplinary record. It looks as though he may have been lying about some other things as well."

The General's face remained expressionless. "So just what are you telling me, Agent Myers?"

"Sir, at this point the Chief is a suspect and we need your permission to press forward with our investigation of him, given his rank and stature on this base."

The General's eyes narrowed as his lips pressed together. The room was silent as they awaited his answer.

"You have it," he said, turning to Franks, "I want you working closely with OSI on this one. Make sure we do everything by the book. And I want you all to assure me that no one, I mean *no one*, is to know the Chief is a suspect. Do I make myself clear? I will not have this man's career ruined. You may very well find he had nothing to do with this. I trust you will use discretion."

The General paused and got up moving to the window. Running his hand through his hair, he stared at the people outside on the sidewalk.

"I want all of you to do everything possible to catch this guy," he commanded. "I don't want any of my people to be at risk. But in the end, and let me be very clear about this, as long as you have proof, I don't care who it is – bring him in."

Chapter 23

One hour later, Emma again sat confined in an interrogation rooms in the OSI building. Across from her sat Tech Sergeant Robert Dort, whom Myers had just asked some of the same questions he had previously asked over the phone to see if Dort had changed his story. He hadn't.

Dort was about average height but everything else about him was thick from his neck to his broad shoulders. The only thing that wasn't thick on Dort was his hair. He had shaved his head bald and it shined under the bright fluorescent lights.

Dort had just told them that his key to the armory had been in his possession the night of the murder, when he paused.

"Hey, speaking of the armory key," Dort offered with a slight Brooklyn accent. "Agent Myers, you had asked last week if anyone had reported a stolen or lost key in the last several months."

Myers nodded "Yes and you said no."

"Well, I forgot, because it was a while ago. But about a couple of months ago, the Chief came to me and told me he had lost his armory key. He asked me to get him another one."

Myers covertly exchanged looks with Emma, and she knew that he, too, was remembering their conversation with the Chief who had been adamant that he had not lost a key. "The Chief?"

"Yeah. It's not that unusual," Dort explained. "So I logged in what had happened and got him a new key."

"Did the Chief ever find his old key?"

"If he did, he didn't tell me."

Emma sensed from the tone of Dort's voice that he didn't hold the Chief in high esteem.

"I'm telling you, that in all my fifteen years in the service, I've never had such lack of support from the top," he said. "As you know, I'm in charge of running the armory, which I may add I'm *very* good at. Those men have tramped on my authority from the get go."

"You know at first I thought talking to you guys would get back to them and they'd come down hard on me," he said, clearly frustrated. "But you know what? The more I thought about it, the more I could give a crap! What are they going to do? Reassign me? Move me to another base? Bring it on!"

Myers put his hand up. "Tech Sergeant Dort, first of all I want to assure you that we are only interested in solving this case. It is *not* our job, nor desire to tell everyone what you have said here.

"Second, I want to clarify something you said. You mentioned the 'higher ups' and 'them.' Who are you talking about?"

"Colonel Carlson and the Chief. They're hands are into everything around here and if you ask me, those hands aren't clean."

"Can you elaborate?" Emma asked.

"Take Teresa Conklin being scheduled to be in the armory that night," Dort said. It was clear that he was agitated. "The Chief had no right to mess with my schedule."

"I'm going to stop you and clear up something," Myers interrupted him. "Did you tell anyone that Conklin was going to take over for the sick airman that night?"

"No. Why would I tell anyone the Chief went behind my back again?"

"Okay. Sorry, please continue."

"Well as I was saying. I was ticked about him putting her on the schedule. Especially since I had told him she wasn't to be on the night shift anymore after she was caught red-handed having people in there. Which reminds me of another thing that pisses me off. I am her supervisor. But when I went to discipline her, I was told *not* to give her an Article 15. Can you believe it?"

When neither Myers nor Emma answered, Dort scowled at them.

"A 15 was more than fair given how many times she did it even after all of those warnings I gave her. It burns my butt that they put me in a manager position and then tell me how to do my job. Let me tell you, I've been a supervisor for years and never once did my superiors go behind my back like these guys do."

"I know you had talked to Agent Myers about Senior Airman Conklin's unauthorized visitors and you told him to go ask the Chief," Emma said. "But it's really important that you tell us everything you know. Who did Teresa have in the armory and why would you tell us to ask the Chief?"

Dort paused wringing his large hands in front of him. "I was given a strict order not to tell anyone that Teresa had been caught letting unauthorized people in the armory."

"The Chief gave you this order?" Myers asked

Dort nodded his shiny head. "He told me he didn't want it to get out that we may have had a breach of security at the armory. Frankly, I think he's full of crap. There was no breach of security! I think it had nothing to do with her letting people into the armory. I think it had everything to do with *who* she let in the armory."

Frustrated by Dort's lack of candor, Myers threw down his pen. "Okay. It's time to tell us everything you know. No more holding back."

"You're sure this won't get back to the Chief or the Colonel Carlson?" Dort asked, shifting in his seat, uneasily.

"I promise I won't reveal who told me this information. We need to know, Dort. One of your airmen was killed and we need to find out why."

"Okay," Dort began slowly, still obviously ill at ease. "Here's what I know. Teresa came here last year, I think in November, from Dyess Air Force Base. I'm thinking this was her third assignment, but you probably already know that."

"Yes, we do," Myers said, scowling. It was, Emma thought, all he could do to keep his cool.

"Sorry. Anyway, they put her under me and I assigned her to work the night shift in the armory. See, it works like this. We put all newbies on the night shift cuz it's a perfect time for them to learn. You know, there's a lot less stuff going on, less guard changes that kind of thing. Anyway, me or one of my guys stayed with her for the first few weeks, just to make sure she knew what to do. I was actually impressed with her. She picked things up pretty quick."

Emma wondered why Teresa Conklin went from a stellar worker to one who broke the rules.

Dort shifted in his seat, his massive thighs scraping against the vinyl. "So, after those first few weeks, I let her fly solo. I even talked to her about putting her on one of the day shifts but she didn't want to move. Told me she'd rather stay on nights cuz it was easier to study. I think she was trying to get her degree. So I let her."

Myers sat back in his chair, studying Dort as he talked.

"Not much happened that first month or so," Dort went on. Now that he had started, he seemed eager to talk. "She did a pretty good job. I mean no one complained cuz they didn't want to do the night shift themselves. Man, they were pleased as punch to give it up to her. Then about two months later I get a call from the Chief. He tells me there's a new policy for weekends, where no guard could work consecutive weekend shifts. Hey, it was no skin off my back. So I changed everyone's schedule, including Teresa's."

Apparently reaching the end of his patience at last, Myers cut in. "You were going to tell us who she let in the armory."

"Hold on! I'm getting to that," Dort promised him. "A few weeks later, I start getting complaints from a couple of my guys from the shift right after hers. They tell me Teresa wasn't finishing her paperwork and they're pissed cuz she left it for them to do. So I told them I'd take care of it. I went down the armory during her shift to see what was going on. You know, see if I could help her out.

"So I went in around midnight, you know since that's right in the middle of her shift. Heck, I'm not much of a sleeper anyway and half the time, don't go to sleep until midnight anyway. When I got there, you can bet I was not happy when I see one of her female friends with her."

"Was this friend a cop?" Emma interrupted him.

"No," Dort frowned. "I'm not sure where she was from, but I don't think she was cop. Could have been though, I suppose.

Anyway, I was pissed and kicked the girl out. Man did I read Teresa the riot act. I chewed her butt for letting anyone in the armory who wasn't scheduled to work."

"What did Conklin say?" Myers demanded, sitting forward and leaning on the desk.

"Huh! She tells me it won't happen again. Gave me some story about a test she had the next day." Dort rolled his eyes. "Said they were cramming. But being the guy I am, I believed her. Thought my warning was good enough. Of course you can imagine how pissed I was when I heard it happened a couple of other times over the next couple of weeks."

"How did you know about these other incidents?"

"One of my airmen who works for me told me that Teresa was bragging about how she was studying during her shift. My airman said Teresa told him she wasn't alone. Well let me tell you. I went straight to the source herself. But of course, Teresa says it wasn't true. I told her that it had better not be true and that I'd better not catch her with visitors in the armory. But it wasn't until a couple of weeks later that I did catch her."

Dort had Emma's full attention now and wanted to hear his answer when Myers asked what he meant.

"Well, I was wired up over something and couldn't sleep so I went for a jog," Dort answered.

"You went jogging at that time of night!" Emma asked, having a hard time believing the massive man in front of her was a runner.

"Yep, I know it sounds kinda weird and it was pretty damned cold, let me tell you. But it helps me blow off steam. Anyway, so I go for a jog around 0100, I think. I usually jog from base housing to the armory and back. But as I ran passed the armory, I saw Carlson and the Chief coming out of it. I knew Teresa was on duty because I had scheduled her. You can bet I was pretty shaken up to see them there; and more than a little pissed they were messing with my armory and one of my guards."

Dort looked at both of them to see if they were following. Myers impatiently told him to continue.

"Anyway," he went on, "they didn't see me because it was dark you know? But I could hear them arguing and let me tell you, the Chief was not too happy. He was yelling about something, but I couldn't get close enough to hear. Didn't want them to see me. So I waited until they took off before I went into the armory to lay into Teresa."

"What did she say?"

"Humph!" Dort snorted indignantly. "This is when I knew that girl was trouble! She started with the tears, bawling about this and that. I can tell when someone's lying to my face," he added, folding his arms over his enormous chest.

"Anyway, I'd had enough of her drama so I threatened a 15 if she didn't tell me what was going on. Well that sure as heck scared her. She spilled her guts. Told me the Colonel and Chief had caught her studying with her friend again. I was like, 'what do you mean they caught you? It's 1:00 in the morning?'"

Emma watched Dort shake his head as he remembered the scene. She, too, had a hard time believing Teresa's story.

"I chewed her ass-sorry Ma'am -up good for breaking the rules again. That's when she tells me she knew, but gave me some bull crap story about having trouble with one of her classes and how this girl was the only one who could help her study. 'So why was the Colonel and Chief here?' I asks her."

"What did she say?" Emma asked glad she wasn't on the end of one of Dort's "ass chewings." She believed that anyone on the receiving end of one of them probably thought twice about breaking the rules again.

"That's when she tells me how this girl and her got into some kind of knock down drag out fight."

"Did you believe her?"

"Yeah, I guess. I did see a scratch on her face. Anyway, she said she was scared and called the Chief." Dort rolled his eyes again. "Now this I believed. That man always tells his airmen to skip ranks and go straight to him if they have any problems. I've called him on it several times, it's pathetic. My people should be coming to me, *not* him!"

"So the Chief *and* the Colonel showed up after she called?" Myers prodded him.

Dort swiped his hand over his bald head. "Yeah. She said she was surprised when the Chief brought the Colonel. Supposedly they told her that they'd been at the office writing some brief they had to give at a conference. I guess her phone call threw the old men for a loop so they both showed up."

"And you still believed her?"

"Ya know, I believed the part where they were up all night working on the brief 'cuz I remember we were working our butts off for that conference, too. But I don't know why they couldn't just have called me," he added begrudgingly.

"Where was the other girl?" Myers asked

"Teresa said the girl took off as soon as she heard Teresa phoned the Chief. I never found out who she was. Anyway, by then I'd had it with her. I told her to report to my office the next morning. I figured I'd deal with her after I ran her story by the Chief."

"And did he confirm it?" .

"Yep. Go figure. The guy told me the same thing, like they'd rehearsed it or something. But I wasn't gonna let them push me around anymore! No, Sir. I told him this crap had to stop. That girl was blatantly breaking the rules. I stood up to the old man. Told him I wouldn't have any Joe Schmoe wandering around my armory. That's when I told him I wanted an Article 15. That girl more than deserved it."

"What did the Chief say?" Emma broke in and saw Dort's face turn beet red. Apparently just remembering the encounter was enough to enrage him.

"Man, he was pissed at me. He told me no way was he going to support a 15. But hey, this wasn't the first time the old man didn't agree with me about punishments. So I demanded he run it by the Colonel and Legal. You know to see what they thought.

"The next day he calls me in and tells me he ran it by them, but get this. He says they both agreed with him. Said a 15 was too harsh. And that's when the old fart ordered me to write her a letter of reprimand."

Emma made herself a mental note to see if anyone in her unit had suggested an Article 15 was too harsh of a punishment for Teresa without running it by her first. She had a suspicion that the Chief was lying again.

Dort paused trying to force back his fury.

"I know the old boy outranks me," he said in a low voice, "but I couldn't stop myself. I argued with him that a LOR was not right. It wasn't good enough. I told him that, with all due respect, I didn't think he should be telling me what to give my airman. I told him I was going to run it by my buds, you know, to see what they thought. I've never seen the old boy so pissed before," he added, snickering. "Cripes, he got all red faced and told me to shut up and do what I was told.

"And that's when he ordered me to not breathe a word about this to anyone. He gave me the bullcrap 'for security' malarkey. So what was I to do? I mean, I got two kids and a wife to take care of. So I shut up and did what I was told. But man, I tell you, I've been pissed about it ever since. And so I must be getting back at the old geezer, talking to you guys. I'm sure he'd be pretty pissed I was talking."

Dort waited while Myers and Emma captured what he had said. The small room bristled from Dort's tension.

"So after this, you took Airman Conklin off the night shift?" Emma prompted him.

"Yes." Dort snorted. "I didn't trust her no more and wanted her where I could keep my eye on her. I also started to dig around a little about my little airman. You know, to see if she had been in trouble before."

Emma stopped writing in mid sentence and looked up at him puzzled. "What do you mean? We looked at her file and the only negative was the LOR."

If Teresa had been in trouble before even at other bases, there should have been more negative paperwork in her file reprimanding her for her behavior.

"You and I both know, Ma'am that not everything is in a person's file. I heard all of these rumors about her from her last base, Dyess; something about her being in some kind of trouble.

127

You can imagine I wanted to find out what she was in trouble for. You know, to see if these rumors were true. Well I must be pretty damned lucky. Cuz it just so happens I used to be stationed with a guy who was a supervisor in Security Forces Squadron at Dyess. I thought maybe he'd know something, so I called him up. When he found out why I was calling, damned if he didn't laugh at me."

"Why?" Myers demanded as Emma speculated what Teresa had done at her former base.

"That's what I asked him," Dort said. "'Why ya laughin'?' He tells me he knows of Teresa's old supervisor, the lucky one before me. Anyway, he tells me my friend, Teresa . . . like she was my friend," his voice trailed off sarcastically.

"What did he tell you about Conklin?" Myers asked impatiently.

"What? Oh yeah, said she was some kind of a wild girl who didn't always play by the rules if you know what I mean. So I asks him if she'd gotten into trouble. He says the word on the street was she had."

"So why isn't there anything in her file?" Emma prodded wishing Dort would just come out with it. Clearly someone was not following the rules by punishing and trying to rehabilitate this girl who was habitually breaking the rules.

"I was getting to that. My friend tells me her supervisor was all hush, hush about the whole deal. Supposedly he wouldn't tell my friend anything, just that she was trouble and they were dealing with it."

"So did your friend know how they 'dealt' with it?" Myers asked his eyebrow raised.

Dort thick lips cracked into a smile eager to reveal his answer. "Damned if my friend didn't start laughing again. He tells me all he knows is that one minute the supervisor is talking about what trouble she is and the next thing my friend knows is that Teresa's been reassigned here to Winburg."

"So they passed off a problem child," Myers said, shrugging. "That isn't very unusual."

It was clear to Emma that Dort was unhappy that they weren't more excited about the information he was giving them. "Yeah, that may not be unusual," Dort said, leaning forward, his eyes bright, "but have you heard of them doing it after only one year on base? I'll bet you . . . ."

"You mean Senior Airman Conklin had only been at Dyess for twelve months out of her three or four year commitment?" Emma stopped him, not bothering to hide her amazement. It was highly unusual for an airman to be transferred before fulfilling their commitment and for Teresa to be transferred after only such a short time was unheard of.

"Now you're catching on," Dort chortled. "See, I was right all along. That girl was trouble."

Chapter 24

About thirty minutes after they ended the interview with Dort, Myers and Emma finished writing up their notes. The stifling room was claustrophobic and Emma longed to escape its confining walls and go outside for a fresh air. Just as she started to open the door, Dan poked his head into the interrogation room and informed them that Teresa's parents were on the base.

"Already?" Myers exclaimed looking at his watch. "I wasn't expecting them until later on tonight."

Dan shrugged his shoulders. "Evidentially they caught an earlier flight. All I know is that someone from Security Forces called me and told me they had an escort pick them up at Frankfurt International a few hours ago and they had just arrived on base. The escort is getting them settled into billeting right now. I told him we'd want to see the parents as soon as possible and he thought we could meet them over there in about two hours."

Billeting was the military term for hotel. Many people who came to Winburg stayed in billeting, some as visitors while others used it as a temporary home while they waited for housing to become available. The rooms were very pleasant and, in fact, rivaled those of some of the major hotel chains.

"Good," Myers replied. "That gives us plenty of time to try to get a hold of Conklin's former supervisor at Dyess. Dort thinks he may know something about Conklin," he explained to Dan.

"Supposedly she was released early from her assignment and we need to find out why. Why don't we all go up to your office and make some calls."

Dan nodded. "I'll tell Agent Manning to page me when she gets word the parents are ready. I'll meet you in my office."

A few minutes later Emma sat on a worn black leather chair in front of Dan's desk, munching on the granola bar Myers had thrown on her lap when she had mentioned lunch.

Myers was seated next to her. "I went through Conklin's personnel file again earlier and got the name of her old supervisor at Dyess from her last EPR. His name is Tech Sergeant Dave Swarsky. I got his number from Air Force Personnel and found out from them he has been stationed at Dyess for about three years and is about to PCS to Mountain Home in Idaho. In fact, he is scheduled to leave Dyess next week and is going on two weeks leave before he gets to Mountain Home. We were lucky to find him before he left on vacation."

As Emma knew, in the military, the acronym "PCS" stood for permanent change of station, a phrase used when a military member was reassigned from one base to another. It was very common for a member to take leave, or vacation, during their move to visit friends and family or just relax before starting a new job.

"We need to tread lightly with Swarsky," Myers cautioned them, "just in case he is still tight-lipped about talking about what happened with Conklin."

After getting their agreement, Myers gave Dan the phone number. A few seconds later, Dan gave a thumbs up sign indicating Swarsky answered the phone.

"Hello, Sergeant Swarsky," Dan said into the phone. "My name is Dan Panchen and I'm an OSI agent stationed at Winburg Air Base in Germany."

Used to people being surprised by his calls, Dan nodded as he listened. "No Sergeant Swarsky. I assure you I'm not aware of any problems with any of your troops. That is, any of your current troops. I'm calling because I'm investigating a case here in Winburg that involves a Senior Airman Teresa Conklin. I understand you were her supervisor about one year or so ago when she was stationed at Dyess."

Dan wrinkled his brow as he listened patiently to the man on the other end. "Yes, I can believe that you are very thorough and I'm sure you put everything in her EPRs and personnel file. But, it's very important that you give me a few minutes of your time, Sergeant."

Emma was glad that earlier Myers had confirmed the fact that all of the commanders on base had met with their troops and given them a short briefing about what had happened. General Brandt had also given a short statement to the Air Force Times, who had called within an hour of the commanders' meetings. The word was out that an airman had been murdered on base and so there was no longer a need to keep it secret, which hopefully meant, in turn, that everyone, including Sergeant Swarsky would be willing to cooperate.

"I'm calling you because I'm part of a team here that is investigating the murder of Teresa Conklin," Dan was saying now. "Since you were her supervisor at her last base, we need to talk to you to find out everything you know about her. When I say 'we', I mean the investigative team. I'm going to put you on speaker phone now so that they can all hear what you have to say, okay?"

"Yes, Sir." Swarsky had a heavy Southern drawl on the other end. "That's okay with me."

After Dan had performed the introductions, Myers took over.

"I know you're busy," he said, "so we'll get right to the point. First of all, I want to assure you that I have read Conklin's personnel file and have seen what you wrote about her in her EPRs. So we can skip all that. What we're looking for are your personal observations. What specifically did she do for you and how was her work performance?"

Emma knew that Myers was starting with an easy question hoping to get Swarsky to open up as quickly as possible.

"Well, Sir," Swarsky said, clearing his throat. "Senior Airman Conklin was a patrolman for me, meaning she drove around base in a squad car looking for breaches of security and answering calls as they came in. Pretty standard stuff, you know disturbances, domestic fights, lights on in buildings after hours, that kind of thing. She pretty much did her job good."

"Can you elaborate what you mean by 'good'?" Emma asked him trying to draw out more information.

"Well Ma'am." He answered slowly as if trying to find the right words. "She came to work on time and she did her job. I didn't hear any complaints about her while she was on duty."

Myers cocked his eyebrow. "You said you didn't hear any complaints while she was *on* duty. Did you hear any while she was *off* duty?"

There was silence on the other end.

Dan leaned closer to the phone. "Sergeant Swarsky? Are you still there?"

"Yes, Sir." He replied clearing his throat again. "I'm still here."

"Did you hear Agent Myers' question?"

"Yes, Sir." Swarsky paused again before replying hesitantly. "Well, I did hear about some things when she was off duty. Several of the other airmen in my shop who lived in the dorms with Teresa starting complaining about her a few months after she came here."

"What kind of complaints?" Myers asked impatiently.

"Um, you know airmen. They're always in each other's business, especially when they pretty much live, eat and work together . . . ." His voice trailed off.

"Sergeant Swarsky," Myers commanded. "I must remind you that we are investigating the murder of Teresa Conklin. You must not hold back information from us. If necessary, we'll order you to fly over here so that we can talk to you in person. I would hate to cut into your scheduled vacation, but will have to if you insist on not being completely open with us."

Myers's words obviously had the anticipated affect on Swarsky.

"No Sir," he replied anxiously. "You don't need to fly me there. I'll answer your questions."

"Thank you, Sergeant Swarsky." Emma said, playing good cop. "So you were telling us what the other airmen were complaining about."

"Yes, Ma'am, like I said, about eight months after she arrived, one of my airman who lived next door to Teresa, came up to me and told me that Teresa was being very loud at night. She said she was keeping her from sleeping.

"To tell you the truth, I didn't think much of it. I've had these complaints before where one person likes to stay up all night playing their music or TV or whatnot, while the other goes to bed at eight o'clock. You can't make everyone happy and I'm not one who has much patience with dorm issues. So I told my airman to go talk to the dorm supervisor and have her look into it."

"So what happened?" Dan asked.

"I actually forgot about it, Sir, until Airman Trace came back to me a couple of days later complaining again. This time she brought another one of my troops with her who lived on the other side of Teresa. They said Teresa was still waking them up at two or three o'clock in the morning. Lots of loud fighting with someone, they said. I asked them if they had gone to the dorm supervisor and they told me they had, but the dorm sup just told Teresa to keep it down."

Emma thought about the information Swarsky was giving them and how it confirmed what Dort had said, that Teresa Conklin was not the stellar, studious airman she held herself out to be. There was a lot more to their victim and her past.

"My airmen weren't too happy and told me something had to be done because they couldn't do their job if they didn't get any sleep," the sergeant went on. "Well, I must admit, I was angry at the dorm super. I was too busy to deal with this stuff, but I also didn't want any of my patrolmen to get into an accident because they couldn't sleep."

In the military, it was not unusual for a supervisor to help a subordinate out with a personal matter and Emma was glad someone had finally stepped in to take care of Teresa's situation. "What did you do?" she asked.

"I called Teresa into my office and asked her what was going on. She told me she had a fight with a friend of hers and she was sorry it got loud. She promised me it wouldn't happen again. I warned her that I didn't want to hear anything more about any fights or loud music or whatever and she needed to fly straight or would be punished."

"And did she stop?"

"It seemed so, at least for a couple of weeks, but then it got really bad. My two airmen came to talk to me again. This time they told me Teresa was definitely fighting with someone. They were both in Airman Trace's room and could hear shouting. They said it sounded like things were being thrown against the wall and someone was threatening Teresa. They told me the door slammed so hard it rattled Airman Trace's wall."

Myers stopped writing, his brow furrowed. "What did they mean someone threatened Teresa?"

"I'll never forget it. Both of my airmen were pretty scared. They said they heard someone shout 'Bitch, you better not tell anyone or I'll make sure you don't'. Sorry Ma'am, but those were his exact words."

Emma looked at Myers and Dan with excitement. Finally, she thought, there was a potential break in the case.

"Were they able to ID the guy for you?" Dan asked eagerly.

The three let out a collective sigh when Swarsky said that they had not.

Oblivious to their frustration, he went on. "They were too scared and didn't leave Airman Trace's room until that next morning when they came to see me."

"Did you confront Senior Airman Conklin?" Myers asked.

"Yes. I called her into my office right away and I could tell she'd been crying. She was really upset. She told me she'd broken up with someone and he'd threatened to kill her. I asked her to give me his name, but she wouldn't. I pretty much tried to force it out of her, but she just wouldn't tell me even though she was really shaken up. I didn't know what to do. I mean that girl was obviously scared out of her mind. So I called Family Advocacy and Mental Health to get her some help."

"Did you tell anyone else Conklin had been threatened?"

"No, Sir."

Myers shoved his pad at Emma. On it he had written, 'Someone threatens to kill Conklin and all he does is send her to the psych ward?"

Seeing how frustrated he was, Emma joined the interrogation with a question about whether or not Airman Trace was still at Dyess, adding that they would like to talk to her. If Myers minded her interference, he did not show it.

"Sorry Ma'am. She's in the desert. She's not scheduled to come back for a couple more months. Course if she was to call me, I could tell her that you want to talk to her."

Emma was determined to get some more information out of Swarsky and continued grilling him. "We understand that Airman Conklin was reassigned to Winburg about twelve months after arriving at Dyess. If I am calculating correctly, this would be about one month after she claims she was threatened. Can you tell me why she was reassigned?"

"I don't know Ma'am," he declared emphatically. "Honestly I don't. All I know is that about a couple of weeks after I sent her to Family Advocacy, I was called into my commander's office and told that Teresa was being reassigned."

"Did the commander say why?" Myers cut in.

"No, Sir. To be honest, I think he was as surprised as me. He just told me that an investigation had taken place which was completely confidential, and that for Teresa's safety, she was being reassigned to Winburg."

Emma mulled Swarsky's words over in her head. She knew that everything with the exception of knowledge of criminal activity was kept confidential by the Mental Health doctors. However, Family Advocacy did not share the same privilege, although many of its advocates begged to differ with her and were very unhappy when she used their information in her criminal proceedings.

Emma also knew from her experience working with them, that Family Advocacy and Mental Health worked a lot with domestic violence. They had programs to protect the violated party and she seemed to remember that one of them resulted in a civilian spouse being sent back home away from their abusive military spouses.

Emma thought she also recalled cases where the program was used to separate military spouses and reassign them to different bases far away from each other. She remembered the couple she had heard about when she first came to her last base who unfortunately hadn't taken advantage of this program.

Both spouses were military and the husband was the abuser. Evidentially, he had threatened his wife on several occasions, but she did not seek professional help for fear it would hurt her career. Unfortunately, one night, the husband carried out his threats and he shot his wife in the head, after which he put her body in the passenger seat of his car and proceeded to drive off at ninety miles per hour until he managed to drive off the road and wrap the car around a tree. When the two bodies were found, he was holding his wife's hand.

Since she had never heard of reassignment of an unmarried airman, Emma jotted herself a note to talk to her friend over at Mental Health.

"Tech Sergeant Swarsky, I need you to clarify something for me," she said now, remembering something that Dort had told them earlier. "We heard from some people at your base, that Airman Conklin was known as a trouble maker. But from what you have said, except for these fights she was a good performer. Do you know why these people would have called her that?"

There was silence on the other end of the phone and Emma was fairly certain Swarsky knew something that he was not telling them. It was her experience that it was hard to get information out of military members who were told to keep quiet, which is the way it should be given their line of work.

"Well, Ma'am," he said finally, "I'm not sure who said that, but I had heard rumors that she liked to party and drink. They said she was kind of wild one, if you get my meaning."

"No, I'm not sure I do know what you mean," Emma told him. "Could you elaborate?"

"Well, like I said, she came into work on time, but I noticed her eyes were red a couple of times like she had been drinking the night before. But, you know, it never affected her ability to do her duty. And I'm not one to believe rumors so I just let it go."

Emma watch Myers roll his eyes and knew he wasn't buying Swarsky's story, but then again, neither was she.

"Did you ever find out who threatened Teresa Conklin?" he asked.

"No, Sir. Again, there were a lot of rumors after she left. People who thought they knew, but I never heard for sure who it was."

"Just so we make sure we have covered all of the bases, why don't you humor us and tell us some of those rumors."

For the second time, the sergeant made no response.

"Sergeant Swarsky?"

"Yes Sir, I'm still here. Well, some people said she had a civilian boyfriend who lived in the local area and that he's the reason she was moved. And um, some people said Teresa slept around with whoever she wanted. They thought one of those people must have gotten jealous and ran her off. The other rumor was it was an officer and that was why she was moved so quickly to Winburg. But I don't believe any of it."

Emma wasn't so sure she was ready to discount the rumors at this point as she still didn't have a clear picture of who Teresa really was and it was entirely possible a jealous lover killed her.

"Well," Dan said, hanging up the phone. "Looks like we may have just found our motive: jilted abusive lover kills the one he cannot have."

"Yeah, but something just doesn't fit," Myers said, frowning. "Okay, so if we go with the jealous lover bit how did he get to Winburg? And maybe more importantly, if he's stationed in Texas, how could he possibly know the ins and outs of the armory here?"

"Because," Emma concluded, "we already knew the killer is very methodical and resourceful. But what we didn't know," she added solemnly, "was how passionate he was about seeing Teresa Conklin dead."

Chapter 25

As Emma walked into the lobby of billeting she spied Teresa's parents, Dan and Mary Conklin, who looked as though they had just stepped right off a Midwestern farm.

Emma guessed that Teresa's father, dressed in dark blue jeans and button down collared shirt, was about fifty. Years of hard work on the farm had kept him lean and fit, although his face, lined and leathery from the many years in the sun, hadn't fared as well. His hand, when he shook hers, was calloused, and his smile was sad.

His wife, Mary, stood beside him, her arm threaded through his as she leaned against her husband for support. She was a slight woman about five feet three inches, whose black high heel pumps made her a couple of inches taller. Her straight blond hair was pulled back in a low but severe bun, revealing a face bare of makeup and cold brown eyes. Whereas wrinkles would have made her somehow seem more human, her tight alabaster skin only made her appear more aloof.

She wore an ankle length black skirt and long sleeve white turtleneck sweater that draped over her slim figure. From the thick black tights on her legs to the high turtleneck, Mary Conklin was completely covered. Emma wondered if her personality was as guarded as her wardrobe. Certainly, in contrast to her husband, who was clearly grief stricken, it was unclear how she was handling her daughter's death. Mary Conklin's icy stare chilled Emma making her pull her hand away. Emma had a feeling Mary Conklin was a woman you didn't want to mess with.

Standing off to the side was a stocky woman dressed in her blues, a staff sergeant whose name tag read "Williams," a sergeant Emma had encountered previously as a bailiff on one of her previous trials. In the military court, the bailiff was an appointed military member usually from the defendant's squadron who was in charge of helping the judge and fetching the jury when it was time for them to enter the courtroom. She also stood at the door of the courtroom making sure spectators in the room were acting appropriately. In cases where the defendant was considered a flight risk or charged with a more serious crime, the appointed bailiff was usually an armed cop who was trained to deal with any dangerous issues that arose.

As a member of the Security Forces Squadron, Williams had handled herself very professionally in the courtroom. Quiet and courteous, it was apparent that she took her job very seriously. Certainly, when she had looked around "her" courtroom, her expression had made it clear that it would be a mistake for anyone to get "out of line."

Emma had also seen Williams around the gym. It was apparent from the strong, well defined muscles in her solid arms and legs, Williams spent a lot of time working out.

While Dan and Myers took the Conklins to a conference room, Emma took Williams aside and asked if she had been appointed as the Conklins' official escort.

"Yes, Ma'am." Williams told her. "I'll also be taking them back to the airport the day after tomorrow."

"We're going to talk to Mr. and Mrs. Conklin in the conference room down the hall," Emma informed her. "You can wait in here. I'm not sure how long we'll be. I hope you brought something to do with you so you won't be bored."

"Thank you, Ma'am," she replied stiffly, "but I'll be fine. I'm working on my PME's so I've got enough to keep me busy."

Emma could understand her eagerness to study, given the fact that PME, an acronym for professional military education, was required for promotion.

"Good," she said, "I'll bring them back to you when we're finished."

When Emma joined Myers and Dan in the conference room, she noted that Mary Conklin was seated at the long oak table, taking in her surroundings with calculating eyes. Emma sat across from her, determined not to let herself be unnerved. As for Mr. Conklin, although his eyes filled now and then with tears, his expression was resolute.

"Thank you again for meeting with us today," Emma began, determined to be as gentle as possible in her approach in an attempt to ease their pain. "I know this is a very tough time for you and I want to assure you we are going to do everything possible to find who did this to your daughter. Anything you can tell us about your daughter will be helpful to the case. We need to find out as much as we can about your daughter; her likes, dislikes, whether she was happy here, happy in the Air Force in general, who her friends were. Anything and everything you can tell us so we can piece together what happened."

Emma had dealt with many reluctant witnesses in the past and judging from the narrowed eyes and pursed lips of the woman in front of her, Mrs. Conklin might prove to be one of her toughest. It did not escape her notice that while she was speaking, Mary Conklin snatched her hand away from her husband's and clasped her hands tightly in her lap.

"Mr. and Mrs. Conklin," Emma tried again, "it may seem like some of the questions we ask you today are irrelevant. But I assure you there is a reason we're asking these questions. Agents Panchen and Myers and I have collectively investigated many cases and I promise we won't ask you any question that is not pertinent to this case."

"We understand, Major," Don Conklin said. As for his wife, she remained silent, her steely eyes boring into Emma.

Emma smiled, grateful to be getting somewhere. "Emma, please," she said.

"As you can imagine, Emma, all this is very difficult for us. We flew hundreds of miles to come get our little girl's body and now we have to fly back home to bury her. But," he added, a shadow crossing his face, "I don't care what it takes. We want you to catch the bastard who did this to her."

Mary Conklin frowned, obviously disapproving of her husband's profanity.

"Mary, we have to help them," he pleaded said in a low voice. "You know we can't let him get away with what he did to our little girl. It rips my heart knowing he's still out there." And, turning back to Emma, said, "We'll tell you whatever we can."

"I want to let you know we're interviewing everyone who is even remotely connected to this case and your daughter," Myers assured him. "But before we get into specifics about what happened, I'd like to ask you about her childhood. As Major Lohrs said, we need to get a better understanding of your daughter. Can you tell me what she was like growing up?"

Tears swelled in his eyes as Don spoke.

"Well, Sir, she was a beautiful child. She is our youngest. She grew up on our farm and loved to ride. She used to spend hours riding with her best friend, Katie, who lived about one mile away. Her dad's farm borders our land."

Emma was sure Mary Conklin flinched at Katie's name.

"Katie and Teresa would ride their horses together and pretty much did everything together. Whenever we couldn't find Teresa, we knew she must be with Katie."

"How about as they grew up?" Dan asked. "Did your daughter and Katie remain good friends?"

Mary Conklin said nothing, but Emma noted that she was clenching her hands so tightly that her knuckles were white.

"Well, you know how kids are." Don wiped his cheeks with his handkerchief. "They get busy with school and church and start to drift apart."

"So your daughter wouldn't have talked to Katie since she was stationed here?" Myers asked. "The reason I'm asking is to see if Teresa might have talked to Katie about any troubles she may have had here or her previous assignment. I have to tell you that no one seems to have really known your daughter here and we're running into a lot of dead ends. We were hoping someone back home might know something."

"Katie and Teresa haven't talked since their junior year in high school," Mary Conklin said, her voice cool and unwavering, "so I doubt that Katie could help you."

Her thin lips shut tightly clearly declaring she would not elaborate any further on what caused the riff between the two best friends. Emma tried another approach.

"We read in Teresa's personnel file that you consented to her entering the military when she was seventeen. Can you tell us why she wanted to sign up so young?"

For a moment Mrs. Conklin looked so angry that Emma thought she might storm out of the room, but her husband spoke authoritatively instead.

"We must tell them everything," he said, placing his hand on her arm. "I know you think Teresa's past has nothing to do with what happened to her. But what if it does? If we don't tell them about her and help them understand who she is . . . was, how will we ever be able to look into each other's eyes, knowing we may have withheld information that would help them catch whoever did this?"

Don waited until his wife finally nodded for him to continue.

"I want you to know that Teresa was a good kid," Don finally said, his voice low. "We're good Christian people, with a strong belief in God and how He wants us to live by His Grace. Our children were raised by the strict hand of God. We had bible study every night before dinner and our kids could read verses from the Bible before they could read anything else."

Mary closed her eyes and nodded in affirmation. Her hands pressed together as if in prayer while her husband went on.

"We never really had any problems with our kids," he went on earnestly. "We turned them over to God and He raised them as He saw fit. If they did get out of hand, we swiftly and justly punished them, just as God intended. It may have seemed harsh to others, but our kids knew God doesn't tolerate sinners. They knew they must repent or face forever damnation in Hell!"

Emma uneasily shifted in her chair, not sure how to respond. Suddenly the couple in front of them no longer reminded her of the wholesome Midwestern couples she had imagined them to be.

"You asked about Teresa's age when she enlisted. Yes, we consented to her entering the military early. It was right after she graduated a semester early from high school," Don went on and Emma could see the pain in his eyes. "Teresa started to run with the wrong crowd at the end of her junior year."

Emma wondered if this wrong crowd was the reason for the break up of Teresa's friendship with Katie. She remained silent watching Don grapple with his next words.

"We didn't know at first." Don went on slowly. "We thought she was still getting good grades, doing her homework, going to church . . . nothing out of the ordinary. She'd always been a straight A student; in the 4H and all sorts of horse clubs. She never did anything wrong. She . . . she was our angel."

Tears came into his eyes again, but his wife's eyes flushed with fury as her husband talked of her daughter's past.

"It wasn't until we got a call from her principal that we learned Teresa had started cutting class. We were shocked when he told us she had even completely skipped school for three days, giving her teacher a fake doctor's note as an excuse. It was . . . it was devastating. Teresa had never been in any trouble. Never done anything wrong, so we didn't know what to do. So we looked to God. He led us to start watching her to see if we could figure out what was wrong. That's when we found out our little girl had completely changed."

Putting his arm around his tense wife's shoulders, Don frowned. "I am sure an outsider wouldn't know anything was wrong," he went on, "But we knew. She started wearing more makeup, always worried about her hair and how she looked. She used her savings, before we closed it, to buy short skirts and tight sweaters. We didn't feel Teresa needed all those things to make her any more attractive to other people."

Myers stole a look at Emma who forced her face to remain neutral. Inside she was thinking it was not at all unusual for a teenage girl to care about her appearance, or for that matter with all of the hormones, to act out against her parents. Lord knows, Emma had gone through all that and more.

"You may not understand or agree with us, Agent Myers," Teresa's mother said stiffly, "but we are God's children and do not believe in dressing provocatively or girls wearing too much make up. We believe such displays are sinful and sinners must be punished. Our children were raised in the church and it is our belief they should strictly adhere to its teachings."

Don agreed with his wife. "At first we thought Teresa was just rebelling against us. But then we found out that she was hanging around with some bunch of rich kids whose parents basically left them alone to do whatever they wanted. There was no supervision whatsoever," he hesitated, clearly disgusted by the memory.

"We found out that they exposed Teresa to alcohol and God knows what else. She started drinking and experimenting with marijuana. When I sat her down and talked to her about it, she told me she only tried it once.

"I didn't believe her," his brow furrowed. "I told her it didn't matter how many times, she sinned and sinners must be punished. I took her out back and she stayed there all night repenting and praying for forgiveness. No daughter of mine was going to shame me or God." His voice rose. "But then I found out that she'd blatantly disobeyed me and had stopped going to church. Well, I just couldn't stand for it any longer. I would not have a deliberate sinner living under my roof!"

Removing his arm from around his wife, Don clasped his hands on the table in front of him and stared at them. His lips moved silently and Emma wondered if, like his wife before him, he was praying.

"I asked God for help," he said finally, looking up. "He told me to keep trying to get Teresa on the straight and narrow and maybe things would get better once school was out for the summer. They didn't."

A tear slowly rolled down his cheek. Teresa's father had obviously been desperate to get control over his rebellious daughter.

"When school first let out, Teresa started going to church with the family again and seemed to be back to her normal self. We were so grateful that everything was okay. We prayed every night that it would remain that way.

"It wasn't until the beginning of her senior year that we found out she had started sneaking out her window at night again. She would take an old pickup I'd parked down at the barn and use it to drive into town to be with those . . . those kids. One day I noticed the front grill of my truck was smashed. It turned out that Teresa had been driving the truck behind my back. She'd been drinking and hit a tree. Thank God she wasn't hurt and didn't hurt anyone else."

Although drinking and driving was pretty serious, Emma couldn't help but feel sorry for the young girl. It must have been really hard to conform to the rigid rules her strict parents placed on her.

"I wouldn't have it!" he exclaimed, and she could see that he was working himself into a fury. "I forbid Teresa from seeing anyone and locked her in her room. I nailed her windows shut so she couldn't sneak out. I even talked to her friend Katie to see if she knew what demon had gotten into Teresa. That was when I found out that she and Teresa hadn't talked since earlier that year. Mary and I couldn't believe it. They had been friends forever. I asked Katie what had happened and practically had to drag the answer out of her."

"She told us that when Teresa started hanging out with this group of sinners," Mrs. Conklin said, her face expressionless, "she started doing things that scared Katie. Don told Katie that he knew about the alcohol and that Teresa had tried marijuana. But Katie told Don that was not all. It seems Teresa did things when she was drunk or high and that's what really scared Katie."

Mary Conklin did nothing to hide the contempt in her voice and Emma wondered if she despised what her daughter had done or the girl herself.

"What exactly was Teresa doing?" Emma asked.

"Not that it is any of your business," Mary Conklin snapped, "but she was having sex, or sleeping around as Katie put it. This had better not get out, do you hear me? If I hear Teresa's reputation has been tarnished by you three, I'll report you to your superiors. You mark my words!"

Clearly appalled by his wife's outburst, Don cut her off. "My wife is just concerned about our daughter. We've been through so much already."

"I assure you what you say here will not be shared publicly," Myers said tersely. "But I must tell you it is very important to our investigation. It may have been one of these people who killed your daughter."

Apparently appeased by this assurance, Don went on. "Katie's a good Christian, from a good Christ centered family and it scared her when Teresa started acting . . . promiscuous." He shuddered as he said the word. "This just wasn't our little girl. It may sound old fashioned in this day and age, but we don't believe in pre-marital sex. And that with the alcohol and everything else, our daughter was sinning in front of our faces and we would not stand for it."

"So you encouraged her to enlist in the Air Force." Emma said gently, not wanting to sound judgmental, even though, given today's society, it was not beyond the bounds of reason that a girl Teresa's age might want to experiment with sex.

"We talked to our clergy and our church counsel and asked for guidance," Don explained, his voice devoid of emotion now. "They prayed for us and agreed it was time to remove Teresa from the situation. She was no longer welcome in our home until she turned her life around and the only way to do that was to get her away from that awful crowd. Teresa needed a place that was more structured and regimented and gave her a purpose again. We had a friend whose brother was in the Air Force and talked to him. After hearing what he and the recruiter had to say, we decided the military was best for Teresa. She needed the discipline and we really respect the people who serve our country."

Emma couldn't disagree with their decision. She had seen the military change many lost and troubled teenagers for the better. Many made the Air Force a career and retired at a young age. Unfortunately, Teresa would not be one of them.

"Did you notice a change in your daughter after she joined?" Myers asked and Emma wondered what he was thinking about the parents in front of him. If he disagreed at all with their tactics, he kept it well hidden.

"Yes. She seemed to love the structure. She actually started talking to us again. She'd call and write whenever she could while she was in basic training. We all went to her graduation from tech school. We were so proud. It was such a relief to have our daughter back. Through the years she told us she how happy she was and how much she loved traveling and living at the different bases."

It was highly unlikely given their previous reaction, Emma thought, that Teresa would tell her parents anything but positive and potentially untruthful news.

"We visited her about twice a year," her mother insisted, as if defending their decision as parents. "She would proudly show us where she was living, and take us around the base. It seemed to be an okay place, although I questioned her living in the dorms. It looked like a place with a lot of sinful temptations."

Emma looked at Mary Conklin and marveled at the lack of emotion the mother showed for her dead daughter. She wondered if Mary Conklin ever once used a kind word towards Teresa or told her she was proud.

"Did your daughter's demeanor change at all when she was stationed at Dyess, in Texas?" Myers asked, directing his question straight at Teresa's mother.

"What do you mean?" she demanded, clearly startled.

"Well, ma'am, we have learned that Teresa may have been dating someone who threatened her there. Do you know anything about this?"

The older woman shook her head vigorously. "No, she never said anything to me, or to my knowledge, her brothers or sister."

"Do you think whoever was threatening Teresa was the one who killed her?" Don demanded.

"We're not sure right now. But I assure you, we are checking into it." Myers answered calmly. "So, she didn't sound like anything was bothering her while she was at Dyess?"

"No!" Mrs. Conklin said vehemently. "We noticed that she didn't call or write as much, but she told us that was because she was taking a full class load."

"Did she tell you why she was reassigned here to Winburg?" Dan asked.

"No, Sir," Don responded. "We thought it was awfully fast, but Teresa told us that they had a special assignment for her. She sounded almost relieved to be moving. She was definitely ready to try someplace new, she told us. We were concerned it would affect her getting her degree, but she told us she could take on-line classes while she was in Germany and that they also had classes here on base."

Myers wrote something on his notepad. "How did she sound after she moved here?"

Don sadly shrugged. "Mostly the same. We really didn't hear much from her. She was so busy. She told us that, between school and working the night shift, she really didn't have any time to herself."

"A couple of months after she moved here, Teresa called to speak to her father, but Don wasn't home," Mrs. Conklin said matter-of-factly. "I was on my way out the door and couldn't talk long, but Teresa told me she was really happy she had moved here. She said things were going really well and she felt like she had a future with the Air Force."

"We wanted to believe her." Don said quietly putting a comforting hand over his wife's.

"But then sometime in the later spring, or early summer," Mrs. Conklin went on, shaking her hand free impatiently. "I knew the devil had gotten her again. She stopped calling again. When we did hear from her, she hardly talked. Of course she never talked to me anyway. But I knew! It was just like the last time. That girl was possessed. I know it!"

"Now, Mary," her husband said in a conciliatory voice. "I think Teresa sounded stressed, like something was on her mind. When I asked her what was wrong, she said it was nothing. She just told us not to worry."

It didn't sound as though Mrs. Conklin had had much time or patience for her daughter's "sinful" frivolities, Emma thought. Even if her daughter had needed help, it was doubtful that she would have turned to her mother. No wonder Teresa acted out against her parents. It would take a saint to live under such extreme circumstances.

Reaching under his notepad, Myers brought out Conklin's journal and pushed it across the table. "We found your daughter's journal in her dorm room," he said. "We've made a copy for you. She wrote in it about every day and I hope that it will give you some comfort. Why don't we leave the two of you alone for a minute? We'll be right back."

The last thing Emma saw before she closed the door was Don flipping through the worn book's pages, engrossed in his daughter's words. Beside him Mary had tightly closed her eyes as her lips moved in silent prayer.

Chapter 26

After ten minutes had passed, they returned to the meeting room. Emma had expected to see that reading the journal would have unleashed emotion but she was completely unprepared for the actual emotion she saw.

Teresa's father was slumped back in his chair, the journal lying open askew in front of him on the table where it had been thrown down.

His wife was standing by the windows, her arms were tightly crossed in front of her chest. Fury, or was it fear, flashed in her bright blue eyes as she stormed back to the table.

"You've read this?" she demanded, angrily.

"Yes, Ma'am." Myers replied, obviously momentarily taken aback by the force of the woman's anger.

"So you knew that she thought she was in love." Mrs. Conklin spat out the words. Her face, Emma noted, was very white. "I expect," she added, "that had something to do with the fact that she had stopped calling us.

"So she *was* at it again," she muttered, giving a heartbroken laugh. "I knew it!"

Completely confused by this turn of events, Emma sought to understand what had caused this reserved woman to so totally lose control.

"I know this is difficult, Ma'am," she said, "but I'm not sure I understand. If you don't mind me asking, what was in the journal that upset you both?"

Mary gave Emma a long look. "I'm sure you saw it," she finally answered sardonically. "It's where she confessed she was in love."

"But why wouldn't you be happy for her?"

"I am not a monster, Major Lohrs! No, don't interrupt me. Of course, I wanted my daughter to be happy and fall in love. The Bible demands we get married and procreate. I wanted this for her. It's not that she was in love that bothered us; it was who she was in love with."

"But she doesn't mention who it is in the journal," Myers said, clearly as puzzled as Emma was. "Do you know? Did she tell you?"

"No. I told you she hardly ever even called us. Supposedly she was so "busy" with school. But there's a hidden meaning in that book," she added, pointing to the black book on the table as though it were the devil itself. "What bothers us is the fact her love was so secret. You mark my works, Teresa was hiding something. You can tell from the words she uses. She couldn't tell anyone about this person, not even write it in her journal. And there must have been a reason. It's just like that horrible time during her last year at home, Don. She was hiding what she was doing then and she is hiding something now!

"Why, Teresa?" She was screaming now. "Why did you do this to yourself? To your family?"

Emma was at a loss for words. In all her years of interviewing people, from drug users to defendants with violent tempers, Emma had rarely encountered a situation like this. Don, however, was apparently startled out of his trance.

"I know this is hard for all of you to understand," he told them. "What Teresa wrote in the journal really concerns us. It brings back bad memories from that last year she was living at home. We told you Teresa had been having . . . extra-marital sexual relations that last year. After she enlisted in the Air Force someone sent a really nasty letter to our house. It was unsigned, but whoever wrote it accused Teresa of having an adulterous affair with her husband.

The woman said she wanted us to know and to keep our daughter away from her husband, or else she would take care of Teresa herself. We didn't want to believe it! But she'd already sold her soul to the devil. So maybe she did get involved with an adulterer."

"Did you talk to her about the letter?" Myers asked.

"Yes. It was while she was stationed at her first base, Mountain Home. Teresa told us it had been over for some time. I preached to her about God's Commandments. That it didn't matter if the man seduced her, that it was a sin and she must beg for God's forgiveness. Every night we all got down on our knees and begged for His mercy. I just knew God could get her through this if she put her trust in Him and let Him guide her to see the error of her ways."

As Emma watched Don smiled sadly at his wife, she wondered if Teresa had really been reformed.

"That's when she said to me 'Daddy, I know I have caused you so many problems. I promise I won't ever get involved with a married man again.' My little girl told me she had asked for God's forgiveness, and 'Daddy, now I am asking you for yours.' I . . . I forgave her. She's my baby. I had to forgive her."

Mary stared out the window behind them and remained silent. It wasn't apparent whether she had forgiven her daughter.

Emma did the only thing she could. She smiled reassuringly at Teresa's father, hoping he'd find some solace in the fact he had done the right thing by forgiving his youngest daughter.

"So do you think whomever Teresa writes about in the journal may have been a married man?" she asked.

"I honestly don't know, Major." Don Conklin told her. "We automatically thought the worst when we read it. I'm so ashamed that we condemned her, thinking she was at it again." A moan escaped his lips. "But why else did she need to keep it so secret?"

Emma remained silent, not wanting to reveal her suspicions that his daughter may have kept it a secret because she was seeing an officer, a crime regardless of whether he was married.

"Whoever she was seeing," Mrs. Conklin said, her voice flat. "It was obviously someone she knew we wouldn't approve of or maybe no one else would approve of for that matter."

Regardless of their beliefs and how they had handled their teenager's wayward actions, Emma's heart went out to this couple who now had to deal with the tragedy of their daughter's untimely death. No parents should have to suffer like that. Her eyes met Myers and she thought she saw a bit of compassion there. She was pleased that he had basically let her take over the interview and she wondered, just briefly, if the compassion he saw there was for her.

"We found a bank statement in Senior Airman Conklin's things," she said. "It's routine for us to call the bank in a death case to see if there are any unusual transactions, like a large amount of money deposited or withdrawn. We didn't find anything unusual but the bank did tell us Teresa had rented a lockbox."

"A lockbox?" her father asked in disbelief. "We didn't know she had a lockbox. What would she need one for?"

"I assure you it is not unusual for an airman who lives in the dorms to rent a lockbox to keep their valuables, like jewelry in," Myers told them. "It is strictly routine procedure to check, but we'd like to see what is in Teresa's. As her parents, you are the only ones who can give the bank permission to open the lockbox for us. If you granted us this permission, we'll inventory the box and then send you anything in it. Unless of course, it is needed for evidence."

"That's fine," Don said wearily. "You have our permission. But, to be honest, I don't think we can handle much more of this."

Bringing the interview to an end, Dan explained that their daughter's squadron would help them with the process of transporting the body back to the States. Although he didn't mention it, the autopsy had been completed earlier in the day. He then explained to them what they could expect in the future regarding the investigation.

"Do you have any questions?"

"Just one," Mary Conklin asked angrily. "Was Teresa all alone when she was shot?"

"No, Ma'am." Myers answered. "Earlier that night, Airman Conklin was studying with a friend, Senior Airman Jaime Kennedy, who was in another room when your daughter died. No, she wasn't alone."

Emma was glad that he could be so sensitive. There were, she realized, depths to this man that she had never dreamt existed. Unfortunately, she found herself becoming attracted to the handsome agent and wondered if this case could get any more complicated.

Chapter 27

"We've got a lead!" Myers exclaimed excitedly as he strode into Dan's office where Emma was rereading Teresa's journal, searching for even the slightest detail they might have missed and Dan was reviewing the personnel files of her past supervisors he had just received.

Throwing Swarsky's file on top of the others, Dan sighed. "I hope it's a good one. I'm batting the big zero with these files."

"I just got a call from a Senior Airman Jessica Harvey," Myers said, waving a small piece of pink paper in the air. "Says she was a friend of Conklin's and worked out with her at least three times a week. Get this! Airman Harvey told me she wants to talk to us about Conklin starting to act weird a few months ago. She's on her way down here now."

"Weird?" Dan asked. "Like how?"

Myers shrugged. "I'm not sure, but at least this girl actually knew Conklin, and unlike anyone else on the base, she seems to know her very well. Let's see what she has to say."

A few minutes later, Myers, Emma and Dan were seated once again in the interrogation room. The door opened and a junior OSI agent announced Senior Airman Harvey's arrival. At first glance, Emma thought the agent had brought the wrong person to them, but the nametag sewed to the front of the BDU blouse confirmed this was indeed Harvey.

Jessica Harvey was a homely young woman whose broad shoulders seemed to swallow her thick neck. Her face was devoid of makeup, and her short hair had been gelled into spikes, she stood with her legs slightly spread apart and her arms clasped behind her back in a parade rest position.

Harvey was very stocky with a flat chest and black eyes that dared them to ask her whether she was indeed a woman. Emma wondered how many times Harvey was mistaken for a man and whether this was an unfortunate card life dealt to her or deliberate one.

"Senior Airman Harvey," Emma began after introducing everyone in the room. "Thank you for coming down here. We understand you were friends with Senior Airman Teresa Conklin and might have some information that could help us."

"Yes, Ma'am." Her voice was as low pitched as a man's. "I do."

"Please, tell us how you know Teresa?"

"Yes, Ma'am." Shifting in her chair, Harvey sat up straight. "You see, Teresa and I met at the gym when she first got here. I go there every day and I saw her there, too. She didn't work out every day, like me, but I was looking for a spotting partner. So after a few weeks of seeing her there alone, I asked her if she would like to spot for each other. We worked out together ever since."

"What was she like?" Myers asked. "Did she have many friends?"

Harvey tilted her head towards him as if sizing him up. "I guess so, Sir. We only saw each other at the gym. Every once in a while I'd see her at the chow hall with another girl. I think her name is Jaime or Jeanie or something like that. Otherwise, it was just her and me at the gym. You know, not much time to talk while you're pumping iron."

Emma found herself wondering if maybe Harvey would lay off "pumping iron" she would look a little less butch.

"When you called, you said Airman Conklin started acting weird a few months ago. What did you mean by that?"

"Yes, Sir. It was around June, I think. Before that Teresa seemed pretty happy. She talked a couple of times about someone she was dating. She said she was in love."

Emma perked up with this information, hoping they might finally learn something about Teresa's secret love life. But when Harvey told Myers she didn't know the identity of Teresa's mysterious lover, Emma's hope faded. It wasn't until Harvey said the lover must have been someone important that Emma felt it return.

"She kept dropping hints," Harvey told Myers, "like she wanted me to figure out who it was. Whoever it was had lots of money, because they were buying her jewelry and things and taking her out to expensive dinners in Amsterdam. She would also say that the person she was seeing had lots of power on base and could get her any job she wanted."

"You could tell she really got off on this you know," Harvey added indignantly. "She flaunted all of this stuff at me and then made me swear I couldn't tell anyone. Like I would have anyone to tell," she muttered to herself.

"So Teresa never told you why it was so important for you to keep this a secret?" Emma questioned.

"No, Ma'am. There were the rumors going around, but I didn't believe them."

"What rumors?" They all asked in unison.

Harvey suddenly looked uncomfortable. "Well, you know, Ma'am. Some idiots said Teresa swung both ways, if you know what I mean. But I didn't believe it." She wrung her hat she still held in her hands. "They were just the same nasty old rumors that are always floating around about some people."

Emma guessed that this young woman knew firsthand the effect of the vicious rumors spread by people who target those different from themselves.

"Why didn't you believe the rumors?" Emma asked softly.

"Because Ma'am. It's hard to keep secrets in the dorm, let alone hide that kind of stuff," she replied. "Everyone knows everyone else's business. Besides, it was just my gut feeling that whoever she was seeing, it was a man . . . and a big man around base, I'm guessing."

"So Senior Airman Harvey, is this what you meant by Airman Conklin acting weird?" Myers broke in. "That she was secretly seeing someone?"

"No Sir. She told me all of this before this past summer. I think it must have been from right after Christmas to around June she was seeing this guy . . .or whoever it was."

"So what happened in June?" Myers asked impatiently.

"I don't know, Sir." Harvey replied, apparently oblivious to his mood. "But like I said before, she was so happy and then all of a sudden she changed. I mean really changed. One day she didn't show up to the gym. Now this was not like her. Teresa never missed the gym, especially when we were planning on working out together. She didn't call or nothing. So I thought maybe she had dissed me, but the next day she came back. I was going to get on her case, but then I saw her eyes." Harvey turned to Emma. "It looked like she had been crying."

"Did she tell you what had happened?" Emma asked, trying hard not to show her eagerness.

"No, Ma'am. She said she was sorry she missed our gym time, but something had come up. She told me she didn't want to talk about it. So we just went about our sets. I remember it was a Friday afternoon and she didn't work out on weekends so I didn't see her again for a couple of days."

Emma watched the young airman glance down at her hands as she talked about Teresa and she guessed Harvey had had feelings for Teresa.

"I figured maybe she had heard bad news from home, or something," Harvey went on, "but I could tell something was still bothering her that next Monday. It was clear something had scared her. I'd never seen her so shooken up. I told her I'd help, but she brushed me off. Said she didn't want to get me involved, didn't want me to get hurt, too. Like anyone could hurt me!"

Harvey was boasting now, Emma thought. She found that she did not know whether to pity or sympathize with the young airman.

"I'm not scared of nothing. And I told her that, but she wouldn't have it. Just acted like she was mad at me. But I knew she wasn't mad. She was just plain scared. The next week she acted like nothing had happened. Told me like it was no big deal. Gave me some story how some old love had came back in her life and it had shooken her up. She told me it was over. 'I'm fine,' she said. Tried to convince me she was back to her old self, but I could tell. She was lying and whoever it was, was still bothering her."

Suddenly Harvey lost her composure. "And now she's dead!" she announced angrily, throwing her hat on the table. "I mean, Ma'am, should I have said something to someone? Maybe Teresa could have gotten help and this wouldn't have happened."

"There was nothing you could have done to prevent what happened to Teresa," Emma assured her. "We don't even know if what happened in June had anything to do with her death. Look at me. This is not your fault. You *are* helping Teresa by telling us everything you know. This is not your fault," she repeated firmly willing the upset young woman to believe her. "But if she told you who this person was, we . . . ."

"No, Ma'am." Harvey said emphatically. "She never said."

"Do you know if anyone else had a problem with Senior Airman Conklin? Anyone who didn't like her?"

"Not that I know of Ma'am," Harvey replied solemnly. "Except that she talked about how the Chief was always on her case. Said the he treated her like crap and let me tell you, she made it no secret that she didn't like him none too much either."

Myers frowned at this news. "When did she start talking about the Chief treating her like this?"

"No sure, Sir. But if I remember it was around the same time she started acting all weird on me.

"Did she say why the Chief treated her this way?"

"No, Sir. Just that he'd better watch it because, if he didn't lay off, she'd make sure he didn't have a job. I told her she was full of it. I mean, a Senior Airman thinking she could get a Chief fired? Whatever."

Emma looked at Myers and remembered how the Chief talked about Teresa. Did she have something over him? Would he kill her because of it?

Chapter 28

By the time they wound up the interviews at 2000, Emma was exhausted. They had uncovered raw emotion and several rumors, true, but the only concrete evidence they had acquired was that Teresa Conklin was a young woman who kept to herself. Perhaps, like her mother, she had been determined not to let people get too close to her.

But before she called it a day, she threw her BDU blouse over a chair and reviewed her notes in an office down the hall where she sought refuge to concentrate on typing up a report for her boss who had called her a couple of times throughout the day to see what she had learned. Unfortunately, she hadn't been able to talk to him at length and after the fourth call, had finally promised she would drop a report of what she learned on his desk before she went home. Franks was unusually persistent to get her notes because he had a meeting with the wing commander early the next day to brief him on the investigation progress, but Emma thought it was odd that he had not requested that any of the people who were actually investigating the case be present during this meeting. However, she hadn't pressed the issue.

Now, pushing a strand of hair back from her forehead, she realized that she must look disheveled. It was, she knew, time to go home, take a shower and crawl into bed.

She was just finishing up when Myers poked his head in the door. "Hey," he said. "Are you hungry? I'm thinking about going for a bite to eat at *Mama's*. I'll even buy."

"Well, how can I pass up that offer?" Emma teased.

For a moment, Emma could have sworn that Myers flushed. "Just so you know," he said a bit uneasily, "I'm also going to ask Dan. I thought we could go over what we learned today and prepare for tomorrow."

It gave Emma some small satisfaction in the possibility that she had made Myers uncomfortable, even if for a second.

"Sounds good," she assured him.

In the bathroom, she splashed cold water on her face, added a bit of powder and lipstick she'd found in the bottom of her purse, and looked in the mirror. Her thick hair sprang from its hold and no amount of tugging could get it back in. It'll just have to do, Emma decided. Besides, she didn't want Myers to think she was trying to impress him.

Fifteen minutes later, after Emma dropped off her report at the legal office, she joined Myers at *Mama's*. Dan had begged off, saying that he needed to spend some time with the family, if they were still up. When she heard that they were going to dine alone, Emma found herself distinctly apprehensive, but her hunger soon overcame any apprehension.

Mama's was a quaint little, stereotypical German restaurant or Gaststätte, with one foot thick stucco walls painted bright white and brown flower boxes under each window. *Mama's* was located right outside the main gate to base and was loved by both Americans and Germans alike. There was a small bar right as you walked in where a couple of locals sat perched on the same barstools they had probably occupied for twenty-five years, when *Mama's* first opened.

A small dining area off to the left was always filled with people waiting for some of *Mama's* famous schnitzel. There were only about ten tables in the whole place, so when one opened up, you grabbed it. In *Mama's* it didn't matter if you knew the people crammed into the table next to you or even spoke the same language. There were no strangers at *Mama's* and the crowded room was always filled with laughter and the clanging of beer steins as people randomly called out "Salut" or cheers.

Even at this late hour, the place was still crowded, the air thick with the smell of fried pork and potatoes. The only available table was in the back, in a corner, and Emma did not hide her amusement as Myers surveyed the tiny table as if wondering how he was going to fold his long legs under it. Emma slid into the chair against the wall and held up her menu as if oblivious to his plight. After several attempts of trying to situated, he finally pulled his chair up to the table, smacking her knees in the process.

He grinned sheepishly. "Sorry."

Emma was grateful for the sanctity of the menu as electricity shot up her legs when he brushed against them. Fearing her face betrayed her feelings, Emma busied herself by looking at the menu.

What, she asked herself, was wrong with her? It was as though she had never been out on a date. Not that this was anything of the sort.

She concentrated on the menu even though she ordered the same thing every time she was here: the schnitzel with asparagus and hollandaise sauce. And then his leg brushed hers again.

"Knock it off!" she heard herself cry out and was immediately horrified.

"Hey," Myers exclaimed. "I said I was sorry. I think we sat in the children's section."

Crimson faced and completely embarrassed, Emma apologized. "No, it's not you," she assured him. "I have this obnoxious habit of talking to myself and most of the time its out loud. Must be the only child thing. No one else to talk to but yourself."

Emma was grateful when the waitress appeared and took their orders.

"So, I still don't know much about you," Myers said after the waitress left. "Other than the fact you're an only child who has always wanted to be a lawyer and likes to speak to herself."

Emma laughed as the waitress returned to set two heavy steins of beer in front of them.

"Well," Emma said, relaxing as the cold ale washed through her. "There's not much to tell. I had the pretty typical small town upbringing. Or at least I think it must have been fairly typical. My high school was small so I got to be in everything, sports, drama, and music. But I suppose I liked the equestrian bit the best. My father kept a horse for me at . . . "

She broke off, suddenly aware that she was babbling,

"Do you ride?" she asked him.

Myers nodded. "I've been known to. In fact, I still own two horses. They're at my parent's place right now. I try to ride whenever I get back there, although lately that hasn't happened much. You look surprised"

"I never figured you for a horse person. Have you found a place to ride here?"

"Actually I have," he said, taking a sip of beer. "There's a place between here and Ramstein that rents horses and they're not old trail horses, either. If you want, I can give you the name of the place or take you there sometime."

Unsure whether he really meant to ask her out or if he was just being congenial, Emma tried to act nonchalant, but when he slipped off his jacket, she found herself distracted by the sheer strength of him.

"So," she said breathlessly trying to regain her composure. "Where does Agent Myers want to go after his time at Ramstein?"

"I'd go anywhere," he answered, his eyes twinkling, "but another base in Europe or in Asia would be the best. I'd like to get more overseas experience before I head back to the States. I think they'll probably keep me over here since I know a lot already about international issues."

Emma raised her eyebrow. "Pretty sure of ourselves, aren't we?"

Emma's heart began pounding deep within her chest as Myers held her gaze.

"I know what I'm good at," he said, "if that's what you mean."

Emma felt a slow heat rush through her, as she realized his meaning.

She was again saved by the waitress, this time setting plates heaping with schnitzel and fries in front of them.

Emma busied herself with her food, taking a bite of the warm breaded meat, savoring its rich flavor.

Myers was easier to deal with or ignore, for that matter, when he was acting like a jackass with attitude, she decided. The man who now sat before her now was much more intimidating. No, she wouldn't admit to intimidation because she had no intention of being unnerved by a handsome face and gorgeous body.

"So, let's recap what we learned today," she said turning her mind from the man seated across from her. "I'm particularly interested in how Teresa came to be stationed here."

"You're going to check with your people over at Mental Health to see how their domestic violence reassignment program works? *IF* we buy she was involved in an abusive relationship."

Emma nodded. "I have to tell you I'm not sure I believe it was a girlfriend who caused Teresa's reassignment from Dyess. First of all, the military's homosexuality policy is something I've often had to deal with over the years. It's even a part of my briefing to new airmen. As you know, the Air Force can't just delve into a person's sexuality unless they openly acknowledge they are gay. We haven't heard any evidence Teresa came out.

"The second reason I have doubts is because even if Teresa had admitted that she had a relationship with a woman, the commander would have no choice but to investigate. It's required by the policy. An inquiry is held to make sure the member isn't just saying they're gay to get an early out of their commitment. There's nothing in her file that suggests an inquiry was held. So I don't think she told anyone or it would be sealed in her personnel file."

"Unless she came out to her shrink," Myers interjected taking a drink of his beer. "Then she is protected by doctor/patient privilege, right?"

"Could be," Emma agreed. "As long as she wasn't committing any violent crime, then her shrink wouldn't have been obligated to tell her commander. If Teresa did have an abusive girlfriend, she somehow kept it hidden and took every advantage of the 'Don't Ask, Don't Tell' policy."

"I know you think you know your stuff," Myers said and Emma thought she caught a glimpse of the old arrogance, "but maybe this girl was really smart and knew what she was doing. Maybe she found a way around your system to get what she wanted. Sounds like from her parents she was a wild child. Of course, I can't blame her being raised in a holy roller place like that. Her parents did say she was 'sleeping around.'

"Maybe she was experimenting with both sides trying to see which one she liked better. Anyway, she gets here and within a month or so starts seeing someone else. Man or woman, we don't know. High ranking Airman or Officer, we don't know. All we do know is she tells her friend that she's in love and she writes the same in her journal, but she can't tell anyone who it is."

"Don't forget," Emma interrupted, "it doesn't have to be an officer to be against the UCMJ. If she was seeing the Chief, for instance, or any airman of higher rank than hers and in her chain of command, this would also be against the rules. We have to keep supervisors from sleeping around or dating their subordinates. It ruins their ability and authority to give them orders."

"At least in the work place," Myers retorted.

Laughing, Emma took another sip of her beer. She was now back in her comfort zone, hashing out bits and pieces of information trying to make them fit together. Strategizing was what she was liked and was good at and it didn't hurt that the man who was helping her was tall, dark, and now for the most part, chivalrous.

"Something happens in June that makes her scared," Myers mused. "Was it the old flame from Dyess? Not sure about that one. What are the odds that person would get stationed at the same base with her, especially if there is a domestic violence profile out on him or her."

"Could be whomever she was seeing dumped her or someone else found out about them," Emma said. "If it's a superior or an officer, she knows she is in deep trouble which could cost her career, not to mention her lover's."

Myers leaned forward. "Then there is the Chief," he said lowering his voice to prevent anyone else from hearing, so close that his warm breath rushed over her. "Why did he have it out for

Conklin? Was he her lover? Did she break it off so he now has it out for her and shuts her up before she can tell anyone else?"

"Could be," Emma admitted. "Don't forget the LOR the Chief ordered Dort to give to Teresa for letting people into the armory. He lied to us about that being her first offense, when Dort said it wasn't. The Chief was also the first person Jaime called after she found Teresa. Why the Chief? Why not 911?"

"There's also the issue of the key," Myers added, his voice deep. "The killer had access to the armory and knew every inch of the place. How did he get in? He had to have had a key. But there are only a couple of people on base who have them and one of them is the Chief."

Emma pushed back her plate. Although she'd only eaten half of her meal, she was stuffed from the huge proportions.

"And isn't it an interesting coincidence the Chief told Dort he lost his key and got a replacement a few months ago," she said. "Looks like Teresa wasn't the only one with secrets."

Myers finished his beer and sat his stein on the table. He leaned back or tried to in the cramped space, his long legs once again rubbing against hers. His brooding eyes met her sending chills up her spine.

"Agreed," he said. "What I think is this. Your Chief has a lot questions to answer tomorrow."

Chapter 29

When they left the restaurant, Emma zipped her Gortex outer coat up and pulled it around her neck against the crisp, fresh night air. There were only a couple of street lights in the tiny village, but the sky was bright with thousands of shining stars glistening against the black sky. Myers was silent as they made their way across the street to Emma's car.

Her head was spinning and Emma was pretty sure it wasn't from the beer or the case they had spent the past two hours picking apart. She felt herself drawn to this man beside her who had the power to both intrigue and irritate her. The truth was that she had enjoyed the evening spent mulling over the evidence, finding holes and trying to discover where they could find the missing pieces. As much as she hated to admit it, she even enjoyed sparring with him. He seemed to read her every thought and now knew exactly what buttons of hers to push to get her riled up. For some time now, there hadn't been a man in Emma's life who was able to stir so many emotions in her at once as he could.

Of course, it didn't hurt that he was so damned handsome. When she first met him, Myers's machismo and cocky attitude detracted from any outer features he had. But now that she had gotten to know him and seen what was on the other side of the wall he built between himself and others, Emma found that his passion for his job and life only increased his striking good looks.

"Sure is a beautiful night," Myers said softly beside her.

Pulling her car keys from her pocket and unlocking her car door, she gazed up at the sky once again.

"I just love nights like these. It looks like you can see forever through those stars. When I was younger, I used to sneak out my window at night and stare up into the stars pretending they were gateway to some new and exciting world I wanted to discover. I swear I'll never grow tired of looking at them."

"I know what you mean," Myers said huskily, not looking at the sky.

Emma turned and, with a shock of sudden surprise found herself lost in the depths of his dark eyes. Myers reached for her hand and brought it to his lips, which were warm and moist against her skin.

"I must say, Major, that I had my doubts when you were put on the case," he said. "But it has been my pleasure working with you. You have definitely made this case more . . . appealing."

Emma felt him pull her towards him and welcomed his embrace. His strong arms folded her against his broad chest, hard beneath his cool black leather jacket. She closed her eyes letting herself relax in his arms. His mouth hovered by her ear and she could feel his warm breath as it tickled her lobe, arousing her senses. To hell with business, she thought as she lost herself in the moment.

"Damn, you are incredible," he whispered in her ear.

Then too soon, he pulled away. His hand still held hers, his dark eyes searching her face in the moonlight.

"I cannot believe I am saying this," he told her. "But we can't."

Trying to hide her disappointment, Emma slowly nodded glad one of them was able to use their common sense.

"You're right," she said. "We can't get involved while we're investigating this case together. Now is not the time or the place."

As she started to get in the car, he stopped her. "So does that mean there might be a right time and place?" he said hopefully.

"We'll see," she told him, risking a deliberately seductive smile.

"Sexy and a tease," Myers whistled low. "You may just be too good to be true."

Chapter 30

I take a sip of the hot coffee letting the steaming liquid warm me as I sit in my cold dark car. When I lean forward to see them better, my breath freezes on the window. Well, isn't that interesting? Looks like it isn't just me those two are investigating.

I know they can't see me parked up here, away from the light, but I don't want to take any chances. But I'm still close enough to clearly see what's happening between the agent and the lawyer. What a joke! Isn't there anyone around here who can actually think with their pants up and not around their ankles? To think I respected her! God, what a waste of talent!

A couple of times I'd snuck into the back of the courtroom to watch the gorgeous Major do her thing. It was hard not to sneer out loud as she raked the poor stupid witnesses over the coals. Damn, I thought the bitch had balls. But now I can see she's just a stupid waste of time like the rest of them. And he's no better-he can't think with anything but his dick. Who does he think he is? Goddammit! My head feels like someone's hitting it with a hammer.

I am so damned tired of these imbeciles running our military and pretending to protect our country . . . our people. I reach for the pills in the seat beside me and chase two down with the bitter coffee. Slowly my head stops pounding.

Now's the perfect time to take out that bitch Kennedy, especially since the Major and agent are obviously too busy with each other to think about me. I watch as the Major drives her car past mine.

This time there will be no mistakes. No mistakes.

Chapter 31

The next day at her office, Emma was still reeling from the night before. She had no idea whether to be completely ecstatic or really uncomfortable. After all, she would be working with Myers until they found Teresa's killer and who knew how long that would be.

She'd taken extra care getting dressed this morning, applying a little more makeup than usual and brushing her hair until it gleamed. Happy with the results, she pulled on a crisp pair of BDUs and drove to work. For some reason the sun shone brighter today.

"Crap!" she silently cursed. "I must be losing it from the complete lack of sleep. I cannot like this guy. I hardly know him and once this investigation's done, he'll be gone . . . off on some other case."

Still Emma smiled as she turned on her computer. It sure felt great knowing some hunky OSI agent found her cute.

"No," she said out loud. "Sexy was the word he used."

"Who said who was sexy?"

Startled, Emma about fell off her seat as Maggie Prane wandered into her office grinning.

"Wow, what's gotten into you this morning, Major?" she said, giving Emma a knowing smile. "A little jumpy, huh? Doesn't have anything to do with that handsome Agent Myers does it?"

"The only thing that agent is . . . is a pain in my ass," Emma replied, dismayed to hear how unconvincing she sounded.

"Uh, huh,' Maggie said. "Speaking of pains in the asses. You do realize the sentencing hearing starts this morning. I know you aren't on this case anymore. Which by the way, have I thanked you yet for sticking me with Captain Mullen *and* now Captain Banks? You know if I've done something to make you mad, you could have just told me."

Emma smiled knowing Maggie was kidding. If anyone was able to handle two young rookies like those guys, she was.

"Anyway, I know you're busy," Maggie said. "But if you have any time today, Captain Banks asked if you could stop by and watch Captain Mullen, you know so you can give him *constructive* comments? Because Lord knows, that child is going to need some serious feedback. You know what he is doing right now?" Maggie rolled her eyes. "He's in his office pacing back and forth practicing his argument over and over and over again. And he's been doing this since 0500! Going to wear a hole in his carpet is what he is going to do? Of course, I am going to wear a hole in his head, if he doesn't stop popping into my office asking me every two seconds whether the hearing paperwork is done. I mean, how many times do I have to tell that child, it was done YESTERDAY!"

Emma laughed.

"I'm not sure I'll be able to drop in on the hearing," Emma said, "but do you want me to come down before it starts and give Mullen a pep talk?"

"Yes, Ma'am. That boy needs something and if you don't do it, that something may be me giving him a swift kick in the behind. And it won't be pretty-let me tell you."

"I have to meet with Lieutenant Colonel Franks in a few minutes and then I'll come down right before the trial starts," Emma assured her.

"And by the way," Maggie said, grinning mischievously, "he's right. You are kind of sexy-even in your BDUs!"

Chapter 32

Sitting in her boss's office ten minutes later, Emma felt anything but sexy. Franks was in a foul mood and had given her the third degree about her synopsis of the investigation. He even snapped at her when she didn't have enough information to answer his barrage of questions. His mood didn't improve when Emma turned the tables on him asking why he supported the LOR for Teresa instead of an Article 15.

"Damn!" he swore softly. "I knew that would come back to bite me and him. One thing you're going to learn fast when you become a SJA some day, Emma, is that not everyone is going to listen to you or give a rat's ass about what you have to say."

Emma had not expected this as she had never heard her boss swear before.

"I told them-Colonel Carlson and the Chief-that I didn't think a LOR was a sufficient punishment for Teresa's actions. I agree with you. The issue wasn't what she had done, but how many times she did it. According to the evidence I was given, the incident referenced in the LOR wasn't the only time she'd had unauthorized people in the armory during her shift."

"Did Colonel Carlson and Chief also have this same evidence?" Emma asked, knowing the answer but wanting to clarify anyway.

Franks didn't mince words. "Of course. You know we see the same stuff that the commander and supervisor do."

Emma made a mental note to tell Myers that the Chief definitely knew about Teresa's other visitors, another confirmation of the fact that he had lied.

"So why didn't they take your advice?"

"I had no clue at the time. I just knew Carlson said I was wrong and overrode my recommendation. Remember, it's his call. As a commander, Colonel Carlson can go against my recommendation if he wants to and, of course, in this situation, he did."

Clearly frustrated, Franks ran a hand through his short gray hair. He looked at her with tired eyes and again Emma was struck by how much her boss had aged over the last few days. His blue shirt hung loosely on his shoulders and Emma was amazed to discover he looked like he'd lost some weight.

"Look, Emma. I'm sorry," he was saying. "I just have General Brandt breathing down my neck about this case, even though, I might remind you, we JAGs are *not* the primary investigators here . . . OSI is."

Emma wondered why the Wing Commander was coming down on her boss about this investigation instead of the real people in charge. Watching his deeply etched face, Emma wondered how long her boss would be able to handle the stress and wished she could do something to help him.

"Why is General Brandt coming down so hard on you, Sir?" she asked. "Why isn't he getting this information from Colonel Carlson or OSI? I know Agent Myers would be happy to brief him."

After a moment of tense silence, he put down the paper he was holding, folded his hands and looked at her intently. For a brief minute, Emma saw her old boss sitting across from her, the patient and kind man who took great pride in nurturing the attorneys under him looked back at her.

"For one thing, General Brandt doesn't know Agent Myers very well and wants one of his own people deeply involved in the investigation to give him updates," he said. And then the haggard look returned.

"There is something else. Something very serious that I cannot get into with you now. All I can tell you is that I have been tasked by the General to look into this other issue. Until it's resolved, I'll be his primary point of contact on this case as well."

Emma had no idea what this other issue could be but could tell it was weighing heavily on her boss. "Is there anything I can do?"

"No, Emma." His voice was grim. "But thank you. You're doing a great job and though it may not seem like it, I do appreciate what you are doing. You know, I told you in the beginning that I wanted you off this case. Well, I've changed my mind. I need someone I can trust giving me information about this investigation. There are a lot of things happening around here and I know I can trust you, Emma. Don't let me down."

Chapter 33

The conversation with Franks was still gnawing at her when Emma ran downstairs to the courtroom. The meeting with her boss had taken longer than she anticipated so she had only minutes to catch Mullen before the hearing started.

The courtroom was mostly empty except for the court reporter, a few spectators and the two prosecutors. As she walked up to them, Emma could hear Greg giving John some last minute advice.

The judges liked to keep the room chilly so that no one, including themselves, would get sleepy. Even so, John was, Emma noted, sweating profusely.

"Hey guys," she greeted then cheerily, although inside she was anything but. "I heard you're ready to go."

"Yep, think so." Greg replied for his co-counsel who couldn't seem to find his voice. "John practiced his argument in front of me last night and it sounded good."

Emma appreciated the fact that Greg was trying to boost John's confidence. She poured him a glass of water and sat down in the chair next to him.

"So how are you doing John?" she asked.

"Okay, I think," he replied, but she could hear the fear in his voice.

"Listen. I know this is your first hearing as lead prosecutor, but I want you to remember something. First, the members do not know this is your first time. They have no clue whether you have argued a hundred times or never before. Plus, this is the first time many of them have been on a panel – or even in a courtroom for that matter. They don't know what to expect during a sentencing hearing. They'll listen to whatever you say, as long as you say it confidently, because you're the prosecutor and in charge of this case."

She was relieved to see her words slowly sinking in. John straightened his shoulders and sat tall in his chair as he listened to her words of advice.

"Second, don't think you have to memorize your entire argument," she warned him. "It's okay to have a couple of notes on the podium to use as your guide. It's okay to use them if you forget your place. Just don't read from them. You will lose all credibility if you read your argument."

Seeing the fear creep back into his eyes, Emma quickly continued. "Don't forget that I've worked with you on this case for the past month and a half. You know the facts backwards and forwards. Otherwise, I wouldn't have recommended you to do the sentencing hearing."

Some color returned to his face as he spoke. "Thank you, Ma'am," he said, and this time she could hear the confidence in his voice.

"You know the facts," Emma repeated. "You know the case. Now go out there tell the panel what you recommend for his sentence and argue the hell out of it."

Just then the bailiff announced that the judge wanted to see counsel in her chambers.

John gathered up his pen and yellow legal pad. "Thank you," he said to Emma.

Emma smiled at him and slowly blew out her breath as they disappeared behind the judge's closed door. Oh boy, she thought. Let's just hope he can make it through this one. Maybe he'll get better with one under his belt.

As she walked past the spectator seats on her way out of the courtroom, Emma noticed a familiar face sitting in the front row behind the defendant's table.

"Hello," she said stopping in front of Staff Sergeant Williams who was dressed in crisp BDUs, her black Security Forces beret on the chair beside her. "What brings you by here? You know the defendant?"

"No, Ma'am." William stood up, smiling. "But I had some time before my shift started and I wanted to come and see another trial. You know last time I was here, as a bailiff, I really didn't have time to really watch what was going on. And when I saw you yesterday, you reminded me of how much I enjoyed the courtroom. So I thought I'd sit in on this one for a little while. I was actually thinking about possibly cross training to become a paralegal."

Emma bid her luck and for a brief second, wished that she could cross train. Her job had suddenly gone from putting the bad guys in jail to finding them. And that was a lot more dangerous.

Chapter 34

Myers and Dan met Emma one hour later in front of the Security Forces Squadron building where they had an appointment to talk to the Chief, who they hoped would be a little more forthcoming this time.

Emma's heart raced as she spotted Myers. Today he wore a dark gray sweater that matched his eyes under a black sports coat and black pants that hugged his narrow hips.

"Morning," she greeted them. "Anything new?"

"You know us," Dan's eyes glinted with amusement. "There's always something new in the exciting world of OSI."

Beside him, Myers cleared his throat. "Actually we did get an interesting call this morning," he said. "Kennedy's escort called and said Kennedy has been hysterical. She's convinced that someone is following her."

There was, Emma saw, as she met his eyes, something new in their gray depths and her stomach did somersaults.

"Did her escort see anything?" Emma asked, praying her voice didn't betray her feelings.

"Nope," he frowned. "She assured me she's been with Kennedy the whole time and hasn't seen anything or anybody."

"The escort thinks Jaime needed a break," Dan interjected, "So we brought Jaime into our office."

"She should feel safer there," Emma said, grateful Dan was with them. "You guys ready to go in?"

As they went inside, Myers briefly touched her back and Emma's heart soared. Still, it was almost a relief when he fell back to walk behind her. There was, after all, business to take care of. Important business. This was no time for emotion. Perhaps as far as this man was concerned, there never would be.

They found the Chief in his office, talking on the phone. As they sat down, Emma took the time to look at the contents of the room which told of a man who had dedicated his whole life to the Air Force. Pictures of the Chief at the various bases to which he had been assigned covered the walls, along with the numerous awards and plaques she'd seen before.

A large display case flanked one wall displaying yet more awards and military memorabilia. A framed cross-stitch of the Air Force logo hung over a black couch sitting opposite the display case. Behind the Chief's desk were two large oak bookcases filled with books on everything from how to be an effective leader in the military to biographies of famous leaders.

The Chief had been an airman ever since the day he graduated from high school. The accolades surrounding him proved he was well thought of and recognized for his achievements and for his leadership.

So why would someone of his stature throw it all away? And for what-a fling? What would possess him to ruin an entire career to which he had dedicated his life? Why would he risk the future financial security he was sure to receive from the full retirement benefits coming to him when he chose to retire? It made no sense which was all the more reason that he give them some answers now.

Today the Chief wore a crisp uniform and was freshly shaven. He had smiled at them when they came in the office. However, braced for a confrontational meeting, they were pleasantly surprised when he greeted them politely and offered them coffee. The hostility he had openly displayed during their last meeting had been replaced by a professional confidence. It was almost as if he had forgotten the gravity of the reason for this meeting.

"So how can I help you today?" he said.

Emma was immediately perturbed at the Chief's apparent lack of concern for the dead airman he had just handed over to her parents the day before.

"We don't have time for any crap today, okay, Chief?" she said crisply. "We have a full fledged manhunt out for whoever killed Airman Conklin and you *will* answer our questions or I'll have you court-martialed for impeding an investigation. Now, unless you have something to hide, in which case I suggest you go talk to the Area Defense Counsel right now, you *will* help us. Do I make myself clear?"

It wasn't very often Emma felt the need to "pull rank" over another to force them to cooperate, or as in this case, to remind another of their subordinate rank to hers.

She had run across many officers and some higher ranking enlisted who often pulled rank as a part of some sort of power trip. As for Emma, she preferred to make her point with an intellectual response.

There were those times, however, when it became necessary. This was one of those times.

The smile faded from his face and a black shadow cast over it. He was obviously not happy to be dressed down, let alone by a younger female attorney. Any feigned friendliness he once displayed was now gone. His eyes were cold as he squinted at her. As for Dan and Myers, it was clear that her abruptness had taken them by surprise. But, she told herself, she couldn't worry about that now.

"I assure you I am not trying to impede this investigation," the Chief said grimly. "If you. . . "

"Good," Emma interrupted him. "Then we'll get started. Agent Myers?"

"All right," Myers began. "Let's start with Jaime Kennedy. Although I shouldn't have to remind you of this, the most important thing right now is her security. Why would you assign a rookie female airman with no training as an escort for Kennedy . . . our *only* material witness?"

"That airman was capable of watching Jaime," the Chief answered defiantly, his blue eyes blazing. "She's a trained cop and I thought she could handle the job."

"So you are telling me that you thought that a nineteen year old escort could provide adequate protection for Airman Kennedy, even though it's quite probable that her life is in danger? Well, I can assure you Chief," Myers continued. "General Brandt did not agree. He has assigned a trained OSI agent to protect her 24/7. I might add the General was not at all happy that you assigned this incompetent escort, especially after Kennedy's dorm room was broken into."

Beads of sweat popped on the Chief's forehead and his eyes darted nervously between them. "The General knows about this?" he demanded.

Emma couldn't contain herself any longer. "You bet he does, Chief," she said. "In fact, we're giving him hourly updates on what is happening. The strange thing is that you seem to be the main subject at every briefing. Why do you think that is?"

The Chief stared at them incredulously. "I don't know," he muttered.

"Why don't you cut this bullshit and tell us why you really left Kennedy unprotected?" Myers asked him.

"Because she is a piece of trash!" the older man blurted out. "She's caused me nothing but problems. She's a disgrace to my squadron and to the Air Force!"

Emma stared at him incredulously. Was he actually implying that he would put one of his airmen in danger because she caused him problems? "What do you mean?" she demanded.

The Chief got up from his chair and turned his back to them in order to stare out the window behind his desk. Emma had to strain to hear his answer.

"She was trouble from the day she came here," he told them. "Jaime Kennedy was quiet at first, but then she met Teresa and they started hanging out together. I would catch them in the armory together during Teresa's shift."

So now they knew Jaime was the unauthorized visitor. The Chief must have read Jaime the riot act for being in the armory,

Emma thought, and that is why she was so nervous when they questioned her.

Emma looked at Myers, who raised his eyebrow.

"I didn't think much of it at first," the Chief went on. "They told me they were studying, and I saw their grades. Both of them were doing well, so I believed them and let it go." He turned back to face them. "Hell, I wish more of my airmen would try to get their degree."

"Is this why you recommended only a LOR when Conklin got caught by Dort?" Myers probed. "Come on, Chief. Don't look at me that way. You know, the LOR issued to Airman Conklin. Why did you tell us the incident in the LOR was Conklin's first offense when clearly you knew this was not the case?"

"I told you," the older man protested. "They were studying. I didn't think that was an offense. It wasn't until I learned they got caught by him when I knew we had a problem."

"Okay," Myers responded clearly not buying the Chief's story. "So tell me what you and Colonel Carlson were doing at the armory during the early morning hours of Conklin's shift a few months ago?"

The Chief sank into his chair, the blood draining from his face. "What do you mean?" he said. "What are you driving at?"

"You know what I mean," Myers told him. "We have information that in late January of this year you and Carlson were seen at the armory around 0100, while Conklin was on duty. What were you doing there?"

Silence filled the room as the Chief stared down at his clenched hands. "She had called me," he explained quietly. "Teresa called me because she had a fight with one of her friends . . . yes, who she let in the armory. It was late and the Colonel and I were just finishing up our briefing for an important strategic planning meeting the next day so we both responded."

"Why call you?" Emma demanded.

"I don't know." He shrugged. "I guess by that time she was comfortable with me. I am a good Chief you know. I'm there for my airmen, for my commander. I do what is needed to make sure they are okay and this squadron runs smoothly. *Whatever* it takes.

And sometimes that means responding at all hours of the day or night."

"So, who was this friend?" Dan asked

"I don't know," the Chief took a sip of his coffee. Some color returned to his face. "She was gone by the time we got there and Teresa wouldn't tell us what happened. I knew then I needed to take more formal action with her, so when Dort came to me, I recommended the LOR. I thought this would scare her. She always wanted to do everything perfectly so I thought the LOR would send the message she needed to straighten up."

Emma probed, "And did it?"

"Obviously not . . . since she is dead." His voice was flat.

"So I think we get your feelings towards Teresa, but why the hostility towards Jaime? You didn't like her because she studied in the armory off hours? You really expect us to believe that?"

"I told you," he said. "She caused problems. Still is as far as I am concerned. She doesn't care who she hurts as long as she gets what she wants."

"So if you didn't like her, why were you the first person Jaime called after Teresa was shot?" Emma persisted.

"I don't know. I suppose because I knew about Teresa having visitors in the armory and Jaime didn't want to get into trouble . . . any more trouble that is."

Emma sat back folding her arms over her chest. Why was this man withholding information from them? Why he was ruining his career over a couple of airmen? It just didn't make sense. She also knew that if she hit him any harder with questions, she would be required to read him his rights knowing full well he might opt to get an attorney and refuse to talk with them. She wasn't willing to take that chance – yet.

"Chief," she said, taking her time now, lowering the tension level, "did you tell anyone, besides Tech Sergeant Dort, that you had assigned Airman Conklin to take the late shift?"

"No," he replied adamantly.

"Do you know why anyone would want Teresa dead?"

He hesitated. "All I know from what I have heard is that Teresa Conklin isn't exactly who she portrayed herself to be. Maybe she made some enemies."

"Do you know who these enemies were?" Myers fired the words at him.

"No."

"Do you have any reason to think her supervisor or any of the higher-ups might have a bone to pick with Teresa Conklin?"

The Chief drew himself up until his back was rigid, his face stony.

"Surely you are not suggesting any of the leaders in this squadron, including me, had anything to do with Teresa Conklin's murder?" he said stiffly.

"Well, since you brought it up . . . did they? Did you?"

"No," the Chief replied fiercely, "and if you are implying I had something to do with this, I'd suggest you better read me my rights. Because unless you do, as far as I'm concerned this interview is over."

Chapter 35

Once Dan's car had left the parking lot, Myers took Emma's arm.

"So, Major. Pretty impressive work in there."

Emma's heart raced and she was pleased by his compliment.

"You mean persuading him he didn't need an attorney . . . yet?" she shrugged. "That's why I'm here, isn't it? To make sure no one's rights get stepped on and to keep you from forcing our witnesses' to lawyer up."

"Well, there is that," he said, grinning. "But that's not what I meant."

Emma's knees went weak as he massaged her arm, and she quickly stepped back, smiling so that he wouldn't misinterpret her action.

"I didn't know you could be such a bad ass," he told her. "You sure did put the Chief in his place."

Emma realized that someone might be watching them, but she found, to her amazement, that she did not care.

"Well, sometimes you boys need to be reminded who's boss."

Myers ran his hand up her arm. "A woman with authority," he murmured seductively before letting go of her arm. "You *are* too good to be true."

And with that he left her, breathless and really ready for this damn case to be over.

Chapter 36

Jaime Kennedy was waiting for them back at the OSI office. Someone had put her in one of the interrogation rooms and before going in they watched her from the adjacent room through the two way mirror.

Jaime looked like hell, to put it mildly. Her BDUs looked as though she had slept in them. Her straggly hair, stringy and unkempt, was falling out of the low ponytail. Black smudges lined her lower eyes, which were swollen from either crying or lack of sleep, or both.

And she was agitated. Emma watched her flit around the room like a trapped bird, not able to sit or stand still in one place for long. There was a can of Mountain Dew can on the table. Emma wondered how many of them she had in the last twenty-four hours. The events of the last few days were obviously taking their toll.

"Where have you guys been?' she blurted out as soon as Emma and Myers walked in the room, Dan having stayed upstairs to make some phone calls. "They've kept me cooped up here for hours. I'm going crazy!"

Emma made a mental note to make sure Jaime continued to receive mental health care. Unfortunately, Emma felt things were only going to get worse before they got better for their only witness.

Myers settled in his chair and stretched his long legs in front of him.

"Settle down Jaime," he ordered coolly. "We're here and you're safe. And let's not forget there's an officer in the room," he added, jabbing his finger towards Emma.

"Right," Jaime said, taking a seat. "Sorry Ma'am."

"It's okay," Emma replied. "Now why don't you tell us why you are here? You called and said someone was following you?"

"Yes, Ma'am. I know he's out there," the young woman said, nervously tucking her hair behind her ears.

"Who's out there?" asked Myers.

"The killer!" She answered rudely as if Myers were completely stupid. "What do you think I'm nuts? I know someone is following me. I can feel it. It's not safe. You know I'm the only one between the killer and jail and that scares the hell out of me. What are you guys going to do?"

"It's okay," Emma said, aware of how essential it was to calm her down. "We'll do whatever it takes to keep you safe. We can even work it out for you to be housed off base, away from the dorms, if you think that will help."

Myers glared at Emma. "Hey now let's not jump . . ."

"You mean it!" Jaime exclaimed excitedly, ignoring him. "You'd get me off this base? I know he's out there . . . on base, I mean. Maybe if I could be somewhere he doesn't know. I'm a sitting duck in the dorms, going to chow hall. You know that. Can I stay with you?"

Emma immediately regretted she had opened her mouth and was completely taken aback that Jaime had jumped to this conclusion.

"Me? Well, I'm not sure it would be any safer at my house."

"But no one knows where you live, right? I mean you JAG's stay off base, away from the punks you put in jail right?"

Emma had never thought of her reasons for living off base this way. But it did make sense. She had to deal with all of the problems on base every day and wanted to escape them at night and on the weekends. Living with the mayhem 24/7, was a price she was not willing to pay.

"It doesn't matter why Major Lohrs lives where she does or where for that matter," Myers broke in. "It's not safe for you to stay with her. She's not trained. She wouldn't be able to protect you if something went wrong."

"Whether or not I could protect you is not the issue," Emma proclaimed. They were, she thought, back to square one. No matter how he tried to hide it, he couldn't help being condescending to her when it came to this investigation.

"What is at issue," she went on slowly, determined not to show her irritation, "is what's best for you. I understand you may feel like everyone's watching you while on base. But that's the point. There are a lot of people to watch you and look out for you. The base is much safer."

"It wasn't for Teresa," Jaime replied, slumping in her seat.

Emma sighed. "You're right. It wasn't for Airman Conklin and I'm sorry about that, really. I don't want anything to happen to you. Neither does Agent Myers." She did not look at him when she said it.

"Right now, let's focus on finding her killer," Myers interjected. "You can help us. We learned Teresa Conklin started acting unusual around June. Do you know anything about this?"

Jaime peered up at Myers through long lashes that were now laden with tears.

"Yes. I know," she answered quietly, willing herself to continue. "Not many people knew Teresa. I mean really knew her. Not like me, anyways. I didn't care what the others said about her. They were just jealous. I mean she was beautiful and smart and really wanted to make something of herself, you know?"

Emma watched as Jaime defended her friend and it was obvious that Jaime knew the rumors about Teresa.

"People are shit!" she blurted out. "Sorry Ma'am, but it's true. They just shit all over a person and then leave them."

Emma was not sure if Jaime was referring to Teresa or herself.

"I liked her," Jaime said, playing with a hangnail. "She was the one true friend I had in this place. And she was so smart. I mean I wished I could get the grades she did. Man she hardly had to study and she'd ace a test. Not me. I had to study my butt off, you know? But she helped me. God, she was smart."

Her words hung heavy in the air as Jaime looked off into the distance, obviously overcome with memories of her friend. And then, suddenly, "But she sure as hell wasn't smart when it came to who she dated!"

Emma held her breath. Had they finally broken through? Was Jaime going to tell them what they wanted to know?

"You promised me," Jaime vented pointing at Emma. "You promised me I could say anything and I wouldn't get into trouble! Do you mean it? Or are you like others around here who make promises and don't keep them?"

"I also told you that you need to cooperate with us," Emma replied, tired of the airman's petulance. "I am not here to prosecute you, that is unless you had a part in this crime. If you had anything to do with the death of Airman Conklin, I will need to advise you of your rights. But to answer your second question," she added crisply, "no, I do not make promises I do not intend to keep. So do you want to continue or not?"

"Sure," Jaime said dejectedly, "why not? What's the worst thing that can happen to me, huh? Oh yeah, I guess I could end up like Teresa!"

Suddenly, Myers pounded his fist on the table. "Listen, young lady," he said angrily. "I for one am tired of your antics. If you know something about this, then tell us! But quit with the "woe is me" routine and quit wasting our time. Now tell us, who was Teresa Conklin dating and does that have anything to do with what happened in June?"

"Fine," she answered defiantly. "I'm going to tell you, because I want to help her. She deserves it. When I first met Teresa early this year, she told me she was dating someone. It was all hush, hush. I didn't know her that well, so I let it be. I mean it was none of my business. But then she started showing up with all of this new stuff: a new stereo, laptop, jewelry, you name it. This was after we hung around and became good friends, so I started teasing her."

Emma was glad Myers finally got through to their tight-lipped witness. Finally, they were getting somewhere.

"'Who's your sugar daddy?' I asked her. No way could she afford those things on her own. But, she still wouldn't tell me. She'd just laugh at me. Tell me I was jealous. I mean I wasn't jealous you know. I sure as hell don't need a man to buy me fancy stuff."

The young airman fiddled with the pocket on her BDUs and Emma wasn't entirely convinced that Jaime hadn't been jealous of her friend.

"Anyways," she finally went on. "I stopped hanging around her for while. I didn't need her crap. Plus everyone was talking about her. Saying she was doing some officer. Hell, I didn't need that. But she kept calling me, begging me . . . saying I was the only true friend she's got. So we started hanging again. Besides I needed her help with my classes."

Jaime bit her lip as her tough façade shattered and tears threatened again.

"Listen to me," Emma told her. "We found a journal in Teresa's room and she wrote about being in love. Do you know if the person she was seeing was the same person she was writing about in her journal?"

"Who knows with her?" Jaime answered bitterly. "She flirted a lot, led people on and then left 'em hanging. But yeah, I suppose it probably was the same person."

"So what happened after you started hanging out with her again?" Myers asked.

"Everything was the same. She would brag about all of the fancy restaurants her guy was taking her too and all the overnight trips he would take her on. I started getting sick of it again. I mean what kind of a punk would date a girl, give her all of these things but never let them be seen together? Why did she let him string her along? So I asked her point blank . . . was he married or what? Why couldn't she ever talk about him?"

Myers perked up. "What did she say?"

"At first she wouldn't tell me. But then, I could tell something had changed. She started acting like she didn't care about him anymore. I mean he was still sending her things; flowers and stuff like that. But she would just get angry and throw them away. When she told me she didn't want to see him anymore. I told her it was 'bout time. He was no good for her anyway. It wasn't like I hadn't been telling her that for months."

"You said that she didn't talk about him at first," Emma said, trying to get the young airman back on track, "so did she ever tell you about him? Come on, Jaime. It's really important that you tell us. They guy, whoever he is, might have something to do with her murder."

Jaime's lip trembled. But, at least, she finally looked Emma in the eye.

"I'll tell you if you promise me I can stay with you until this thing is over," she said, her eyes locked on Emma's. "We could have my escort, Agent Sanchez, come and stay with us, too. It would be safe. I know it. At least safer than here."

For all of the toughness she tried to portray, Jaime Kennedy was really a scared young woman underneath and Emma knew she was serious. And she also knew that she was even more afraid than she let on.

"I mean even if he didn't kill her," Jaime continued, "and I don't know if he did or not, if he found out I knew about the two of them he would come after me. I know it. I know he hates me."

"Who hates you, Jaime?" Myers frowned. "Are you talking about the Chief?"

"Ha! The Chief! What a putz! Yeah, he hates me. There is no doubt about that one and the feeling's mutual, I can tell you. I don't trust that guy one bit."

Emma didn't want to lose momentum in finding out about Teresa's former lover, but she also wanted to find out what Jaime knew about their prime suspect – the Chief.

"So if you don't trust the Chief, why was he the first person you called when you learned Teresa was shot?"

"Cuz he was the shit head who put her on that shift in the first place," she answered furiously. "It was his fault she was there. Teresa didn't trust him and neither do I, but she was always calling him. I didn't get it. I'd yell at her 'Why do you call him, when you just told me you don't trust him?' But, Christ, she would just laugh it off. Told me I wouldn't understand. I was too naïve. She could be such a bitch."

As though aware that she had let herself go too far, she made a visible attempt to rein herself in before she continued. "She would have wanted me to call him, that's why I did it. Don't ask me why, cuz I don't know. Maybe you could ask the old man himself. But no, I'm not talking about the Chief, although I wouldn't put it past the bastard to kill her."

The young airman finally broke down crying and buried her face into her hands and Emma felt her despair.

"You have my promise," Emma said firmly, not daring to look at Myers. "You can come and live with me . . . with Agent Sanchez," Emma added staring directly at Myers daring him to disagree with her.

"Thanks," Jaime replied, wiping her face with the back of her hand. "After a while, Teresa told me that he was married and that's why they had to keep it quiet. But she wouldn't tell me who he was because if anyone found out, his career would be over. I knew it had to be an officer. Anyways, you were right about June. That's when she wouldn't go out. She'd just work, study and go to the gym. She acted like she was really scared and I figured it was him, so I told her if she didn't tell me who was bothering her and what was up I'd go to the IG myself."

The IG, or Inspector General's Office, was responsible for investigating personal complaints against military members, including those alleging improper conduct by an officer.

"What did she do?" Myers asked.

"I shouldn't have done that," Jaime moaned. "I shouldn't have threatened her. I didn't know. She was so scared. I mean, really scared. I've never seen anybody like that. She made me swear I wouldn't tell anyone about her dating an officer. She swore it was over by then anyway. Said I was right and she had called it off. She said if he wouldn't leave his wife and really be with her then she didn't need him." She took a deep breath. "Teresa didn't want to take no back seat to anyone so she left him."

"Who was she scared of?" Emma probed. "Was it him, this officer?"

"No," Jaime told her, "at least that is what she told me. It wasn't him. She could handle him is what she said. It was someone else. Someone she knew from a previous base that she had seen."

Emma caught Myers's eye and she leaned forward. "Did she tell you who this person was? What they were doing here?"

"No, Ma'am. She just said they were bad news. That she needed to watch her step. And she did for a while. She kept to herself. Wouldn't even go to chow. I would bring her food to her room. But a few weeks later everything seemed back to normal. She seemed herself again. Told me the problem was taken care of. They had talked it out and not to worry. So I didn't. I mean, she acted like nothing had happened. Just went about her business like nothing had happened. But something did happen, didn't it? She died!"

It was difficult to calm Jaime down, but Emma managed to do it, thankful that Myers gave her free rein. But the witness was still recalcitrant, claiming that Teresa had never given her the officer's name, and that, although she was probably seeing him after June, she hadn't talked about it.

"Okay," Emma continued. "Now what about the person she was so frightened of, the one she knew on from another base. Do you know if it was a man or woman?"

The fear in Jaime's eyes was unmistakable.

"No, Ma'am," she stammered. "I don't know anything about it. I mean, there were rumors. But, hell! Can't two girls be friends without people thinking they're lesbians?'"

Her defensiveness seemed to indicate to Emma that she had been on the receiving end of such rumors before, but she ignored that and assured Jaime that she was not on a witch hunt, but that they had to know the name of anyone who might have posed a threat to Teresa, all the time chafing at the fact that the don't ask, don't tell rule kept her from being more direct.

When Myers told the young woman that she could go, Emma was ready to discuss what they had or had not learned. But instead, he muttered something about her taking Kennedy under her wing, clearly angry at her for agreeing to take Kennedy home with her. And then, without waiting for her answer, he walked out the door.

The last words Emma heard him say were, "Better watch your back!"

Emma threw her pencil on the desk and rubbed her throbbing temples. What had she gotten herself into?

Chapter 37

After taking three Tylenol and gulping down a 7-Up for lunch, Emma decided she sorely needed a breath of fresh air and a change of scenery. So she walked the few blocks to the medical clinic to talk to her friend about the domestic abuse relocation program.

Her shoulders felt tight from the tension of the past few days, Emma raised her face to the sun, letting its warmth wash over her, and tried to relax. Although used to a rigorous pace with courts, clients and briefings, the stress and anxiety from this investigation was taking its toll. The base was fairly quiet and Emma was happy she didn't see anyone with whom she would feel obligated to stop and chat.

The Medical Clinic on base was like any other clinic found in the civilian sector with the exception that the base psychiatrists, psychologists and social workers also had their offices here. True to Air Force form, it was a long beige building with a huge parking lot.

A double sliding door automatically opened as Emma stepped on the black rug in front of it. As usual, the waiting room right inside the doors was crowded with military members and dependents waiting to see the family practice doctors. Emma made her way back to the Mental Health Clinic.

Whenever she visited this clinic, for some reason Emma felt like she was intruding on the private lives of those who sat in its waiting room.

Emma didn't have to wait long for her friend, Dr. Nancy Martin, with whom she had worked closely many times before.

Nancy Martin was prior military and like many others, had decided to stay in Germany after she retired. Happily embracing civilian life, Nancy loved to wear loose fitting clothes after many years of crisply pressed form fitting uniforms.

Today she wore a large red and gray tunic that hung loosely on her tall slender frame. Black flowing pants and black heels completed her outfit. Her long, graying hair was pulled neatly back in a low pony tail and glasses hung from a silver chain around her neck.

Nancy was a very intelligent woman, who actively went to bat for her clients and their rights. Nothing riled her more than when a supervisor tried to circumvent a process to punish a military member who was under Nancy's care. She was a champion of the underdog and was not afraid to take on a commander for a cause, regardless of his or her rank. Emma had seen her in action and was glad she was never on the receiving end of one of Nancy's crusades. On the contrary, Emma and Nancy had developed a good working relationship over the last couple of years and now Emma considered Nancy a friend.

"It's so good to see you," Nancy gushed as she gave Emma a hug. "Please sit down and tell me what brings you to my part of the world."

Emma took a seat on a soft brown leather couch, quite unlike the standard military issue found in most military offices. But then was nothing in Nancy's office looked like it was standard issue. Soft sage green walls and thick beige carpet created a comfortable, almost Zen-like atmosphere. Instead of the normal plaques and awards, the walls were bare except for one painting that looked like a replica of a Monet.

There was, in fact, nothing in her office to distract a patient. The top of her small oak desk was bare except for a closed laptop. Lush green plants were scattered throughout the room, the bigger ones on the floor and the smaller ones strategically placed on an end table or a small shelf.

Nancy sat across from Emma in a small antique chair she had bought for a song in an old antique store in a neighboring village. When asked why she chose to sit in a straight backed chair instead of a more comfortable one, Nancy replied it made her really sit up and listen to her patient.

"And besides," she would add with a laugh, "it's good for an old woman's posture."

After pouring Emma a cup of tea from the green ceramic pot, Nancy crossed her legs at her ankles and waited for Emma to reveal the purpose of her visit.

"I'm sure you heard what happened last week to a Security Forces Airman in the armory?" Emma began, taking a sip of her tea.

Nancy nodded sadly. "What an absolute travesty! I couldn't believe it when I first heard . . . to think a murder here on our base!"

"I know. It's really disturbing." Sitting her cup on the coffee table, Emma leaned forward. "What you don't probably know is that I have been assigned to the investigation and have been helping try to catch the person who did this."

"Hot damn!" Nancy exclaimed. "About time they got smart and recruited some real talent."

Grateful for the compliment from a woman she had long admired, Emma thanked Nancy.

"That's what brings me here," she continued. "We're trying to find out more about the victim's background: who she was and why would anyone want to do this to her. It seems she kept to herself for the most part."

"You want me to try to do a profile on her?" Nancy asked.

"No. At least not yet. We're slowly piecing bits we have learned from her few friends, family, and supervisors together. There is one piece that has us stumped though and I'm hoping you can help."

Emma now had Nancy's full attention. "Of course, I will help in any way I can . . . ethically that is."

Nancy was also a champion of doctor-patient confidentiality and would not reveal anything unless her client consented or it was required by law. She had come to blows with several of the attorneys in the legal office for refusing to reveal pertinent information for a trial even after they produced a court order. Although Emma guessed she was not aware of it, Nancy was called by some "Hard ass Martin."

"We've learned that the victim, Senior Airman Teresa Conklin, was previously stationed at Dyess and after only one year was transferred here," she said, watching Nancy closely for any clue that she might recognize the name. But if she did, her friend gave nothing away.

"What we don't understand," she went on. "is why she was transferred so quickly. It appears she was in a relationship that turned ugly and so she was moved here for her safety. I know there is some kind of program, a domestic violence program, which will help a military member or civilian spouse relocate away from the abusive spouse and was hoping you could tell me more about it."

Nancy put her cup on the table. "Yes, you are right, although technically it's not a program. But there's a system in place used in extreme cases to relocate abused military members or their dependants. As you know we don't have any authority over civilians. So if the civilian spouse is the abuser all we can do is turn him or her over to the authorities and see if they'll handle it. But in really bad cases, we can ask the General to bar him or her from base. Now nine times out of ten it's the dependent who is abused, so we can send them back home through the system if necessary."

"Doesn't an investigation take place if someone says they're abused?"

Nancy nodded. "If abuse is alleged, we assign a Family Advocacy caseworker to assess the situation and investigate the incident. Safety is our number one priority so we make sure the victim is protected at all costs. The caseworker and other Family Advocacy officials also interview the alleged abuser, after, of course, their rights are read."

"We then take all of this information to a multidisciplinary committee, which is comprised of legal, chaplain, law enforcement and other medical staff," Nancy continued. "This committee then determines if the alleged abuse is substantiated or not. If it's substantiated and involves an abusive military member, then we take the information to his or her commander to act accordingly."

Emma was familiar with this stage of the process as part of her job as Chief of Military Justice entailed recommending punishments for military members charged with spousal or child abuse, but she said nothing. The important thing now was to pick Nancy's brain.

"Sometimes," her friend continued, "the abused civilian spouse moves back home because the military member is in jail or punished, but most of the time they chose to remain here while their spouse gets treatment. So you can see the system you mention is rarely used. It's reserved for those case where we must protect the abused spouse and get him or her away from the situation as quickly as possible."

"What if the victim and abuser are both military members but not married?" Emma asked.

Nancy frowned. "I would say it's highly unusual. Personally, I've never heard of it happening."

Emma couldn't help showing her disappointment. How was it, she wondered, that every lead that she pursued seemed to go nowhere.

"Now, now, my eager beaver," Nancy patted her hand. "Just because I have never heard of it before doesn't mean it cannot happen. If the committee felt a military member was in imminent danger, then they might have recommended that the abused member's commander she be transferred to another base."

Emma perked up. "So it *could* have happened in this case. Teresa could have been relocated here away from her abusive military partner."

Nancy smiled thoughtfully. "Yes. It could have happened. But if it had, my office would have been involved. The receiving base is required to be notified of a domestic situation so they can deal with it and provide the appropriate assistance to the relocating member. As the receiving base for your airman, I should have been notified and I can assure you I was not. I wouldn't forget a case like this," she added.

Wanting to make sure she left no stones unturned, Emma decided to ask a favor of her friend.

"Do you think you could find out from your counterparts at Dyess if they know of her case?" she asked. "Before I tell my boss we still don't know why Teresa was transferred here, I want to make sure someone didn't just forget to follow procedures and notify you."

Emma was relieved when Nancy agreed. "That's why I said you should be on this case!" she added, taking out her planner. "You are so thorough. I'll make a couple of calls and get back to you. I am assuming this is high priority?"

"Yes. Thanks, Nancy. I really appreciate your help."

"Don't thank me yet. Wait to see if I can actually get information out of them."

Chapter 38

Emma left the Medical Clinic and headed towards the Community Savings Bank, located across the street from the legal office, where she was to meet Myers to open Teresa's lockbox.

A fighter plane fired up over in the distance on the flight line, its loud engines booming. Emma stopped and shielded her eyes from the bright sun watching the magnificent aircraft fly away into the sky. But instead of the exhilaration she usually felt at such a sight, she was overcome by a sense of uneasiness. Was the murderer here now? Emma glanced around uneasily. Was he watching her right now? Emma shook her head chiding herself for being silly.

Suddenly a bell chimed as a door opened a few feet from her. Startled Emma took a step back and then quickly recovered as a Lieutenant Colonel passed through the door carrying his dry cleaning.

"Sir," Emma saluted him.

"Major."

Emma quickly lowered her hand willing her heart to stop beating so fast. What was going on with her? This case really had her riled up. Then it hit her. She had always hated the unknown. And this time the unknown was dangerous. She looked around the almost empty sidewalk. It seemed as though no matter where they turned, they were met with silence. No one wanted to tell them anything. Didn't they care the murderer was still out there and that there could be another victim?

Emma stopped and took another breath. Of course they knew that was the problem. She turned towards the wing headquarter building which she could barely see in the distance. They know. After all, a lot of high ranking people were involved in this case: Colonel Carlson, Chief Peterson, her boss, and General Brandt. They all knew something and they were the ones closing the doors. Was this some kind of good old boys' club where they were all protecting each other?

She decided, suddenly, that she had had it. She was going to get some answers. No more secrets. No more lies. She would start with her boss and demand he tell her everything he knew. Emma knew it could cost her, perhaps even her job, but she didn't care anymore. She was assigned to this investigation to find the murderer of Teresa Conklin and she owed it to the other military members on this base and to herself to do just that.

Emma felt better with a renewed sense of purpose. Above the tops of the buildings, Emma could make out the large window of the General's office, and found herself wondering if the General could see her. And if he did, did he realize that she wanted answers and that no matter how many hurdles were put in her way, she was going to get them.

Chapter 39

Myers was standing inside the main entrance to the bank waiting for Emma. It was clear that he was tense, and Emma found that she was glad to know that she was not the only one this case was getting to.

"Find out anything?" he asked.

"Not much yet," she replied. "I did learn, as we suspected, that it's highly unusual for an unmarried airman to get transferred away from an abusive partner. But, my friend thinks there is a slight chance it can happen. She says she hasn't heard of Teresa's case, but she's looking into it."

"You believe she'd tell you if she knew about Conklin?"

Even though she wasn't sure who to believe anymore, Emma told him, grudgingly, that she thought that Nancy would come through for them.

The head teller at the bank, an indifferent woman in a navy blue suit took them past a long line of people waiting to cash checks and change U.S. money into foreign currency for their visits to other countries. A TV monitor hung above the line displaying the current exchange rates for various European countries and the U.S. Everywhere the sounds of drawers closing and crisp money being counted out loud could be heard.

They settled themselves in a small room while the teller went to get Teresa's lockbox.

"Believe it or not, I think I like your interrogation rooms better than this one," Emma remarked surveying their small quarters which had barely enough room for both of them to fit in the two chairs that sat in front of a counter running the length of one of the walls.

"Remind me to bring a hostile witness in here to interview them," Myers said, grinning as he tugged at his tie to loosen it, "a couple of minutes in this place and they'll be spilling their guts just to get out of here. I hope you're not claustrophobic."

Once again, in close quarters with him, Emma found herself intensely aware of his physical presence and the scent of his cologne. She found herself wanting to run her hand through his thick wavy hair, which was absurd, of course. She was relieved when the teller returned and set a long narrow metal box down on the counter in front of them.

"Just let me know when you are done," she said. "The button's by the door."

It was so hot that Emma could feel sweat forming on her upper lip. It helped to peal off her Gortex coat.

"Well, let's see what she's hidden in here," Myers said, opening the box. "Well, I'll be damned. Take a look at this!"

Inside the box were two rows of little black and gray boxes; some short, some long and all neatly lined side by side. Emma wasn't a big jewelry wearer since there were restrictions on what kind of jewelry you could wear in the military, but she knew jewelry boxes when she saw them. And there were lots of them in here.

Inside the first box that she opened was a beautiful dark blue sapphire ring about the size of her pinky fingernail. Tiny diamonds surrounded the blue stone which sparkled in her hand. "Man, this is gorgeous!" she exclaimed.

Myers was examining an opal ring in his hand. It was perfectly round and absolutely stunning. He held it up for Emma to see.

"The Air Force must be paying our young airmen a pretty good salary these days," he observed.

"Must be better than officer pay," Emma replied as they opened the rest of the boxes and found three more rings: a ruby, peridot and blue topaz, all large and beautifully mounted in different settings.

There were also five necklaces, most of them were gold chains with pendants hanging from them.

"Okay, now I'm getting jealous!" Emma said, holding up a silver rope of diamonds.

"He must have bought that to match this," Myers replied, showing her the matching bracelet. "I'll give him one thing. He's got good taste."

Emma stared at the gems spread out on the counter. "I don't get it. Why buy her all of this stuff when she can't wear it anyway? She wouldn't be able to wear most of this stuff with her uniform. It's against regulations. And if she tried to wear it around the dorms, someone would surely notice and call her on it. There's a small fortune in these boxes. So why did he buy them just so they could stay in this lockbox? It doesn't make sense."

Myers thought for a moment, scratching his chin. "Maybe he got off on her wearing it when they were alone? But sure looks like he was crazy for Conklin . . . or obsessed. That's the only reason I can think of he would buy all this stuff."

"You think the Chief could afford all of this?" Emma asked.

"I don't know, but I bet a high ranking officer could."

Ignoring the comment about her salary, Emma started to replace the boxes, only to notice a thin black book at the bottom of the lockbox.

"What do we have here?" she exclaimed, taking it out and flipping through it. "I'd say we just found another of Teresa's journals. And this one actually might tell us something."

Emma held the journal so that Myers could read it over her shoulder, leaning so close that his breath tickled the back of her neck. She remembered last night when he almost kissed her. If she just moved her head slightly her lips would touch his.

"Okay," she said shakily. "Let's see what she has to say."

The journal began when Teresa moved to Winburg. The first few pages recounted nothing more than her first impressions of the base. And the fact that she was lonely, even though she was excited about being in Germany. On the sixth page, however, she wrote enthusiastically about working out and how she'd lost some weight. And she was even more expansive about having signed up for some classes so she could finish her B.A.

"Maybe this will finally make mom proud of me!" she'd written.

As they flipped the pages, the trivial entries made Emma wonder if they had hit a dead end yet again. But then they hit the jackpot when she turned the page to December 2, 2005, one month after moving to Winburg.

Dec 2, 2005

He made a pass at me today! I know it! His hand brushed mine and I could feel his eyes on me. I know he likes me. God, he is so handsome! And everything else I want in a man – sophisticated, worldly and powerful. I knew when Sergeant Dort put me on this assignment, that I'd see him every day. Some stupid project with all of these people from all over the base Dort thought would be a "good opportunity for my career!" God! Opportunity I'll say! Every day I get to be with him – watch him, want him! And now he wants me! I am so excited – I love it here!

Dec 13, 2005:

I can't believe I haven't written for 11 days. But God what an 11 days! It's been incredible. I was right! He likes me. About a week ago I was making coffee in the break room and he came up behind me. I could feel his breath on my neck and I almost passed out.

He told me he was proud of me for going to school and of the work I had done for my squadron. I couldn't even talk – just nodded or said yes, Sir! What an idiot! He must think I'm a complete moron. When he walked away I almost wanted to cry. I had blown it. He approached me and I'd blown it.

But you'll never guess what happened – the next day he called me into his office! I couldn't believe it. I thought for sure I must be in trouble or something especially after I had acted. Boy was I wrong. He closed the door and had me sit down on the couch next to him. I could hardly breathe.

He asked me if I liked it here. I told him yes – but it sometimes got lonely. That's when he asked me if I was dating anyone. Can you believe it?!? I told him no – that I hadn't met a lot of people yet – on account that I worked the late shift and was working when everyone else went out. He said that was a shame – that maybe he could help me out or something so I didn't have to work every weekend.

"A pretty girl like you shouldn't be without a boyfriend – someone to love you." When he said that I about flipped! I knew he was hitting on me – he was coming on strong and I loved it! So I played his game. I leaned forward and thanked him – so he knew I knew what he was up to. That's when he started acting a little nervous. Like he had never done this before. It was so exciting. He told me he'd like to help me out and maybe we could meet in a couple of days to discuss it. I told him sure and then left his office.

I saw him again a couple of days later on Friday night– the same day I was given a day off from working the night shift. I knew he was behind it! I mean I had been working the shift pretty much every weekend and all of a sudden Dort comes in and tells me I can have this weekend off. He says there was a new policy that we only could only be scheduled every other weekend. It was so cool. I knew he did it for me.

So I was working out and all of a sudden he came out of nowhere as I was walking back to my room from the gym. It was so dark he scared the shit out of me. But then I saw it was him. His eyes – they're so nice, so kind. He's so strong – he's got a great body, all muscles!

He asked me how I was doing. I wanted to throw my arms around him and thank him for what he had done. But I didn't – I just told him I had the weekend off and was really glad to have some time to go explore the area. I mean I made sure the door was wide open if he wanted to do something – and he did. He told me if I ever wanted to know of some good places to visit around here – just to ask him. I said yeah – sure I would do that.

He was so quiet but his eyes were intense – it was dark but I could tell. He kept looking around to make sure no one else could see us. Just then a couple of guys came up the sidewalk and he said he had to go. It sucked – I watched him walk away. SO close! But I know he wants me.

So I didn't see him for the next few days and I was bummed. Was that it? Did I dream it? I know when a guy is hot for me – and this guy was mine. Maybe he got scared, I mean it is kind of dangerous – him and me. But God, how exciting!

I was getting pretty bummed – until yesterday. I was working on this assignment again and he asked me to come into his office. There was no one else around- everyone was at lunch. I knew it! He wasn't so nervous this time – just strong and powerful. I just wanted him to take me in his arms and hold me. He says to me that if I was interested there was a neat restaurant about 1 hour from here in a small village down south. I said – yeah – I love trying new places. He asked me if I would like him to take me there. My stomach was doing flips – but I kept my cool. I told I would like that. He asked me when my next night off was and I told him next week. He then asked me if I could get into town – I said yes.

*So he told me to meet him at the bus stop on the walkplatz
in downtown Winburg about 7:00. I could hardly walk out
of there my knees were so weak! Hot damn! I think I may be
in love.*

Emma stopped reading. "It sure didn't take him long to come
onto her. Whoever he is, he's either really stupid or thinking with
something other than his head." She tapped the side of her head.
"I mean the one up here."

Myers moved his chair slightly so he could face her. "She was
very attractive, but shit. Enough to ruin your career over? Let's see
what happened on their date."

Dec 16

*Tonight was one of the most wonderful nights of my life.
It was everything I could have dreamed of and more. He is
incredible. He picked me up in his beautiful car and drove
me to this tiny village.*

*It was so romantic. I asked him how fast his car could
go and he floored it. He was showing off and I loved it. I
kept squealing like a little girl every time we went around a
corner. It was so cool! We got to the restaurant and it was so
elegant. I hadn't been to a place like that for a while. I wore
my short black skirt and red shirt – it was tight and gave
him a little peek of what I had to offer. I think his eyes about
popped out when I took off my coat.*

*He was such a gentleman. He even held my chair out for
me and everything. We had wine and I got a little tipsy, but I
didn't care. This was my night and nothing was going to ruin
it. Not even the fact, he was married or an officer. I didn't
care. He was a big boy and I'm a big girl and he knows what
he is getting into. And me – I can take care of myself. Besides
it's nice to finally be treated with respect. I deserve it!*

We forgot about everything and just laughed. He told me all about where he grew up, what he had done with his life. It was so inspirational. I mean he has worked so hard and gotten so far. I was just so proud of him. I told him I wanted to get my degree and become an officer too. That made him smile – he said he would help me. I know he meant it.

We ate and afterwards danced – it was fabulous. As we were driving back to Winburg, he pulled over on the side of the road and asked me if he could kiss me! What a gentleman! I grabbed his shirt and pulled him to me. He is such a good kisser!

The wine and his kisses made my head swim. He put his hand up my shirt and I let him. It had been so long since a man – a real man and put his hands on me. It felt so good and I just melted into him. But I didn't want to give it all up at once – so after a while I stopped him. I told him I didn't want to make love with him in a car on the side of the road – at least the first time. He was so gentle – said he understood. Said I was the sexiest thing he'd ever seen and I deserved to be treated like a princess. And for the rest of the ride back he held my hand and called me his princess.

I didn't even care that he had to drop me back off at the bus stop. I know no one could see us drive on to base together – it didn't matter. He is the best and I cannot wait until the next time I see him!

The next pages were filled with descriptions of their affair: the out of the way places they visited together; the quaint, quiet restaurants they frequented and the places they had sex. Teresa was very explicit in her description of their first time making love. The graphic nature of the entry made both Myers and Emma awkward. The room suddenly got even hotter.

Ready to move on, Emma flipped through the next pages in which Teresa also detailed the gifts her lover bought her. It started out as flowers or a book of poems, nothing that could be traced back to him, like a card with his handwriting. He then got bolder right after Christmas and bought her a piece of jewelry, a sapphire ring, probably the one Emma had just looked at.

It was after receiving the sapphire when Teresa wrote how safe she felt with her lover. In the same entries she also briefly mentioned having friends study with her in the armory.

> I told him today I've been having a friend, mostly Jaime, come in and keep my company during my shift. It is so damned hard to stay awake. I let him know we just study – but it really helps me. I'm not going to stop either. My grades are improving and I'm going to get straight A's. I just know it.

Beside her Myers chortled. "Wouldn't Dort have loved to have this evidence to support his Article 15 against Conklin? She's actually flaunting the fact that she was getting away with it"

Emma turned the page.

> He is so WONDERFUL! He doesn't see any problem with me studying in the armory. In fact, he's proud of me – that I am taking my studies seriously. (Wish Dort would get his head out of his ass and see it this way).

The next entry read:

> He protects me from people on this base who want to hurt me. They're just jealous of me I know, but it feels so good that he is there for me. He's my savior. I teased him tonight in the car that maybe he should come by sometime while I'm on duty. I whispered all of the things we could do together there. Man, did he blush. But God, wouldn't that be exciting!!

The pair started going on weekend trips together whenever his wife was out of town and Teresa wasn't working. Over the next several weeks, there were few mentions of her lover's wife. She did write about the secrecy and how it was getting so hard. He loved her, she wrote, but couldn't be seen with her in public and this was really getting to the young airman.

By late February of '06, it became clear Teresa was taking the upper hand in the relationship. She wrote of wanting to spend more time with him, to be with him every weekend.

Emma almost felt sorry for this man who started spending more money on his young lover to placate her: extravagant trips, expensive clothes, electronics and jewelry.

By early spring, Teresa was calling his wife the "bitch" who soon became an object of hatred for Teresa, someone she would like to get rid of. In mid March, the young airman made the ultimate demand: that her lover leave his wife or else.

He pleaded with her and told her he couldn't, that if people found out about them, he would be finished and kicked out of the Air Force. He professed his love for her over and over again, promising her that when he retired they would be together and he sealed this promise by presenting her with a diamond necklace and matching bracelet.

"Shit, was he in deep!" Myers swore. "She had him by the balls and she knew it."

The diamonds seemed to appease the young woman for a while and she went back to writing about their time together and how in love they were. It was in April when her tone again changed.

It appeared that one of his friends had somehow found out about the affair and advised him to end it. Teresa made no secret about how angry this made her, but once again, there were no names. Instead, she called him "The Snitch."

Once she learned the Snitch's weakness of his dedication to her lover, she blackmailed him. If he went to anybody about them, she said, "I'll take you both down!"

For the next few pages, Teresa went on and on about how she would get her revenge by going to the Inspector General and telling him that she had been taken advantage of by an older man, an officer. And, she said, she would hand "The Snitch" over to the authorities, as well, by explaining his role in getting her better shifts and clearing her lover's calendar for their trysts.

Emma paused. Senior Airman Harvey's comments about the change in Teresa came back to her. But hadn't Harvey said that was in June? But if she remembered right, Jaime had told them that Teresa had assured her in the spring that things were over between them. Struggling to get the timeframe right, Emma went back to reading.

Teresa made sure her lover and the Snitch understood who was boss by informing them she had also been telling one of her friends about the affair.

> *No names and not all of the details, but I'll give them enough so I have witness if those two nark.*

"It must have been Jaime that she told," Myers said. "The timing corresponds to when Jaime said Teresa told her she was dating a married man. She knows too much," he added, his voice low. "Not only is she a witness to the murder, but she knows about Teresa's affair."

For the first time, Emma could really understand the gravity of Jaime's situation and why she was so scared.

Although she didn't write about specifically breaking it off with him as she had told Jaime, Teresa's journal entries made it clear that she had made him suffer by keeping him at a distance and taken great pride in doing so. And he apparently had become distraught.

"I wonder," Myers said, "if his despair led him to murder."

"Not yet, anyway," Emma replied turning the page. "It looks like she hooked back up with him."

Emma read aloud the next couple of entries in which Teresa explained that she started to pity him, and that she no longer cared about the elaborate gifts he sent her.

And then, in the middle of June, the tone of the journal changed.

> *Oh God! Trapper found me!*

> *I was walking to my dorm room and Trapper was right there, smiling at me like nothing happened. Shit! I about puked! Did Trapper get reassigned? Here on a visit? I thought I had left all of that bullshit behind in Dyess. I shouldn't have gotten involved with that shithead in the first place.*

"Who's Trapper?" Myers interrupted.

"Not sure," Emma replied flippantly, and then, when he looked askance, "Sorry. It's just that it is a bit claustrophobic in here."

"Actually, I'm rather enjoying it," he said with a grin that made her flush. "Trapper," he went on, "must be the abusive partner. The timing matches up with when Harvey said Teresa started acting weird. But we can talk about that later. Go on reading."

It became apparent Myers was right and the writing made it clear Teresa and Trapper had been dating and it had turned ugly. Teresa detailed their volatile relationship in the next several pages. She wrote of how she and Trapper couldn't let anyone know they were seeing each other. How no one knew what was going on between them and if anyone found out they would be in trouble.

"Another secret partner?" Myers proclaimed. "Good Lord, this girl doesn't know how to have a real, legitimate relationship, does she?"

Emma felt his eyes on the back of her neck. "She doesn't know what she's missing," he said in a low voice.

Heat seared her face as she read on. The relationship lasted about six months before the abuse started.

At first Trapper had threatened her verbally but the physical stuff followed soon after. Pages were filled with the hitting, kicking, and punching; all on her chest, back and stomach so the bruises could be covered by her clothes. Suddenly, for no apparent reason, Teresa wrote that she had reason to believe that things would get better and much to Emma's surprise, they did. Trapper stopped hurting Teresa and the young airman once again fell "madly in love" with him.

"So why the transfer here?" Myers questioned. "If this Trapper was no longer abusive, how did she get transferred here so quickly?"

They read on hoping to find the answer, but what they did find was not clear. Both of them assumed the abuse started again, but could find no mention of it in the rest of the journal. Instead, Teresa boasted how she had tamed the "wild beast" and that the abuse had stopped.

Trapper is putty in my hands!

Several entries described how Trapper was now "a pussy cat" and would "bend over backwards" for Teresa.

Knowing, as she did, what the girl's fate had been, Emma found all this extremely hard to read, particularly as it seemed a game to Teresa, to see how much power she could hold over someone else. The only abuse that appeared to take place during the rest of her tour at Dyess came from Teresa, who completely demeaned and degraded Trapper in her journal. The young vixen bragged about threatening Trapper to "do what I want or I'll leave your ass!"

Only one short excerpt alluded to her transfer to Winburg.

I did it! I'm out of here. Away from Trapper for good. That will teach 'em not to mess with me!

Emma was confused. "I thought Harvey said Teresa was scared of this person? Sure doesn't sound like she was scared when she moved here. So looks like our theory of her getting transferred here through a domestic abuse program is out the window."

"Beats me," Myers replied. "But I know one thing for sure. She really knew how to work the system . . . and the people around her. I don't think I would put anything past that girl. Looks like if she wanted something, she was going to do everything and anything to get it."

Emma's back ached from sitting in the same position for so long. She stood up and handed the thick journal to Myers. "Here, it's your turn to read."

"She's now back to when Trapper came here to Winburg," Myers explained as he skimmed the next few pages. "That's interesting. She doesn't say much more about Trapper and it certainly doesn't appear she was frightened by him. Man, for someone who is so graphic about everything else, Conklin has very little to say about this guy. She just writes about handling the situation and not worrying about him anymore. Says she's too busy dealing with her lover. Listen to this."

"Besides, he is really starting to be a pain in the ass. I think I should probably break it off with him, AGAIN!. But he keeps sending stuff – great stuff. And then there's the Snitch. He keeps threatening me not to talk to anyone.

Thinks I'll spill the beans. What a moron! The Snitch's even put him up to asking me – more like begging me – not to tell anyone about us."

Myers turned the page and starting reading again.

I am SO PISSED! He and that damned Snitch are really getting on my nerves! They've been acting so weird these past few weeks. They keep on me about whether I'm going to talk. Who do they think I am? But hey – I'm not stupid. I know how to work this. I'll let it hang over his head for awhile – let it hang over the Snitch, too. Let them sweat! I have nothing but time. I am going to start keeping this journal in my lockbox though – just in case. You can never be too careful around these guys. Besides, now I can go look at my jewels every week. Man if my parents only knew about my stash! Wouldn't that really rock their bible thumping world!

"That's it," Myers said as he closed the book. "That's her last entry, dated two weeks ago. So what we now know is that she was dating this Trapper guy, it became abusive, but then things turned around again and she liked him. Somehow, she got herself transferred her by way, we used to think, of the domestic violence program, but now we're not so sure. What we do know, is soon after coming here, she hooked up with an officer who was married and who wouldn't leave his wife but kept Conklin happy on the side by buying her expensive gifts. Then this guy, Snitch, found out, and both guys get worried she's going to spill the beans and ruin their careers."

"She was so naïve," Emma shuddered. "She thought she was so in control, but she was really just a young, stupid, naïve girl."

"But she was playing with fire and she knew it," Myers added putting a hand on her shoulder. It was, Emma thought, a comforting gesture. She imagined him wrapping his strong arms around her, sheltering her from all they had uncovered. Neither of them moved.

As she thought about seeing Teresa lying on the armory floor, Emma felt really emotional. It was a lot to deal with the murder of a young woman and even more so when you learned about her secret life.

"Guess not everything or everybody is as they appear," she said quietly, knowing from the look in his eyes that he knew what she meant and for a moment she felt more connected to him than ever.

"We've got to get going," he said, his voice hoarse. "We need to take all of this back to the office so it can be logged as evidence. This is not going to be easy on her parents, you know."

Emma remembered all too vividly how the Conklins, each in their own way, had denounced their daughter's behavior in regard to her affair with a married man. And now they were to be faced with glaring proof of another instance of her promiscuity.

"From an evidentiary standpoint this is gold, you know," Myers told her. "What it all boils down to is that she was having an affair with a married officer and that there may have been an accomplice."

"That gold," Emma pointed out grimly. "will also destroy several careers."

"I know," he agreed. "What a mess! My guess is we're talking about Carlson."

Emma believed he was right but wasn't ready to jump to any solid conclusions yet. "We can't assume anything. Besides even if the Colonel was her lover, it doesn't mean he killed her."

"Unless she threatened to talk," Myers argued. "He would have been ruined. His life would have been over. Who knows what a man in his situation would be driven too?"

"Don't forget about this Trapper person." Emma shot back. "We know he was abusive before maybe he became abusive again. Maybe he came here and found out Teresa was seeing this officer and got crazy jealous."

"Now counselor, who's doing the assuming now?" Myers retorted. "Who said Trapper was a man? What I can do is have Dan find out everyone who was transferred here in the April/May timeframe of this year. Maybe that would help narrow down who Trapper is."

Emma helped empty the contents of the lockbox into a black bag Myers brought with him and closed the lid. Just as Emma was about to press the button to notify the teller they were finished so they could get out of the godforsaken room, Myers's cell phone started ringing. After listening intently for a moment, he clicked it shut.

"You know how right after this we have an appointment with Carlson?" he said. "Well it seems instead of meeting us at his office, he told Dan to meet us at the firing range. Appears he has back to back meetings out there and is going to squeeze us in."

Emma frowned, suddenly not so eager to leave the protective room. Although she decided not to say so, the firing range was, she thought, an interesting place to interview a suspect in a murder case.

Chapter 40

The shooting range was located on the northwestern perimeter of the base. All military personnel, unless exempt, were required to annually qualify on a weapon. Even Emma, as a JAG, was required to shoot a M9 and qualify to carry the weapon.

But this had not been her first experience with a gun. When she was a kid Emma's dad had taken her to hunter safety classes. He had also let her shoot pop cans out in an overgrown field on their acreage with his small pistol. She still remembered how clumsy she had felt the first time she had held it. But, not wanting to disappoint her dad, she had concentrated really hard on what he had told her to do and, to her delight, she hit the can he had set on a tree stump with the first shot.

Her dad's instruction had come in handy when she had entered the military. During her officer training, Emma and the other JAGs in her class were taken to the shooting range at Maxell Air Force Base in Alabama to first qualify on the M9.

All shooters were first required to clean and assemble their gun before they could go out on the range. After a quick instruction, Emma had her gun ready to go in no time. However, a few of her classmates weren't so adept.

At first everyone in the room laughed it off and after a few tries, most finally got it. For Emma, it had given her considerable satisfaction to put on her headgear, stride out to the range, wait for the Tech Sergeant's final instructions, and then, with a thrill of excitement, aim her pistol at the outline of a human figure. When she squeezed the trigger and hit the spot designated as its heart, she had found herself wishing her father could see her.

Today, Emma was greeted with the rat-a-tat-tat of bullets propelling towards the targets as she got out of her car.

"You ready for this?" Myers asked, slamming the car door behind him. He was scowling and she wondered if he was dreading what they had to do as much as she.

"We don't have much choice, do we?" she replied.

Suddenly, his eyes blazed. "Dammit, you do have a choice. You don't have to do this. One person is dead, Emma, and that man in there might have done it. He could be dangerous. All I know is that I don't want you getting hurt. If he thinks you know too much, God knows what might happen."

"Watch my back then," she said, forcing herself to smile. "I really appreciate your concern. But I have to do this. I'm in it too deep now. We both are. We need to find out who did this to her and why. And that man in there might just hold the key."

She looked into Myers eyes and could see he would support her although she was sure it would be reluctantly.

Inside, they went straight to a large Plexiglas window which fronted the observation area. On the other side of the glass was a long concrete slab running the entire length of the building. Ten stalls separated by wooden partitions constructed from two by fours, lined the edge of the slab. These structures not only created a division between each stall but also gave the shooter something to "hide" behind as they aimed at their target. A shooter occupied every stall. Behind them, a trainer walked back and forth, making suggestions and correcting stances.

Suddenly a man's voice came over the loudspeaker and all at once nothing else could be heard, the deafening noise drowning out all sound.

Holstering their weapons, the shooters walked out to examine their targets. Emma couldn't tell which one was Carlson since they all were dressed in BDUs. It wasn't until they started walking back towards the glass that Emma could begin to make out faces.

"There's the Colonel," Myers said, pointing. "Third from the left."

The hair prickled on the back of Emma's neck as she saw the target he was holding. There were two tennis ball size holes on the black outline where the head and heart should have been.

"Well he's a good shot!" Myers exclaimed, taking the words right out of her mouth.

They waited until the trainer gave the all clear signal before going outside. Now that they had taken off their protective ear and eyewear, Emma recognized several of the marksmen. Four were officers in Carlson's squadron. She guessed the rest of the men who were enlisted were also under Carlson's command.

It was not unusual for a commander to request he test with members in his own squadron. This practice created camaraderie and allowed the commander to see how his troops fared on the range.

The Colonel was joking with one of his officers as they approached. As soon as he saw them, his smile faded.

"Agent Myers, Major." Handing his gun to the officer next to him, he said, "Captain Shard. Would you mind please putting this away for me? I'd appreciate it."

When the Captain had gone, Carlson leaned against the wooden wall and slowly took off his glasses and stared at them. This was not the same man who just a couple of days ago had been so devastated by the death of one of his troops. Emma was taken aback by this apparent metamorphosis.

Emma, having worked with Carlson for years, could clearly recall the times he helped put one of his own troops behind bars for the crimes they committed because justice required it. He was a well liked commander who spoke passionately about the military, declaring his pride for it and his country. In all the time she'd known him, Carlson had been nothing but professional to Emma, even if he wasn't always courteous.

Now, however, any courtesy seemed to be gone and she knew that she could be looking into the eyes of a cold blooded killer. But she had no solid, concrete proof the man standing before her killed Teresa Conklin and she was determined to get the facts from him.

No one spoke a word until the last man left the field, leaving only the three of them. The wind picked up, blowing tiny swirls of dirt out on the range.

"You'll have to make this quick," Carlson finally spoke. "I have a meeting that I can't miss on the other side of base in twenty minutes."

"Fine, Sir." Myers assured him. "We just have a couple of things we need to clear up."

"Humph!" Carlson snorted cynically. "I heard you cleared a couple of things up with the Chief and now he feels like he is a suspect."

His accusing eyes turned on Emma. "So what are you going to do now, Major?" he demanded. "Tell me I'm a suspect? What kind of shit are you filling people full of? Jesus, you are ruining careers here and you don't even care!"

"Sir, I can assure you we have accused no one of this crime, including the Chief," Myers broke in. "I'm not sure what he told you, but *we* have kept this entire investigation confidential. We haven't told anyone about what we have found except for Lieutenant Colonel Franks and General Brandt."

Emma was thankful that Myers had taken over. He spoke to the senior officer confidentially and it was clear he was not overawed by the older man's rank.

"If there is a leak of information," he went on. "I suggest you talk with your Chief."

"Let me tell you something, Agent Myers. You had better watch whose toes you step on. I won't have you spreading vicious rumors all over base. Do you understand?" He aggressively took a step towards Emma. "And do *you*, Major?" the Colonel snarled.

Carlson looked as though he hadn't slept for days and Emma detected alcohol on his breath.

Myers took this opportunity to step between them. "Sir," he said. "I must respectfully ask you to back away from Major Lohrs, *now!*"

For a moment the Colonel looked as though he did not understand, but then he backed away. It occurred to Emma that he had not realized what he was doing.

"I'm sorry," he muttered apologetically. "You can't begin to imagine the stress I have been under these last few days, what it's been like to have one of your own murdered so viciously. That poor young girl! Such a waste!"

He walked to a bench and sat down wearily.

"I just got done talking to her parents." His eyes clouded over as he bent his head and Emma strained to hear him. "Christ! I hope I never have to do that again."

Emma's heart beat rapidly as she watched the older man rub the back of his neck. Although it happened so fast, she could not believe the man she had worked with over the years had almost attacked her.

"I'm sorry," Carlson said again. "Please just ask me what you need to. I don't have much time."

Determined not to be intimidated by him, Emma spoke first. "Sir, I believe you have a key to the armory. Tell me, has it been in your possession the entire time since you received it?"

"I keep it on my ring with my car keys," he replied, pulling a key ring from his pocket. "It is and has been with me at all times."

"Are you aware that the Chief lost his key a few months ago?"

Carlson didn't flinch. "Yes, I was just made aware of this. The Chief came to me this weekend. He wanted to tell me before you two did. He said someone had broken into his office a while ago and taken his key and a couple of other things."

Emma's eyes shot to Myers. This was the first time either of them had heard the Chief's office had been broken into. Why hadn't he told them earlier? This complicated things a bit since they didn't know who took the key . . . if the Chief was telling the truth this time.

Carlson looked past them at the blowing dirt. "I remember when this happened, sometime this summer. I told him to file a report, but didn't think much about it after that. In fact, I thought I remember he told me they had caught the guy who did it. It was a local who was on the cleaning crew."

"Do you know if he got the key back?" Emma asked.

"No, I'm not sure." He sat up straight. "But the Chief is very careful with his things. He wouldn't do anything to harm the security on this base."

Myers changed the subject. "Sir, do you remember an LOR that was given to Airman Conklin in February of this year?"

"Hell, Agent." Carlson spat out the words. "Do you really think I can remember every single piece of paper given to my troops?"

Unfazed, Myers continued. "Let me see if I can refresh your memory. Senior Airman Conklin was letting unauthorized visitors into the armory while she was on duty during the late shift. She was caught several times and her supervisor, Tech Sergeant Dort, recommended an Article 15."

Emma could have sworn that Carlson clasped his hands in his lap to keep them from shaking.

"Well," he said staring at Myers. "If she was doing this then it sounds like a 15 might have been appropriate."

Myers zeroed in on his target. "That was exactly what Dort thought, until he was told no."

"No?" Carlson asked. His cool demeanor was unconvincing. "What to you mean?"

"You and the Chief told him you wouldn't support a 15 and ordered him to give her a LOR instead," Myers said, his eyes never leaving Carlson's face.

"I assure you," the Colonel stated indignantly, standing to his feet. "If there was concrete evidence of her behavior, I would have supported a 15." He paused to catch his breath. "Like I told you, I don't remember this incident. But I know if Sergeant Dort didn't present any concrete evidence to me, I would have had no choice but to not support his decision."

"I'm sorry I can't be of more help on this one," Carlson said, extending his hand to Myers. "Now if you'll excuse me, I don't want to be late for my next appointment."

Dumfounded, Emma and Myers watched him walk inside.

"Well, for a man who didn't want to be a suspect," Myers declared to Carlson's retreating back. "He sure left us no choice but to consider him one."

"My God," Emma sat down on the bench stunned. "If he didn't kill her then he's got to be covering for the Chief. I've got to tell Colonel Franks. And we have to let the General know, too."

"Let's get out of here and call it a day," Myers said, taking both her hands and pulling her to her feet. "You've had enough for one day."

It was now late in the afternoon and as they reached Emma's car, they heard the faint sound of loud speaker next to the wing headquarters building signaling the beginning of retreat. Every night at 1630, the beautiful sounds of the military ritual could be heard all over base signifying the end of the official workday.

Emma stopped and turned around. Standing straight and proud, she saluted the red, white and blue flag blowing gently in the breeze above the building they just left. Cars on the road behind them pulled over and stopped in reverence. The setting sun shone brightly on the flag as the melody of the national anthem hummed in her ears.

The parking lot was empty except for Emma and Myers, who stood straight beside her, covering his heart with his right hand. After the last note played, Emma dropped her salute but didn't look away from the flag.

In that brief moment Emma was revived. The ceremony was performed each day to increase morale and esprit de corps, as well as heighten mission effectiveness and for Emma, it did just that. She pushed aside the frustrating events of the day, knowing exactly why she was here.

Over the years, Emma had received a lot of flack from people who said she wasn't a real officer because she wasn't on the front lines with the men and women who went to battle. But she had learned to shrug the comments off, even though she was often tempted to tell them about the young women who had been brutally assaulted, or the nineteen year old airman who had clung so tightly to her after he broke into her office, his mind fried from the meth habit he so desperately wanted to kick.

Then there were the countless other young men and women, her clients, who looked to her as a mother, teacher and friend when no one else was there. And finally, there were the sobbing widows whom she helped sort out the estates of husbands who were never coming back.

But Emma had never talked about that side of her job, about the private moments between her and the people she helped. So she may not be dodging bullets on a front line somewhere. But she was contributing. She was making a difference. It didn't matter what other people thought.

"I'm okay," she told Myers now. "Thanks for caring."

"It's my job," he teased, sporting a boyish grin. But he flushed when he said it.

Still smiling, Emma opened her car door. "Why, Agent Myers," she said coyly peering up at him over her car door. "If I didn't know better, I'd say you're blushing."

"Me? No." Myers answered in a deep manly voice. "Real men don't blush."

"I was just thinking about how you're going to handle your new roommate," he said, opening the passenger door. "It makes me angry thinking about her staying with you."

The smile quickly faded from her face as he got in the car.

"Damn!" she swore softly. She'd forgotten she agreed to baby sit Jaime Kennedy tonight. "Who says I'm not out there on the front lines!"

Chapter 41

While Myers went into the OSI building to get her new roommates, Emma stayed in the car and called her boss on her cell phone. Luckily he was still in the office. However, his mood had not changed. Emma braced herself for his reaction to her news.

"Sir, I wanted to let you know we just talked to Colonel Carlson."

"Good. What did he have to say?"

Emma contemplated her next words. "Well Sir, it was more of what he didn't say?"

"Okay, now you have my attention."

"Agent Myers and I went there to ask him about his key to the armory, and the LOR he recommended for Senior Airman Conklin. But before we could say anything, he basically attacked us. He accused us of leaking information about the investigation and spreading 'vicious rumors' were his exact words."

For a long moment there was silence on the other end of the line and then he cleared his throat and said, "Was he physical? Did he hurt you?"

Touched by his concern, Emma decided not to tell her boss about Myers having to ask the Colonel to back away from her.

"No, Sir," she assured him. "But he was really mad. To tell you the truth, I've never seen him like that before."

"I'm so sorry, Emma," Franks said softly.

Emma was unsure of why he was apologizing. "It's okay, Sir. I'm fine. But I do need your help."

"Anything."

"Based on the Colonel's actions today and his responses to our questions, I have to inform you that Colonel Carlson is now a suspect in this investigation. We're going to have to tell the General."

Once again there was silence.

"I understand," her boss said finally. "I'll call the General right now and set up a meeting with him for early tomorrow morning. Do you think you can have your brief about Colonel Carlson done and on my desk by 0630? Then we can talk in the morning. Now go home and try to relax. I'm sure this has been a rough day on you. Wait, you're not going to be alone are you? I want someone there with you . . . just in case."

Again deciding not to tell her boss the entire truth, she told him that she had and then, just before hanging up, heard him say something that sounded like "How did it come to this?"

He hung up leaving Emma wondering what he knew but wasn't telling her.

And why hadn't he acted surprised when she had told him that Carlson was a suspect? Come to think of it, the fact that the Chief was on the list hadn't seemed to surprise him either

For the second time that day, Emma knew it was time for her to confront her boss. If he wanted them to solve this case, he needed to spill what he knew. As she dropped her cell phone into her bag, Emma knew that was exactly what she'd demand tomorrow when she met with him.

Chapter 42

A sharp rap on her window startled her. Outside Myers, literally loaded down with suitcases, was struggling to juggle them.

"What's all that?" she said as she rolled down her window. "Looks like you're moving in."

"Open the trunk, will you?" he huffed. "Although I wouldn't mind," he added before he disappeared behind her car.

Emma popped the lever and felt her car groan under the weight he deposited in the trunk. At the same time, Jaime, wearing a bright pink sweat suit with matching pink tennis shoes, came sauntering towards the car. On each shoulder were two overstuffed gym bags.

"Good grief," Emma moaned. "How much stuff does this kid have? I'm not sure my place is big enough for her."

Following behind Jaime was Agent Amber Sanchez, impeccably dressed in a black pencil knee length skirt which revealed slender calves and a cream blouse which accentuated the curvaceous woman's amble bust, pulling a small neat black small suitcase behind her. Although Emma recalled seeing her earlier, she had never formally met the stunning agent before.

"Hey, look on the bright side," Myers said, laughing, clearly enjoying Emma's chagrin. "At least Amber didn't bring everything she owns."

Not waiting for her answer, he got into his black BMW and pulled behind her. Seeing him still grinning in her rear view mirror, she put on her sunglasses and then silently groaned when Jaime opened the back door of her car and threw her bags into the back seat before squeezing herself in with them. Agent Sanchez appeared at her window and announced that she was going to ride with Myers.

"It'll give you girls a chance to talk," she said, giving Emma a knowing look.

Twenty minutes later they arrived at her house and Emma leaned her head on the steering wheel as Jaime, still talking nonstop, got her things out of the trunk.

How could one person talk so much? And wasn't this the same girl, they had to pry information out of a couple of days ago? Jaime obviously felt comfortable with Emma now as evidenced by the thousand times she thanked Emma for letting her "shack up" with her.

Emma had broken several traffic laws as she raced through the villages, intent on nothing except getting this woman out of her car. It hadn't helped she could see Myers and Sanchez in her rearview mirror laughing and enjoying the ride the whole way here. Not that she was jealous. Thankfully she lost Myers in one of the neighboring villages as she had stepped on the gas, blowing the speed limit.

The trunk slammed and the door behind Emma opened. "I've just about got all of my stuff. Thanks again for letting me stay with you. I really appreciate it."

"It's okay," Emma muttered as she got out of the car. "I'm just glad you're safe. But please, you don't have to thank me anymore. Just be honest with us. That's all the thanks I need."

A shadow quickly passed over her younger woman's face. "Sure, I will. I mean I am . . . being honest with you, I mean," she stammered.

Emma said, "Right," but she was unconvinced.

After finding room for Jaime's mountain of stuff, Emma settled the airman on the couch, placing a tall stack of DVD's and some magazines on the coffee table in front of her.

"I'll throw in a frozen pizza and bring it out to you," she called out, firmly closing the kitchen door behind her. Emma could hear her guest still chattering in the next room and was now grateful that her landlord had put a door to every room.

A moment later, Myers and Sanchez joined her. Getting three beers from the fridge, Emma invited them to have a seat at the table.

"At least she can't hear us," she remarked falling into her chair.

"Don't you mean at least we can't hear her?" Sanchez said, tossing her thick mane of hair back over her shoulder.

"Touché." Emma clinked her beer against Sanchez's. "Here's to a hard day. Thank God it's over."

Myers sat silent, watching the exchange.

"You know, it may not be over," he said solemnly. "You two are in danger out here."

"Come on Myers," Emma moaned, pushing his beer towards him. "Lighten up. That's why I've got Agent Sanchez here . . . to protect me."

Myers frowned, obviously unconvinced.

"Look," she said, trying to assure herself as much as him. "I'm okay. We've got a couple of suspects but we know who they are. Now we just need to find the evidence to pin this thing on one or both of them. Now relax and have a drink with us before you go."

"It's not the suspects we know about that worries me so much," he told her earnestly, his grey eyes piercing hers. "It's the ones we don't know about that really bother me."

Chapter 43

Having changed into jeans and a t-shirt and let down her hair, Emma put a frozen pizza in the oven and got herself another beer. By the time the spice smells of tomato sauce and pepperoni filled the kitchen, her mood had improved considerably.

Every once in a while she checked on her guest, who had made herself quite at home. Sprawling out on Emma's overstuffed green couch with two empty cans of pop tossed on the coffee table in front of her, Jaime was so engrossed in her movie that she barely acknowledged Emma when she opened the kitchen door. No doubt, Emma thought, all that talking had worn her out.

When she set the pizza on the table, Myers eyed it appreciatively. "I always did like a woman who could cook," he said, a smile forming on his lips.

"Why thank you. I learned from the best . . . DiGornio's."

After taking a couple of slices to Jaime, Emma sat down at the tiny table and the three of them dug in. They had asked Sanchez to stay to discuss the case to see if she could see anything they were missing. The hot food warmed her stomach and satisfied her hunger. But it didn't stop her mind from wandering back to the case.

"What a day!" she said, "I've sorted out everything we learned today. I'm now convinced that Carlson was Teresa's lover. I know I said before we shouldn't make assumptions, but the journal, the jewels, the secrets—it all seems to add up. And based on the way he was today, I'd say he has the ability to become violent. It would make sense then that the Chief was the Snitch.

"I agree," Myers said solemnly. "And what that means is our situation may have just gotten more dangerous."

"What do you mean?"

"These men are two of the highest ranking officer and enlisted men on base. They run the Security Forces Squadron and are highly influential."

Sanchez grimaced. "Don't forget they are highly trained to protect themselves," she said.

Myers put his hand over Emma's. "I know you've worked with these men and it may be hard for you to imagine them hurting anyone. I also know you believe in the whole innocent until proven guilty theory and we don't have any concrete proof against them . . . yet. But, especially after how Carlson reacted today, you need to watch out. That man has a temper and could be very dangerous."

Emma realized that the fact that he was being protective of her mattered. A lot.

"I think it's time we put surveillance on Carlson and the Chief," Myers said, turning to Sanchez. "Go call Dan and have him put his men on them tonight. I want them watched at all times."

As Sanchez called Dan, Emma remembered something she had seen earlier this morning on her calendar. "I've got it!" she exclaimed.

Usually she was more organized than this, but the investigation had distracted her so completely that, until now, she had forgotten about the Wing Commander's Quarterly Awards Banquet.

The awards banquet was held once every quarter and gave commanders and supervisors the chance to recognize the outstanding achievements of their troops. There were several categories of awards ranging from young airmen to Company Grade officers.

Late last month, she had nominated Master Sergeant Prane for an award and she had a good feeling Maggie would win. Emma needed to be there to cheer her on.

The banquet was a celebration, usually held at the Club, to which military members, dressed in their finest dress blues, brought their spouses and dependents. Squadrons sat together at the different tables cheering their nominees on. The cops were known to bring sirens while the Communications people brought loudspeakers and various other technical gadgets.

It was a fun night and Emma always looked forward to it. She had actually been the recipient of the Company Grade Officer Quarterly Award a couple of times. She was especially excited about this banquet because she would have a chance to support a paralegal who worked her butt off and deserved the recognition.

"Tomorrow night is the Quarterly Awards Banquet at the Club," Emma told Myers and Sanchez, who was now off the phone. "I know Colonel Carlson and Chief Peterson will be there as all commanders and First Shirts are required to attend. Maybe we could sneak into their offices while they are gone and see what we can find."

Myers raised his eyebrow. "Don't they call that breaking and entering, Ms. Lawyer?"

Emma shrugged innocently. "Not if their offices aren't locked."

"No, it's too dangerous," he said sternly.

"Listen," Emma persisted. "I know this is a little unusual, but Franks talks to the General tomorrow. We can get him to authorize the search and get spare keys from his Exec."

When Myers shook his head, Emma found herself instantly defensive. Sure, she liked to think that he was protective, but she could take care of herself and she wanted to prove this to him.

"When else are we going to get the chance to do this?" she demanded. "You can't ask for a more perfect opportunity. They're both going to be so busy with the banquet, which by the way goes on for hours, so there's plenty of time to search both of their offices. Plus, their offices are right across the street. All we have to do is have you and your guys up front, keeping an eye on the cops, while I sneak over across the street and have a look around."

"Wait a damn minute!" Myers exploded. "Let me get this straight. You think you're going to go over and break into Carlson and Peterson's offices while I sit back and just twiddle my thumbs! You're crazy!"

"When else are you going to do this?" Emma retorted. "You want to wait? Well, why don't we just tell Peterson and Carlson we're coming, how would that be? So they can hide or destroy anything they have. Come on, Myers, you know I'm right. I nominated my paralegal for an award and it's customary for me to go buy her a drink right after dinner before they start the awards. No one will even think twice when I get up to leave with her and go to the bar. But instead of staying in the bar, I'll run across the street and search their offices."

"No!" Myers glowered at her, crossing his arms over his chest. "If anyone is to do this, it will be me or Dan."

"*You* will do it? You don't think that will raise suspicion? Carlson and Peterson are not stupid. He knows that his actions today will cause him to be watched. You know as well as I do that if you or Dan leaves the banquet tomorrow, Carlson and Peterson are going to know something's up. You'll tip them off and probably mess up the whole thing. It's got to be me. They won't ever suspect me."

"She's got a point, you know Myers," Sanchez broke in.

Emma nodded indignantly, grateful for the other woman's support.

"We can work out a plan," she told him. "Like I said, you guys sit around the Security Forces' table and I'll sit with my office. We'll eat dinner and once it's time for the nominees to leave, I'll slip out after they start the awards. Before then everyone gets their drinks and talks so there's plenty of time for me to run across the street. I'll have keys so it won't take me any time to get in, quickly search through their offices and come back. You won't even know I'm gone. More importantly *they* won't know I'm even gone."

Emma could see Myers frown as though mulling over her plan, trying to find loopholes.

"Come on Myers," she prodded him. "You'll be right there and so will all of the rest of your agents. You're going to know if Carlson or Peterson leave and you can follow them. When else is the whole base going to be practically shut down and everyone will be in one place where you can keep an eye on them?"

The room was silent. Myers cheek twitched as he clenched his jaw. Emma had had years of experience making persuading arguments and she felt confident that he'd agree to the plan, even if he didn't want to.

"What am I doing?" Myers rubbed the back of his neck. "Christ, I'd hate to be on the stand with you grilling me."

After a few more minutes of tense silence, he raised his head, his worried gray eyes drilling into her, and Emma knew she had won.

"You stick to the plan, got it?" he demanded. "I want you in and out. So help me God, if you're not out of there by the time we assign, I'll personally come across the street and drag your ass back to the Club. Do you understand?"

Although Emma was pleased that Myers now had enough confidence in her to let her lead this important part of the investigation, she didn't want to appear boastful so she just nodded.

The three of them spent the next hour developing the plan. They were just finishing when Jaime poked her head in the door.

"Hey, I think I'm going to take a shower. Do you mind?"

"You can use the one in my room," Emma said calmly, although inside her mind was reeling from the planning session.

After she had gone, Myers turned to the two women. "You've got to watch her tonight. I'm still not happy she's staying here. You'll *both* need to be on the alert. Remember that girl in the other room is the one person who stands between the killer and Leavenworth."

Chapter 44

They were just finalizing the plan when Myers' cell phone rang. He took the call which lasted only a few minutes on the front porch. When he returned, his face was flushed with excitement.

"You'll never guess who that was," he said leaning against the counter. "Remember the Airman First Class who complained to Sergeant Swarsky? The one who lived in Conklin's dorm at Dyess."

"I thought she'd been deployed," Emma replied.

"She was," Myers said, "but Swarsky talked to her earlier today and he told her to give me a call. She was full of information about our victim. It seems our Sergeant Swarsky didn't tell us everything about Conklin. Luckily Airman Trace was more than willing to give me the scoop. It was pretty obvious she didn't like Conklin, at all. She was more than happy to give me all the dirt about the fights between Conklin and her partner. It seems that they were a regular occurrence at the dorms."

"Interesting," Emma cut in. "I didn't get that impression from Swarsky."

"Me neither. But now it seems that after the first couple of fights, when neither the dorm supervisor nor Swarsky would do anything about it, Airman Trace decided to take matters into her own hands. She and her friend Airman Carmichael met in Trace's room and leaned against the wall to see if they could hear anything."

Emma knew dorm room walls were notoriously thin.

"Trace said pretty soon they heard things crashing against the wall so hard it even knocked one of her pictures off her wall. Someone was threatening Conklin, yelling at her that they were going to shut her up for good if she said anything. So now our little detectives were scared and held up in Trace's room and didn't leave until the morning."

"That jives with what Swarsky told us." Emma recalled.

"Right. But what he didn't tell us was that Trace and her friend sneaked out of their room early the next morning and sat in Trace's car which was parked a few spaces down from her dorm room in order to scope out Conklin's room."

Emma held up her hand. "Wait a minute. I'm not following. I thought Teresa's partner left in the middle of the night. Isn't that what Swarsky told us?"

Myers sat down at the table. "He said Trace told him they heard Conklin's door slam. But that's not the whole story. Trace told me that around 0500, Conklin's door opened and out walked Conklin. She was still in her pajamas and even from their car they could see she had been crying. Trace told me Conklin's face was pretty banged up. So our little detectives crouched low in their car waiting to see if anyone else comes out of the room."

"And . . .," Emma said impatiently.

"And . . . a second later, out walks the partner."

"Now wait a minute." Emma sat back. "How do they know it was her partner? It could have been a friend trying to console her."

"Okay, Ms. Lawyer. I'll give you the proof. Trace said as soon as the person comes out the door, Conklin started crying again. Then before they knew it the partner looked around to make sure no one was looking and embraced her. Trace said Conklin's arms just hung at her sides and looked like she wanted to just run away."

Emma was skeptical. "I'm not sure that is proof. Why did the boyfriend make sure no one was looking?"

Myers didn't answer her right away, savoring in the suspense. "Because, Ms. Lawyer. It wasn't a boyfriend . . . it was her girlfriend!"

"Whoa!" Sanchez exhaled sharply.

Emma looked at Myers hard, her prosecutorial mind whirling.

"Are you trying to tell me those rumors about Teresa liking both sexes is true? Because I still don't buy it. Sounds like we have a case of a pissed off dorm buddy who wants to get her neighbor in trouble because she can't sleep. I wouldn't take that one to court."

"Okay, Ms. Lawyer," Myers replied, clearly ready to meet the challenge. "What if I told you Trace saw this woman knocking on Conklin's room several times before that night trying to get in?"

"Still not buying."

"What if Trace overheard Swarsky tell another supervisor that something had come down from Family Advocacy and that the commander told him Conklin was going to be shipped out."

"Still not enough. We already guessed that was the case."

Unfazed Myers leaned back in his chair, crossing his arms in front of his chest.

"Would it be enough if she also overheard Swarsky say he'd heard the reason was because of another girl?"

He had her attention now, but Emma was still skeptical. She'd been in her job way too long to start believing gossip and she'd seen the damage it could do.

"Still sounds like rumors," she said. "Besides, if Teresa had openly admitted she was gay, they would have investigated per the policy."

"You tell me, Ms. Attorney." Myers countered, obviously enjoying playing the devil's advocate. "What if she didn't openly admit it, but instead said she was being stalked or scared by this girl. That's not enough to warrant an investigation, is it?"

"You're right," she admitted. "In your scenario there is not enough to generate an investigation. And per the 'Don't Ask, Don't Tell' policy the commander or supervisor are prevented from delving into this relationship to see if it is, in fact, homosexual."

Emma mulled over the evidence.

"Okay, Agent Myers, say you're right and this is how she got transferred here. That still doesn't mean they were lovers. Does your Airman Trace know where this girl is now?"

Myers got serious. "No. Trace hasn't seen her around, but then again she made it clear to me she doesn't hang around with 'those type of people.'"

Myers shrugged. "Hell, for all we know she got out. But I still think it's pretty coincidental, don't you, that Conklin had a girlfriend who beat her up and threatened to keep her mouth shut so Conklin gets reassigned here AND is murdered less than a year later."

"I suppose you could be right," Emma told him. "But as far as finding this girl, we've hit a dead end, right? If we don't know who she is or where she is where do we go from here?"

The smile crept back on Myers's face. "I didn't say we didn't know who she was?"

"What do you mean?" Sanchez broke in.

"Seems our little detectives took a picture of this mystery woman. Trace will be gone for a few more weeks, but she said she could have her cohort in crime find the picture and email it to me. I should have it tomorrow."

Emma couldn't help but laugh at his smugness. Myers was really pleased with himself and she had to admit, this new lead was plausible. But instead of feeling comforted by this, Emma was overcome by a sense of foreboding. All of a sudden, there were now not just one, but three people who could have wanted Teresa Conklin dead which made finding the murderer that much harder.

Chapter 45

An hour later, Emma waved to Myers as he backed out of her driveway and headed back to base. The night air smelled slightly of wood burning from her neighbors' chimneys, but the small village itself was eerily quiet.

Not ready to go back in quite yet, Emma peered up at the sky where a full moon hovered over her, noting that the comforting stars were in hiding behind the thick clouds. Emma shivered in her thin t-shirt as the wind swirled the fallen leaves, scattering them about her feet. Her neighbors' houses were dark and suddenly she felt alone.

As she closed the heavy garage door, Emma realized that she was glad for Sanchez' company. She didn't want to be alone and Jaime didn't count. Speaking of her charge, Jaime had already claimed the guest bedroom downstairs, and as far as Emma knew, was asleep.

Hurrying upstairs, Emma latched the deadbolt on her thick oak front door, and waved to Sanchez who was bunking on the couch and went into her bedroom. For the first time since she had lived here, Emma crossed over to the French doors in her room which she usually simply locked on the handle and slid the deadbolt. Somehow that extra step made Emma feel a little more secure.

She quickly washed her face and examined herself in the mirror, dismayed to see the dark circles under her eyes. What she needed was a good night's sleep. After brushing her hair and putting on her flannel pajamas, she hopped into bed and pulled the covers up to her chin. Her room was still, the moonlight peeking in through her blinds. In the other room, she heard Sanchez turn off the TV. The house went quiet. As she thought about what lay before her, Emma found herself hoping that this was not the calm before the storm.

Chapter 46

"Damn!"

My fist is throbbing from having punched that concrete, but I have to know where that bitch is! I broke the goddamned streetlight. I'm in a position to see her bedroom. But there's nothing.

Nothing!

Tonight was the night. No more dicking around. There's no way I'm going to let that conniving bitch live any longer that I have to.

If it hadn't been for that gorgeous bitch of an OSI agent they've assigned to her, I could have got her last night. And the beauty of it is that she knows I'm watching her – I can see it in her face. She's so scared she knows I'm coming for her. It would have been perfect. But then . . .

Shit, where is she?

Christ, I don't have time for anymore of this. This is getting out of control. I've got to take care of things now. They are learning too much.

My hand pounds as I think of the bitch that got me into this situation.

Teresa screwed her way to the top. She didn't care who it was as long as she got what she wanted. Not like me. I did everything I was asked to do, even when the cocksuckers made me work the worst shifts. I went by the book and I climbed all the way up the ladder by myself.

Hell, if my folks could see me now, they wouldn't believe it. I did it in spite of them. Drunken ass of a father beat the shit out of me when he was home. And my mother. When she wasn't whoring around, she was out at the bars, finding her next trick. Who needs them?

Who needs her? The uniform is better off without her in it.

But there's still one more who must be taken care of. I look again at the dark dorm room and a plan forms in my head.

Don't worry, I'll find you. It will all be over soon.

Chapter 47

Bright and early the next morning, Emma prepared for her meeting with Franks, telling herself that today was different. She no longer cared about confidentiality and secrecy, everything that had kept her from the truth for five days. No, this time she wanted answers and she intended to get them, no matter what the price.

She had showered before the other two got up letting the cold water wake her up. Having slept fitfully all night, Emma was at least glad to see the eye cream had done its job.

After applying light foundation and mascara, she padded to her closet wrapped in a towel and pulled out her navy blue pants and long sleeve light blue shirt. Today, he was going to know she mean business, she thought as she snapped her tie around her neck and pulled on her service coat.

Emma looked at herself in the mirror and found that the sight of the two rows of multi-colored ribbons adorning the dark blue coat signifying the various medals and awards she won over her career bolstered her resolve.

Last night, she had strategized with Myers on how to approach Franks. He had wanted to come with her, to give her support during her confrontation with her boss, but she had said no.

"He's my boss," she had told him firmly. "I have worked my ass off for him for three years. I deserve to know what he is hiding."

Myers put up an argument, but Emma wouldn't budge any more than she had over the search of the offices. She knew precisely what she had to say and do and no one – not even Myers – was going to stop her.

"Thanks, but no thanks," she'd said, trying to keep her tone light. "This is something I have to do alone. There has to be a reason he hasn't been straight with me. So this is something he and I need to work out on her own. Besides," she'd teased, "he might get intimidated with you in the room."

And finally, he'd relented. "But you call me as soon as you walk out of his office," he'd demanded. And she had agreed.

Now sitting in her car in the parking lot which was empty except for her boss' Volvo, Emma was even more determined. It was still dark when she used her key to enter the building, the only light coming from Franks' office. After hanging her mess dress she'd brought for the ceremony tonight on the hook behind her door, she braced herself and marched off to confront her boss.

Without waiting for him to respond to her knock, Emma pushed open his door to find utter chaos. Papers lay strewn over his desk and the coffee table. Unread newspapers were thrown into a pile on the floor. Behind his desk two uniforms desperately in need of pressing were draped over a coat rack. The man who owned the office looked no better. Sitting hunched over his desk, Franks was busy searching for something in the large pile of papers in front of him, his eyes bloodshot from lack of sleep.

For a minute, Emma felt her resolve weaken. Her knees trembled as she sank into the nearest chair. What was happening? If her boss, her fearless leader, was losing it, could she remain strong? As the older, more experienced officer, he should be guiding her, telling her everything would be okay.

But as Emma watched the man in front of her, it hit her like a ton of bricks everything was not okay.

Was it only a few days ago that her biggest worry had been some kid who tried drugs? Emma almost felt like laughing. How ironic was it that she, the one who tried to protect the base by putting wrong-doers behind bars, couldn't find the one wrong-doer who could end up killing again . . .maybe even killing her.

But when he finally spoke, Franks sounded like someone emerging from a trance.

"I'm sorry."

For the first time in her career, she lost her cool in front of a superior officer as the last five days of frustration overtook her sense of propriety.

"Sir, what do you mean you are sorry?" she demanded. "I've been out there busting my ass trying to find out who did this all the while knowing you've been keeping something from me. You said that you're trying to protect me, but all you've really done is keep me from the truth. So please tell me, Sir, how that is protecting me?"

Emma stopped, her breath ragged, her heart racing. No matter how upset or frustrated you get with a superior officer, you must never show it. You must never be disrespectful, no matter what.

Emma held her head up, her eyes never leaving his as she waited for his response.

Instead of reproaching her, however, he sighed and said, "You're right. I have been lying to you."

Emma remained silent as he came to sit beside her and put his hand on her arm.

"Emma," he said, "I thought I was protecting you. You see there are so many things that go on around here you never see, never know about. That's what makes this so damned hard to explain. As I'm sure you can guess, some of these things have to do with politics, some are classified as top secret, and some . . .." He paused. "Well, some become personal and those are always the toughest to deal with. Those are the ones you can't tell anyone even when they begin to affect you professionally and personally."

Concern filled her as Franks confirmed Emma's suspicions that whatever he was dealing with was affecting him personally. Based on her experience with military top secret matters, Emma knew she might not ever know exactly what was going on, but right now she was worried about him and hoped in some way she could help.

"Are you in some kind of trouble, Sir?"

"No, Emma," he told her, running one hand through his already tussled hair. "But sometimes it feels like it. I know you have been really frustrated with me lately . . . for my lack of candor." For a moment he smiled wistfully. "And I can't blame you for becoming upset with me."

"Hell, I deserved it," he said, waving her apology away. "There are so many things I wanted to tell you, but you'll just have to understand that you couldn't be privy to what I knew. And so I kept it from you."

At that moment, Emma felt fear. Whereas before she was upset that her boss had not been truthful, this was now replaced by sheer trepidation, knowing that there was something far bigger out there . . . something she could not know. What scared her most is that it may have something to do with the killer.

"Damn!" he cursed. "That's why I tried to get you off this case to begin with. In fact, when Colonel Carlson brought up the idea, I warned General Brandt, but he wouldn't budge. He wanted you in the thick of things . . . an innocent bystander . . . to report what was going on with the investigation. He assured me we'd pull you out if things got dangerous."

His words rang in her head and she wondered if he were alluding to things getting dangerous with the Colonel. "I'm sorry, Sir, but I don't understand."

Franks turned towards her taking both her hands in his. "You were on this investigation to be our eyes and ears, if you will, Emma. The General wanted to know exactly what was revealed through the investigation and felt you were our perfect mole."

Emma's mind spun as she listened to him tell her they had used her. But surely her boss wouldn't let anyone put her in harm's way?

"I still don't get it," Emma persisted. "Why couldn't he get the information from Colonel Carlson or OSI? They are required to tell him everything they learn through the investigation."

Suddenly her own words sank in. "Unless they are part of the investigation," Emma said solemnly, as the truth hit her. "I told you last night over the phone Colonel Carlson was now a suspect, but you already knew that didn't you?"

"Yes," he answered gravely.

All at once, bits and pieces of information gathered in the course of the investigation began to piece themselves together. Emma remembered being in the General's office that first day where Captain Angeles had said something to her about the Colonel. She searched her boss' weary face.

"The Colonel has been under investigation for some time now hasn't he? But not just for the murder of Teresa Conklin?"

She saw the truth in his eyes even before he spoke.

"Yes, Emma. I couldn't tell you before, but since it's come to this, I have no choice. Besides, from what I've read from your briefs, you would eventually find out anyway."

Franks paused and squeezed her hands, his voice beaming with pride. "You know, you really are good. And I don't just mean the trial work."

He pulled his hands from hers and stood up, slowly pacing the room.

"I have been part of a small team who has been investigating Colonel Carlson for adultery and fraternization for some time now," he began, his voice once again serious.

Now it all made sense. All the pieces fit together. She had been right. Colonel Carlson had been Teresa's lover, the one she wrote about in her journal. He was married and having an affair with an enlisted member.

"I didn't want you on this investigation," Franks went on, "because I was scared for your safety. I also didn't want Carlson to somehow use you as a scapegoat and ruin your career to save his. I'm sure he wanted you involved to throw us off his trail, because he knew he was the first person I would suspect."

Thinking about the significance of what she just learned, Emma's mind raced. She had been used by a man who she now thought was their main suspect. The killer had been meticulous, the same as the Colonel had obviously been in using her to throw off the investigation. And hadn't she personally seen his rage at the firing range?

"Teresa wrote in her journal that she was trying to break it off with Colonel Carlson, but he that wouldn't let go," she said slowly.

"Maybe he killed her because he couldn't have her. Or maybe because she was going to tell someone about their affair."

Franks stopped pacing and turned to stare at her.

"You must be careful, Emma," he warned. "I've known Colonel Carlson for a while and I can't believe he would kill anyone. But then again, I wouldn't have believed that he would cheat on Karen, either," he added sadly.

"I'll be careful, Sir." Emma assured him, rising. It was, she knew important that she tell Myers what she had uncovered as soon as possible. "OSI has him under surveillance," Emma added, "and he'll be watched tonight at the awards ceremony."

She filled him in on the plan to search the Chief and Colonel's offices during the banquet.

"Good Lord, I almost forgot about the banquet!" Franks exclaimed. "I'll be there, too. If you need anything, just give me a signal or something and I'll be there. And listen, you're letting the OSI handle this, right? *They* are the professionals and know what they are doing. I don't want you anywhere near Colonel Carlson or the Chief. Do you understand?"

Emma saw the worry in his eyes and knew she could not tell her boss that she would be searching the Colonel and Chief's offices during the ceremony.

"Yes Sir, I understand," Emma lied as she closed the door behind her.

Walking out the back door to her car, she once again looked up at her boss's window. The sun was rising and its rays glinted off the building. She caught Franks staring down at her and waved. He waved back and disappeared.

It was not until she was driving away that Emma realized the extent to which this latest encounter had shaken her. Perhaps, this investigating business was better left to someone like Myers. All in one day, she had not only insulted a commanding officer, she had lied to him as well. It was not the sort of defense any judge would buy, but then again, she would not have to worry about that if the killer got to her first.

Chapter 48

Emma was just about to pull in the parking lot of the OSI building when her cell phone rang. She pulled over to the curb to answer it.

"I'm not sure what to make of it, but I have some news for you." Dr. Nancy Martin began. "I called my friend at Dyess Mental Health to see if she knew anything about your airman. I figured I could find out something, you know doctor to doctor. But that strange thing is she was pretty vague."

"What do you mean?"

"Well, she definitely knew who I was talking about, but she wouldn't or couldn't give me any specifics although she did confirm that Teresa Conklin was transferred here under the program. She also said there was another military member involved and that abuse was a factor. But that's it. When I asked her who the other military member was, she clammed up on me, said she was not able to give out that information."

Emma could hear the frustration in her friend's voice. And she understood. This investigation had already resulted in so many dead ends that she was becoming immune to them herself. But she imagined that, given Nancy's tenacity, she wasn't used to such a roadblock.

"I was blown away," Nancy continued, "'Come on,' I said. 'The poor girl's been murdered and we need to know who this person was who abused her.' But she wouldn't budge. She informed me if we needed the information, we would need to go through the appropriate channels to get it. In other words, go to the higher ups and get them to order the release of Teresa's file."

"Crap." Emma replied. "That could take days."

"Tell me about it. Someone down there doesn't want your Airman's file released."

"Or released to the wrong person," Emma muttered, thinking of Carlson and the Chief, Teresa's commander and First Shirt.

"What do you mean, 'the wrong person?'" Nancy demanded.

"Never mind," Emma said quickly changing the subject. "What did you find out on this end?"

"Nothing. Blank slate. And here I thought I was privy to everything in my office."

"Another roadblock, huh?" Emma asked although not surprised.

"Yes," said Nancy angrily. "I tried to look up her file, but it was nowhere to be found. I did confirm, by looking at my calendar, that I was in the States during the first three weeks she was here. I was teaching at a conference in California. Anyway, it appears Dr. Schmidt took her case in my stead."

Emma groaned aloud. Dr. Schmidt was head psychiatrist at Winburg. Unlike Nancy, he was active duty, a Colonel. Emma had only worked with him a couple of times, but each time she'd found him to be very stiff. He played by the book or at least what he thought was the 'book.' He also liked to pack his sentences with medical jargon to throw off his audience. Emma found him and his terminology pompous and stayed away from calling him as an expert in a trial. She didn't want the panel to be as turned off by him as she was.

"Let me guess," Emma interjected. "Dr. Schmidt wouldn't talk."

"Bingo," Nancy replied derisively. "That arrogant SOB could care less a young girl had been killed. He said he wouldn't compromise his integrity by releasing the information without the proper paperwork."

Emma thanked her friend for trying. "I owe you one, Nancy," she added.

"No you don't," came her reply. "Now I'm on a mission. I'm going to find out what's so secretive about this file, if it kills me." Nancy paused. "Bad choice of words."

Thinking about what she had learned today, Emma warned her friend.

"Listen," Emma said seriously, with what she had learned today still haunting her. "Watch your back on this one. There's a lot of things going on around here. Be careful.

"Besides," Emma continued, recalling Airman Trace's promise to email Myers a picture of Teresa's former girlfriend, "I think I may have another way of finding out who this abusive military member is."

"When you find out, make sure you tell me. . . . that is, if you can."

Emma hung up the phone and hoped her friend's unintentional play on words didn't come true.

The parking lot was now crowded as the work day had begun and it took Emma two passes around the building before a spot finally opened up behind the building next to a group of tall trees which were bright with autumn color. Emma marveled at the beauty of the autumn leaves against the blue sky. As she locked her car, she was surprised at how many sunny days they had had in a row, quite unusual for a German fall.

As she walked away from her car, Emma had the strange sensation again that she was being watched. Whirling about, she looked behind her towards the trees. But there was nothing there. Everything was still except for the birds and the sound of the wind blowing through the trees.

Emma stood there for a moment as if she would catch a glimpse of something or someone behind one of the huge oaks. In the distance she could hear the light rumble of cars passing by on the main road.

Suddenly, a loud roar filled the air. Emma jumped and then laughed nervously as she recognized the sound of a F-15 taking off on the runway several miles away.

Glancing one more time towards the line of trees, Emma turned and briskly walked into the building. Once inside she felt safe. But as she looked out the glass front door, she couldn't shake off the feeling that someone was out there watching her.

Chapter 49

Upstairs in his makeshift office, Myers was talking on the phone, with his feet up on the desk. Immaculately dressed, he looked like he just stepped off the cover of GQ even though Emma knew he'd left her house past midnight and couldn't have gotten much sleep. He wore a charcoal gray suit with a dark blue collared shirt underneath. A matching dark blue tie hung loosely knotted at his neck.

How did he do it? She marveled smoothing back a strand of hair.

"Hey there," a voice behind her whispered loudly. Dan plopped in a chair beside hers. "He's on the phone with Headquarters OSI, setting up something for tonight. Some of his buddies are coming down here to attend the banquet. They'll be undercover. You know, to make sure we have enough coverage just in case we have to take him down."

Emma nodded feeling like she was in a movie. Surveillance, 'taking people down' and undercover operations were not something Emma was used to. For some reason she didn't share in Dan's excitement.

Instead, all she could think about was how tonight someone might lose their job, and more importantly their career. Maybe tonight people would find out how a high ranking officer had committed unthinkable crimes right under their noses.

As a defense counsel, she'd learned that, despite what they did, there were real people behind the crimes they committed. Nine times out of ten her clients had been pretty messed up, but human nonetheless. Mostly she found the general public tended to forget the other "victims" of the crimes: the loved ones, the parents, the spouses, all of whom ended up hurt and devastated. So as she thought about tonight, Emma couldn't feel a little sad. Although the sadness was underscored by her desire to see justice served.

"Okay, all set." Myers announced as he hung up the phone. Swinging his long legs to the floor, he stood up, stretched, and asked who wanted coffee.

"You know I couldn't have done this investigation without him," Dan confided after he had left the room, cup in hand.

"We're not done yet, you know." Emma countered, still not daring to believe that tonight they would somehow manage to catch Carlson or Peterson in an incriminating act.

"I know," Dan told her, and then, unable to contain his eagerness, "But we're close. It had to be one of them."

Emma was half listening to him prattle on about how they were going to bring their suspects down when she saw the photographs of Teresa Conklin, half buried among the papers on Myers' desk. Rising, she went to look down at the all too familiar face and wide blue eyes.

"She needs us to find out who did this," she heard Myers say in a low voice behind her and felt his hand on her shoulder.

Emma nodded not turning around. "I know," she replied.

"If we don't bring in whoever did this to her, there will be no justice for her . . . or for her family. Dammit," he swore softly. "That's why I didn't want you on this case. You shouldn't have to deal with this."

"No, I *do* have to deal with this," she said, turning to face him, touched by his concern. "She didn't deserve to die. I'm ready to do whatever it takes."

"You're sure?" he replied still searching her eyes.

"So what did your boss say, Emma?" Dan interrupted them.

"We were right," Emma told Myers. "It was Carlson. He was having an affair with Teresa."

Myers's lips were tight. "So the Chief is his snitch sidekick. And your boss knew this, because he was in on the investigation."

"Yes. That's also why he wasn't surprised when I told him last night Carlson was a suspect."

"So that's why Carlson and the Chief didn't go with your boss's recommendation for the LOR," Dan volunteered. "He didn't want her to get in trouble."

Emma nodded. "Everything falls into place. It's just like Teresa said in her journal. They were having an affair. He bought her extravagant gifts. She got tired of him and tried to leave and then was murdered."

"But we still don't know for sure if it was Carlson or the Chief who killed her," Myers mused, "so we . . . ."

Dan finished Myers' sentence. "Watch both of them tonight and see what they do."

For the next four hours, the three laid out the facts of the case on big charts that now covered the walls in Myers's office. They twisted what they had learned every way they could think of, making sure they didn't falsely accuse anyone. The problem was that, even with Teresa's journal, they had no concrete evidence. No smoking gun that pointed to the Colonel or the Chief.

What it all boiled down to was that, at this point, they really didn't even have enough circumstantial evidence to use in an arrest. Both the Chief and Colonel had alibis for that night: both had said they were home in bed with their wives.

But the three of them didn't give up. They knew there had to be something.

Although they had discussed getting a search warrant from the General, they all decided it was wiser not to get a warrant. If they did, word could get back to Carlson or the Chief and they couldn't risk any alteration of evidence.

They also knew the men wouldn't risk keeping anything linking them to Teresa at their homes, for fear their wives or children would find it. So that left their offices.

Their plan was fairly straight forward. Myers's men would strategically place themselves around the banquet room so all exits would be covered. Agent Sanchez would escort Jaime to the banquet and would sit at the same table as Myers and Dan, one close to the Security Forces' tables.

Before the awards were presented, Emma would leave the room with Maggie. Myers would get the keys from Captain Angeles later in the day and give them to Emma. After buying Maggie a drink, Emma would run across the street and let herself into the building.

When Myers tried once again to talk Emma out of it, she brushed his arguments aside and turned up her negotiating skills.

"Carlson already knows the Chief is a suspect and by now knows he's one, too. They'll already have spotted your men at the banquet and hightail it out of there is you guys start disappearing," she added, even though she knew that, with several hundred people attending the banquet, there was no way that either of them would even notice Myers' men. Emma hid behind a confident bravado that she was far from feeling.

Finally, she wore them down. "But if you're not back in twenty minutes," Myers warned, "I'm coming to get you."

"Fine. Now are we done here?" she asked on her way out the door, eager to escape before they changed their minds. "I have to brief Franks and then get ready for the banquet. Brighten up, will you guys. Everything's going to be all right."

But as she hurried down the corridor, she wondered if anything would ever be all right again.

Chapter 50

By mid afternoon Emma decided to relieve her tension by going for a jog. The afternoon clouds had moved in and she felt the dampness of a coming rain against her face as she ran. Usually in tune with her surroundings, she was surprised when she came to the edge of the flight line, her two and one half mile marker and realized that she had been so preoccupied that she hadn't even realized how long she'd been running.

The run back was no better. A light rain started to fall, seeping into Emma's long cotton t-shirt and jogging pants. But she didn't care. The freedom that she felt with each stride was a Godsend.

After showering and changing into a fresh sweat suit back at the gym, she returned to her office, expecting everyone to have gone home to get ready for the banquet, Emma was surprised to see a light on in John Mullen's office.

"Hey there," she said popping her head in the door. "What are you still doing here?"

John gestured to the neatly stacked papers lying in a wire basket on top of his desk.

"I'm just trying to finish up a couple of things. Man, you never told me how far behind I'd get on my daily work while I was in trial."

"Oh yeah, I forgot to mention that," she said grinning. "So tell me, how'd it go yesterday? How was your first sentencing hearing?"

"Good," he replied sheepishly. "Actually great. The jury awarded the sentence I had asked for."

"Congratulations," Emma replied, giving him a high five. "I knew you could do it. You worked hard and it paid off."

"Well, I couldn't have done it without you or Greg . . . or Master Sergeant Prane. I have to ask, is she that tough on everyone or is it just me?"

"Everyone," Emma assured him. "But hey, I've got to get ready for the banquet. Are you going?"

"I don't think so," John replied wearily. "I've been here late every night and am ready to just have a night at home."

"Understood. You should probably take the night off because now that you're a pro in the courtroom, we'll have to assign you more cases."

Emma went upstairs to change. After drying her hair and applying makeup, Emma curled the ends of her hair and plied it loosely on her head. It was nice to feel feminine after days of wearing combat boots and camouflage.

Still in her sweats and sweatshirt, Emma went down the hall to her office to get dressed. She used the long mirror that hung on the back of her office door to help her. Although still confident she was doing the right thing, Emma couldn't help but feel a nervous excitement.

Emma remembered the first time she had put on her formal uniform. She'd worked for what seemed like hours, making sure everything hung perfectly. At that time, the only thing adorning the short matching blue jacket had been a silver pin symbolizing she was a JAG. Today, shiny medals hanging neatly in a row against the dark blue glinted back at her in the mirror.

Suddenly she felt incredibly proud. It never ceased to amaze her how the little things like a uniform, or standing for the national anthem before a movie on base, and returning a salute to the airman guarding the front gate, caused such a patriotic surge in her.

Emma knew her mission tonight was incredibly important and she that would do anything to achieve it. "When you think of your country and the mission first, before yourself," her OTS instructor had once said. "That's when you know you are truly an officer of the United States Air Force."

Although over the last few years, she had felt she lived up to these words, tonight she was the first time she was truly ready to lay down her life for the mission.

Chapter 51

White lights adorned the tall green topiaries that filled the lobby. While Emma waited in line to be checked in, she listened to the jazz being played by a military ensemble band drifting out of the ballroom, and wished that this evening was going to be free of danger.

"If this were another time and place, I just might ask you to dance."

Smiling, Emma turned to Myers. "That seems to have become our motto," she said, "another time and place."

"Damn, you look incredible," he said, his eyes caressing her.

"Thank you, Sir." She answered brazenly. "You don't look so bad yourself."

His black suit fit him perfectly, accentuating his muscular shoulders. One lock of his dark hair, glistening ever so slightly from the rain, fell over his forehead in a way that made her want to reach up and push it back. Emma felt herself flush as she saw the look in his eyes and knew for a certainty that he meant for there to be another time and place.

"Why don't I buy you a drink?" he said, his voice husky with emotion.

Emma nodded, not trusting herself to speak, and let him lead her through a sea of dark blue uniforms, pausing every now and then to greet someone, to the bar where Kyle was waiting for them.

"There she is!" he said, moving over to make room for her to join him. "I was just wondering if those bad asses over at OSI were keeping you working late again. And speaking of which . . . Agent Myers, so glad you could make it."

Emma ordered herself a merlot. Kyle was still fumbling in his pocket when Myers laid a twenty on the bar.

"I'll take care of it," he told Kyle, grinning. "After all, it appears we bad ass OSI agents owe Major Lohrs." And to the bartender, "I'll have the same."

"A wine drinker, huh?" Kyle ribbed. "I didn't know there were any of those in the OSI."

"Personally, I always appreciate the finer things in life," Myers told him, his eyes on Emma who, suddenly uncomfortable, looked around the room.

She spied her boss and his wife at the other end of the bar.

"I'll be right back," she said leaving the two men to themselves.

"Good evening, Sir . . . Sharon."

"Emma, sweetie!" Sharon Franks exclaimed wrapping Emma up in her arms. "How are you?"

Tonight the boss's wife wore a deep cranberry jersey dress with a short-cropped gold-beaded jacket draped over her arm. Her short hair had been curled and coiffed and barely moved as she hugged Emma.

"It seems like I haven't seen you for ages," she said, holding Emma at arms' length. "Every time I come to the office, you're not there. Really Jim, you cannot work Emma so hard. She's a young attractive girl and shouldn't be cooped up in some courtroom all day long."

"No really, Sharon," she answered playing along. "Colonel Franks can't keep me out of the courtroom. I really love it. You should sit in sometime. See us in action."

Sharon squeezed Emma's hand. "Oh sweetie, I'd love to. Maybe I'll get to one of these days."

Emma knew that she would do no such thing. Sharon Franks didn't like to see any of the "bad things" that went on around base, preferring to focus on the good and Emma understood. Being exposed to the "bad things" skewed your perspective, something that definitely happened to Emma after this last week.

Suddenly, Sharon waved to someone behind Emma.

"Thanks for not letting on about the investigation," Franks said as his wife dashed off to greet someone named Ruth, embracing her with the same enthusiasm with which she had greeted Emma. "She is great friends with Karen Carlson. I don't know what this is going to do to her when she finds out."

"Is Carlson here yet?" she asked, her voice low.

"He and Karen just came in," he said over the rim of his glass. "They're behind you over by the crud room."

Emma moved beside her boss and saw the Colonel, handsome in his dark blue uniform, looking at ease as he entertained the group surrounding him with some story. Karen, tall and slender in a black crepe dress with an uneven hemline, was looking up at him and laughing. She was, Emma thought, stunning, but definitely not a trophy wife. Emma wondered if she knew the truth about her husband, and found herself pitying this woman who had remained by her husband's side for over twenty years. Like many other commanders' wives, Karen Carlson had made her husband's career her own. She dutifully attended every banquet and holiday party. She actively volunteered for several organizations on base, including the Red Cross and several children's organizations. Her own children adored her, as did the many people whose lives she had touched over the years. It saddened Emma to think that, after tonight, her life could suddenly become a tragedy.

"She'll be okay," Franks said beside her, reading Emma's thoughts.

Emma turned to him, surprised that he could so accurately read her thoughts.

"Don't get me wrong," he explained. "If Kent killed that girl, it will be devastating. But Karen's strong. She's a fighter and she'll do whatever it takes to protect her family. But it's going to hurt. Damn him!"

As Emma continued surveying the room, her eyes came upon the Chief. Although his boss looked comfortable tonight, the Chief was clearly uneasy, sitting stiffly in his seat, now and then tugging at his tie.

A petite brown haired woman, Emma guessed to be his wife, sat next to him, wearing a dark blue three quarter sleeve dress with a slight v-neck exposing her white skin. Too afraid the Chief would catch her looking at him, Emma turned back to Franks and saw over his shoulder, Myers beckoning to her.

Back at the bar, Greg and Chase, who had joined Kyle were engaged in an animated conversation centered around what pub they were going to try this weekend. Myers held his own in the ultimate search, suggesting pubs around the Ramstein area. Intrigued, Greg and Chase hung on to his every word while Kyle waved off the competition's suggestions.

"Where are we going to stay if we go down there?" he complained. "I'm for sure not driving back that night."

"Not a problem," Myers explained. "You guys could stay with me or you could get a room on base."

Kyle scowled. "I vote for the room on base," he muttered in his drink.

"Looks like you boys are playing nicely," Emma said, rolling her eyes and ordering another glass of wine.

Behind her, chimes sounded announcing dinner was being served. While the others made their way into the ballroom, Myers took Emma's elbow and held her back.

"You sure you're ready for this?" he asked one more time.

"Would you buy the cliché 'as ready as I'll ever be?'" she asked him. "Because if you won't, there's no need for me to bore you with any others. Did you see Carlson?"

"Yes and my guys are already on him and Peterson."

Emma was impressed. She hadn't even spotted 'his guys' yet.

"So one more time," Myers went on his voice low. "You'll come in here with Master Sergeant Prane and then sneak across the street during the ceremony. You'll be back here within twenty minutes at the latest and be in your seat by the time the nominees are being announced."

"Right." Emma knew it would take the General twenty minutes to deliver his speech tonight as she was certain he'd comment on Teresa's death to console and reassure his troops. Then he would attempt a few jokes to lighten the mood before the awards were handed out. The actual awards program started with the young airmen nominees and continued by rank, so she knew she'd have plenty of time to slip back to her table before the senior enlisted awards were announced.

"If you don't come back, I'm coming to get you," Myers told her, following her into the ballroom where they parted ways at the door, Myers taking a seat beside Dan at a table close to the stage where the General and his wife sat at a long table covered with a white linen cloth. Flanking them, were the Vice Commander and Senior Chaplain on base, Colonels Winn and Hoffmeyer, their wives and several local dignitaries. A podium stood at the corner of the stage.

Emma found the JAG table on the other side of the room. The rest of her colleagues were already seated when she arrived and she was able to slip into a chair between Maggie and Marsha Sloan. Not being in the mood to listen to any flippant comments about Myers, she was relieved not to be sitting next to Kyle.

Just as she sat down, the lights dimmed and the faint sound of sharp clicks could be heard from the back of the room. Everyone turned as the Honor Guard, two men and two women, all sharply dressed, marched slowly in formation into the room. The man leading the Guard carried a rifle as did the woman bringing up the rear, while the two in the middle proudly carried the American and Air Force flags. Their back and arms ramrod straight, the Guard glided in precise unison on the balls of their feet. The only sound in the crowded room came from the taps on their shining black shoes which clicked with each step.

Just short of the stage, the formation stopped, and in answer to a command, began to slowly rotate until they faced the crowd. At once the National Anthem filled the giant ballroom and the crowd rose to their feet in respect, the civilians covering their hearts with their hand.

When the final note of the anthem drifted away, another short command filled the air. Once gain, the formation rotated until they faced the stage, at which point the two Guardsmen with rifles stood at attention as their comrades, carrying flags marched towards the stage.

"If you would all join me in a toast," the Emcee announced, as they all rose, "to the President of the United States."

"To the President!" everyone cried.

"To the Joint Chief of Staff!"

"To the Chief!"

"And to the men and women who could not be with us today."

Despite being distracted by what she would soon be called on to do, Emma was touched with the Prisoner of War ceremony that followed, one of the many ceremonies that had become familiar over the years. But tonight she could not allow herself to be caught up in the spirit of the evening. There was too much at stake. What was important was that Myers and Dan, along with the Carlsons and the Petersons, were sitting at the tables near the front so when it was time to leave, she should be able to do so without being seen.

The dinner passed at whirlwind speed. Emma watched, ever vigilant, everything that was going on. At the same time, she kept Myers in her peripheral view, waiting for any sign that their mission was aborted. As the Emcee introduced the General, Emma walked through the plans one more time before excusing herself and going in the direction of the bar, only to double back and slip out a side door and into the night.

Chapter 52

Outside, the rain had stopped, replaced by a heavy damp fog that draped itself around her. The street lights cast eerie shadows. Resisting an urge to look back at the brightly lit club, Emma hurried across the dark, lonely street.

The Security Forces Squadron loomed in front of her like an old abandoned warehouse. At the front door, Emma stopped and listened. The night was still, silenced by the fog, except for the faint sounds of laughter coming from the club behind her.

Emma reached into her pocket and pulled out a key ring that held three marked keys. Earlier Myers had put different colored florescent stickers on the keys so Emma wouldn't have to fumble in the dark. And dark it was, the single light above the doors having been unscrewed before the banquet by an OSI agent to avoid the possibility that someone at the club would see Emma going in the front door.

Relief rushed over her as the key turned smoothly in the lock. Peering over her shoulder to make sure the street was still empty, she slipped inside, locked the door behind her and switching on her pencil thin flashlight, made her way up the front stairs.

Luckily, both the Colonel and Chief's offices faced the back parking lot, away from the street. Otherwise, there would have been a chance that someone from the club would have seen the light. Emma swallowed her trepidation. Although she'd been in this building many times, tonight the shadows flickering on the walls made it seem like an unfamiliar place.

With only seventeen minutes left to go, Emma unlocked Carlson's office first and went directly to the filing cabinet behind the Colonel's desk and rifled through the well organized drawers only to find nothing out of the ordinary. After which she searched the desk drawers.

She was about to give up when she saw a dark green binder shoved partially out of sight on top of a small bookcase behind the desk. It was his planner. She quickly flipped through the pages, stopping briefly at dates that matched those in Teresa's journal. Again nothing.

About to give up, Emma turned to the letter "C" of the address section and skimmed the page over the various addresses of friends and relatives. Turning the page, Emma thought she'd hit another dead end. Then she spotted the numbers "06/22" at the bottom of a blank page.

Confused, Emma pondered the number. Of course! It was a date – June 22. Teresa Conklin's birthday.

"Boom!."

Emma flew out of her seat and flipped off her flashlight, her heart pounding in her throat. Emma heard the sound again and making her way back to the window, she peered outside. Below her the parking lot was empty.

And then, suddenly, something moved by the dark green dumpster in the middle of the lot. Emma took a deep breath and released it slowly as she saw an animal, possibly a raccoon, meander away.

Alarms rang in her head and Emma looked at her watch. Ten minutes left. It was time to check the Chief's office. Emma put the leather binder back on the bookcase and rushed out of the room, pulling the door behind her.

The Chief's office was one door down on the right. Unlike the last time she'd been in here, books were now thrown haphazardly into the one bookcase in the corner and files were stacked on the desk.

After quickly searching the bookcase, Emma moved on to the file cabinet next to it. The first drawer held supplies: tablets, pens, staples, nothing of any importance. Emma didn't have any better luck with the second drawer which was clearly the Chief's junk drawer. Extra black socks, pins, ribbons and other uniform paraphernalia lay piled on top of each other.

Sliding the drawer shut, Emma moved to the final two drawers. She quickly scanned over the file folders which appeared to be of Security Forces Squadron's personnel and thumbed to the "C's". Her pulse leapt as her eyes landed on a folder marked "Senior Airman Teresa Conklin."

It was her personnel file. Although it wasn't unusual, First Sergeant's typically didn't keep copies of personnel files leaving that up to the member's immediate supervisor.

Emma thumbed through a couple of more pages before she came upon a printout of an email from Tech Sergeant Dort to the Chief. Emma ran the thin strip of light over the lines.

> *Sir, I strongly urge you and Col. Carlson to reconsider your decision to give Senior Airman Conklin a letter of reprimand for these offenses. I do not think this is a fair or just punishment for an Airman who continues to break the rules. I will not be able to keep a secure armory if people are allowed to come and go as they please. Again, I respectfully ask you reconsider and support my position of an Article 15. I await your reply. TSgt Dort.*

It was, Emma thought bitterly, amazing that the Chief hadn't been able to remember the LOR incident while, at the same time, keeping emails about it.

The next few documents were letters from various people complaining about Teresa and her apparent lack of respect for the rest of the squadron and her job.

The last document was another letter. When Emma recognized the writing and saw that it was from Teresa herself, her heart began to race.

> *Chief, I am writing you again because I know you hate it. And because I know you aren't stupid enough to keep this so*

I'm going to keep sending you letters. That way I don't have to talk to your face. GET OFF MY BACK! Do you hear me? I've played the nice girl and now I'm pissed. This is none of your business. And if you keep bothering me, I will make your life a living hell – just like you've made mine. Don't mess with me – I mean it.

Besides you know he'll always be on my side – not yours so why fight it?

Your friend.

Emma quickly stuffed the folder back in the drawer. Since she didn't have a warrant she couldn't take anything out of the office, although it was very tempting. As she slammed the drawer shut, Emma knew time was close to having run out. She pulled out one drawer after another and was about to give up hope of finding anything else when she saw a photograph of a beautiful young woman, laughing at the camera. Dressed in cut off jean shorts and a tank top she was posed in front of what looked like a Bavarian castle, one arm around the shoulders of another young woman.

Senior Airman Jaime Kennedy.

The world stood still as comprehension hit Emma with such force she felt the breath knock out of her. It was the picture that had been stolen from Jaime's dorm room. But what was the Chief doing with it?

The ticking of the wall clock brought Emma around. She had two minutes to get back in her seat before Myers came looking for her.

Throwing the picture back in the drawer, Emma slammed it shut, ran to the door, flipped off the lights and locked the door. And then, just as she was about to run for the exit, she remembered. She hadn't locked Carlson's door.

"Shit!" she swore as she turned away from the exit and ran the other way.

The hallway was dark and Emma anxiously fumbled with her keys. She was racing against the clock and was losing.

"Come on, get a grip," she steadied herself.

Emma had a lot to prove to both herself and to Myers. There was no way she was going to fail now.

Kneeling on one knee Emma put the keys to the single strand of light coming from the Colonel's secretary's open office to her right. Straining to see the colored tape, she spotted the blue one.

"Thank you, God!" she exclaimed, sliding the key in the lock.

"Please don't lock the door on my account."

Chapter 53

"Don't let this gun frighten you, my dear," Colonel Carlson went on smoothly and fear gripped Emma, immobilizing her. "I saw some light in the building and thought someone had broken in so I got my gun. Imagine my surprise when I found you here with keys, no less. So you're the lawyer. You tell me, isn't it still trespassing when you enter a place you *don't* belong? Well," he added, gesturing to the door with the gun, "why don't we both make ourselves at home in my office? After all, that is why you are here right? To search my office."

Emma blinked as the bright florescent lights came on overhead and took a seat on the couch as he instructed. Watching Carlson lock the door behind him, Emma tried not to panic.

"Shame on you, Major," he went on. "You know you have to have a search warrant."

Emma found her voice. "I did," she bluffed. "The General knows I am here. I got the keys from his office."

In an instant, his face was distorted with fury.

"He wants to ruin my life, my career," he said muttered, looking past Emma as though he had forgotten her. "He doesn't care what I've done for this base, for my country. He could give a damn!"

"So you know that you were being investigated because of your relationship with Teresa Conklin?" Emma asked, trying to sound calm, as though this were an ordinary conversation. Perhaps, just perhaps, if she could engage him intellectually, he would not give way to the rage she could see was building in him. All she needed was time, she told herself, time for Myers to get here.

"Of course, I know," Carlson answered. And then, lowering his gun, he looked at it as though he had never seen it before.

"I loved her, you know," he continued. "No one understood. They just wouldn't let us be. They destroyed everything we had." And then, his voice broke. "Oh, God! What have I done?"

Emma shot up. Now was her time to escape.

But he was too fast for her. Raising the gun, he aimed at her. "Sit down!" He screamed. "You're not going anywhere!"

Emma knew then that she was dealing with a mad man and the realization shook her to her very core.

"You're the only one who really knows about Teresa and me," he told her. "In the months he's been investigating, your incompetent boss hasn't come up with one shred of concrete evidence against me."

"So you are the only link," he said, and in that moment Emma realized that he was going to kill her. There was clearly only one thing to do.

"That's not true," she said, sliding into her role as prosecutor. "It appears Teresa was smarter than you think. Evidently, she became quite scared of you and so she made sure that if something happened to her, there would be evidence left behind."

"You're bluffing," he spat out the words. "I made sure there was nothing linking the two of us."

Emma felt a surge of confidence. Her ploy was working. She saw the apprehension in Carlson's eyes. She'd caught him and wasn't going to let go.

"Oh, really?" she said. "Well, how do you explain the journal I found in a lockbox rented to Teresa Conklin?" She paused, letting the full impact of the words sink in. "It's all about you. Where you took her, what you bought her and more importantly how you wouldn't let her go."

Carlson sucked in air as though she had punched him in the stomach and slowly sank into a nearby chair.

Taking full control now, Emma charged on.

"It's over, Sir. We know everything, including the Chief's role in this."

He looked at her bewildered. "The Chief?"

"Yes, Sir," Emma replied. "We know the Chief aided you in hiding the relationship. . ."

Carlson cut her off. "No! I told him to stay out of it, but he wouldn't. He kept telling me to think of my family, my career, everything I'd worked so hard for in my life. But he didn't understand. Without her, I didn't have a life."

Emma remained silent.

"I tried everything. Jewelry, flowers, love." A short bitter laugh escaped from his lips. "But my love wasn't good enough! She wanted me to divorce my wife and quit my career. I told her to wait. I only had two years before I could retire and take care of us. Two years!. Then I'd be free to marry her and give her a good life. The life she deserves. But that wasn't good enough."

The gun trembled in his hand and Emma watched as he moved his finger back and forth over the trigger. Desperation filled Carlson's face and she wondered if it was the same desperation that had pushed him too far with Teresa. Watching tears that had started to run down the older man's cheeks, Emma prayed that now it wouldn't overcome him again.

Emma had taken the mandatory annual suicide prevention training. But this was real. Fighting back terror, she spoke to him slowly, authoritatively.

"It's not over, Sir," she said. "Your wife loves you, and your children love you. You still have your whole life in front of you. You will recover from this. You've been trained to deal with traumatic situations. Don't forget the many years you've devoted to your country. I assure you no one else will forget. They're going to take all of this into consideration. This is not the end. I can get Lieutenant Colonel Franks to recommend that you be retired early at a lower rank. I'm sure the General would support this."

"That's not true and you know it," he replied, calmly now, his eyes not leaving the gun. "Everything I worked for will be ripped away from me. My wife and kids will never speak to me again. I've given my soul to the Air Force and I'll be damned if I'm going to walk out of here anything less than the rank I worked my ass off to get. No, there's no hope for me."

Suddenly someone pounded on the door, and she heard Myers' voice. "Emma, are you in there?"

"Please Sir," she implored softly knowing that it was important that she establish eye contact with him . . . connect with him. "Don't do this," she said, "You will make it. We can get you help."

Smiling sadly at her, he nodded. "I'm sorry."

"Emma, dammit answer me!" Myers shouted again.

The door handle rattled.

Emma kept her eyes on the Colonel's.

"It's okay," she said again softly. "Everything's going to be okay."

"I know," he replied, no longer crying, his face strangely peaceful.

At the same moment, someone threw themselves against the door. Emma turned to call out for them to wait.

And when she did, she heard the explosion.

Chapter 54

"Don't look," Myers told her as she buried her face in his chest, his strong arms tight about her as he rocked her back and forth. "It's okay. It's okay."

"Oh, my God!" she sobbed. "He's dead, isn't he?"

His deafening silence affirmed her worst fear.

'It's okay," he said again. "We need to get you out of here."

Out in the hallway, Myers gently lowered Emma to the floor. Closing her eyes, she leaned against the cool wall. She heard people rush past her into the Colonel's office.

"He admitted to his affair with Teresa and it appears he may have killed her," she said wearily.

"That doesn't matter now," he murmured, stroking her hair. "The important thing is that you're all right. When you didn't come back, I thought I'd lost you. Carlson managed to escape my guys when he went to the restroom. I panicked when they told me. And then, when I got here and couldn't open the door, I went ballistic."

"What the hell is going on here?" Emma heard someone shout. "Where's Colonel Carlson?"

Emma raised her head in time to see the Chief running down the hallway, red faced, his eyes blazing.

Myers stood up and put his hand against the Chief's chest. "You can't go in there, Chief," he said.

"Like hell I can't!" the older man replied, pushing past him. And then, pausing in the doorway, "No! Oh God, no! Why?" the Chief moaned still staring through the open doorway. "Why did he do this?"

Outside Emma heard sirens wail and a few minutes later two cops came running down the hall. Emma recognized one of them as Staff Sergeant Williams. The other was a lanky male Staff Sergeant. Her boss was right behind them with Jaime Kennedy, wearing her mess dress, on his heels.

"What the hell are you doing here?" Myers asked her.

"Agent Myers," Franks explained uneasily, "when you left, Agent Sanchez asked me to sit with Senior Airman Kennedy so she could assist you. Everything was okay until Airman Kennedy said that something must have happened to Major Lohrs because she hadn't come back on time. I had to make sure Emma was okay."

Motioning Jaime and Sergeant Williams to one side, Myers explained what had happened to the Colonel to Franks.

"You shouldn't be here," Myers said, turning to Emma. "Sergeant Williams will take you and Jaime back to your house. I'll talk to you when I'm done here."

Emma watched the Chief across the hall.

"Myers," she called to him and he came to her. "We need to talk to the Chief. Look at him. He's in shock and no wonder. There are some things I have to tell you. Important things."

Myers nodded and went to the Chief. It was not until he walked past her that Emma saw that her shoes were spattered with the Colonel's blood.

Chapter 55

The Chief had made no protest when they took him to his office. Still clearly in shock, he remained silent when Emma took Teresa's file from the cabinet and put it, together with the letter and the picture, in front of him on the desk.

"It's time to come clean," Myers told him. "You need to tell me everything you know about Carlson and Conklin now. Starting with why he killed her."

This got the Chief's attention. Suddenly he looked about. "Why *he* killed her? No, no, you've got it all wrong. Colonel Carlson didn't kill her. He couldn't have."

"I'm afraid you don't know your boss as well as you thought," Myers said. "He told Major Lohrs all about Teresa Conklin right before he shot himself."

"Oh my God!" the older man cried. "Why did he do that? I told him everything would be okay. He just needed to ride this whole thing out and then it would have been all right."

Emma glanced at Myers. Together they waited, silent, until he regained his composure.

"Colonel Carlson didn't kill Teresa Conklin," he protested. "I know he didn't."

Emma leaned forward. She was tired of this bullshit. "Okay. Then why don't you tell us who did?"

"You know, Chief," Myers added, "you are our next main suspect. And the evidence in front of you doesn't help your case any. Why don't you start by telling us why you have these?"

The Chief looked up from the photograph. "I had to keep these," he said slowly. "I needed to have evidence against her. Against both of them. They were blackmailing him.

"Who?" Emma asked.

"Dammit! Pay attention. Teresa and her little friend were blackmailing the Colonel. Those little bitches! I told him she was trouble. He just couldn't stay away. It was like she had some sort of hold on him and wouldn't let go. He wouldn't listen to me. His career, everything would be ruined all because of that little whore."

Over the Chief's head, Emma saw Dan quietly walk in the room and stand by the door. Thankful for a witness to a potential confession, she signaled for him to remain.

"When he wouldn't listen, I went straight to her," the Chief blathered on, oblivious to anything except himself. "Told her to stay away from him or else I'd make sure she was kicked out of the Air Force. That's when she started threatening me. Me? Can you believe it? A little bitch of an airman was threatening a chief! That's when I started keeping some letters, just in case she tried anything."

The Chief clapped his hands and laughed bitterly. "Of course, she already had him wrapped around her finger and she knew it. The LOR. Making sure Dort put all 5's on her EPR to keep her happy. Changing of the weekend schedules so they could spend more time together . . .God! It was all so sick. He was so whipped! He told me to leave her alone. They would work things out. Damn! What a disgrace . . . both of them! They didn't deserve to be in uniform."

Emma watched the Chief as his face became distorted with anger and suddenly wondered if this obvious hatred for these two women played a part in the murder.

"But he wasn't himself," he continued his voice returning to normal. "He was blind and I knew he couldn't make it through this mess without me. I had to protect him. Getting that picture was one of the ways."

"What do you mean?" Myers asked him and Emma saw that, although he was refraining from taking notes, his concentration was total.

"They were trying to ruin his career?"

"Conklin and Kennedy?"

"Yes. Colonel Carlson wasn't the only one Teresa Conklin was running around with," the Chief muttered. "He might have been blind, but I wasn't. I know two lesbians when I see them. Always sneaking around in the armory during her shift. Studying, my ass! I tried telling him about the two of them, but he wouldn't believe me. I even took him to the armory late one night just to catch the two of them together."

Emma recalled what Dort had said about catching the two men at the armory. "But he didn't believe you?" she asked.

"Of course not!" the Chief exclaimed. "So I took the picture to keep her damned mouth shut. If she tried going after the Colonel, I was going to bring her lesbian ass down!"

"That's why you ordered the rookie airman escort for her, isn't it?" Myers demanded. "You didn't care what happened to her because with her and Teresa gone there were no other witnesses to the affair."

The Chief glared at him. Emma couldn't believe that the man in front of them would kill to protect his boss.

Myers studied the picture of the two women with their arms around each other. "So you think these two were in on some sort of blackmail scheme against Carlson?"

"Of course they were! Teresa wasn't stupid. She kept trying to break it off with him. She knew full well he was hooked and wouldn't let her go. She must have told him she'd talk, because I caught him buying her all sorts of expensive jewelry and electronics. That little bitch got everything she wanted!"

Remembering what she had read in the journal, Emma explained what Teresa had said about the gifts. "She made it clear that she had no intention of blackmailing him," she said. "She didn't ask for anything. But Colonel Carlson kept buying them. He was desperate to hang on to her."

The Chief appeared dumbfounded. "He did it on his own?"

"Yes," Emma told him, "because, you see, he really loved her."

"Why didn't he tell me?" the Chief said, his face a mask of disbelief. "Why did he let me think she was going to ruin him?"

Emma thought she heard remorse in the Chief's voice, but wasn't sure. One thing was for certain, the evidence was now mounting against him.

"So," Myers pressed on, apparently thinking the same, "when the sick airman called you that night, you assigned her to the night shift. It was the perfect opportunity for you to shut her up for good. Right?"

"No!" The Chief cried out. "I didn't kill her!"

"It's all coming together," Myers said grimly, "The gig is up, Chief. Read him his rights, Dan."

When, as soon as he said that, the Chief sprang from his seat, pushing Dan away, Myers raced around the desk to tackle him.

"Cuffs, NOW!" Myers yelled throwing all of his weight on the older but stronger man.

Picking himself off the floor, Dan slapped handcuffs on the Chief's wrists. No longer able to use his hands, Peterson kicked at them. It took the both of them to get him back into the chair. The Chief's face flared, his eyes furious as Dan read him his rights.

"Get these damned things off of me!" he shouted.

"Not a chance, Chief." Myers gasped. "We need to take you down to the office for more questioning. And, Emma. I want you safe at home. Now!"

He flung open the door.

"Listen, Williams," he said to the Sergeant outside the door. "I want you to drive the Major and Senior Airman Kennedy home." And to Emma, gripping her arm, "I'll be with you as soon as I can. And for God's sake, don't do anything foolish. We've put you in enough danger already."

Chapter 56

It was not until they arrived home that Emma realized exactly how exhausted she was. Excusing herself, she stripped off the bloodstained clothing, showered and put on a sweat suit.

On the drive home, during which Sergeant Williams and Jaime had been silent, she had tried to piece what had happened together, but all she could seem to remember was the expression on the Colonel's face just before he had shot himself.

She was just coming out of her room and going into the kitchen when she heard the two women's voices raised.

"But," Emma heard Jaime say, "I know I recognize you from somewhere."

"No, I don't think so," Williams answered.

"Where have you been stationed?"

"All over," came Williams reply, her voice now terse. "I've been at Dover, Colorado Springs, Dyess, and Fairchild.

Emma filled a teapot and the sound of the water momentarily drowned out their voices. She turned off the water and reached for a cup.

"Look!" she heard Williams say, "I've told you I've never seen you before. Drop it will you? Christ, maybe you should take a psych class like your friend. You are a nutcase! How did they let you in the Air Force in the first place?"

Emma caught the tea cup before it dropped on the counter. How did Williams know that Teresa was studying psychology? In fact, how did she know Teresa at all? Her mind raced back to the textbook she saw lying on the desk that night in the armory . . . Psych 101.

Just then, she heard Jaime cry out and her eyes searched the kitchen, resting on steak knives in a wooden block on the counter. Putting down her cup, she quietly reached for one of the knives.

"That's far enough," a voice said behind her. Turning around slowly, Emma found herself staring into the barrel of a gun.

Behind Williams, in the living room, Jaime lay, apparently unconscious on the floor.

"She made a big mistake trying to figure out how she knew me," Williams said in a low voice. "I thought she was too dumb to do it. You on the other hand. You're a different story. You obviously figured it out. What a pity! I tried to keep you out of this. But now you both have to die."

"Why are you doing this?" Emma demanded, her eyes steady on the gun.

"Don't give me that," Williams snapped, "After all you've learned about our precious Teresa, you know why she had to die."

"No, I don't. Why don't you tell me?" Emma said, trying to keep the fear out of her voice as she saw the madness in this woman's eyes.

"Here I thought you of all people would understand," Sergeant Williams said scornfully. "That's what you do. Put people away. If they break the law and dishonor our service, you lock them up or kick them out. You can't tell me her screwing the Colonel didn't disgust you! She was a whore and a disgrace to our uniform!"

Emma was scared by the wrath she heard in William's voice, but her only hope of survival was to remain calm.

"Yes," she replied firmly, "what she did was against the law. But death is not a punishment. We would have taken the appropriate measures to see she received a fair trial."

"Give me a break!" Williams cut her off. "You think she was worth wasting all of that time and money on? She was a lying, backstabbing bitch. No, she got her fair punishment."

"You can't go around playing the vigilante," Emma told her. "You talk about dishonor, but where is the honor in that?"

In a flash, Williams was on her, pressing the gun to her temple.

"What do you know about honor, Major?" she hissed, nostrils flaring. "You think you know it all? You're nothing but an office quack. You sit there in your fancy office making judgments about people, but you don't know. You've never been out there . . . on the front lines where people are getting killed all around you. You've never seen the scum who are along side you wearing the same uniform. They're supposed to be protecting you? They should be at home with their mommies and daddies. They have no business being here. Just like *she* had no business being here! She didn't care about her job . . . her mission. She only cared about herself. That's why she screwed everything that walked. Don't you dare tell me that bitch didn't deserve to die. She screwed with my head and ruined my life. Teresa Conklin didn't deserve to live."

Drawing a shaky breath, Emma pushed her hand gently against the barrel. She would have to conciliate this woman or she was going to die.

"Please, Sergeant Williams. Please put the gun down. I'm not going anywhere, but I can't listen to you with that thing pointed at my head. You're right. I haven't been on the front lines. I haven't seen what you have seen. And more importantly I haven't been hurt by someone like Teresa hurt you. I can't imagine how hard it was for you. It must have torn you apart when she requested reassignment here."

A single tear ran down the woman's cheek and she hastily brushed it away with her sleeve. "Yeah," she said hoarsely. "How did you know . . . about us I mean?"

"You told me." Emma answered truthfully.

Something Williams had said to Jaime let the final piece of the puzzle snap into place. Williams was the former lover from Dyess. She was the one Teresa wrote about in her journal, the one who had shown up one day at Winburg, frightening Teresa. Williams was the one who had broken into the Chief's office and stolen the key. She had used it to scope out the armory and oil the hinges on the cabinet doors.

Once her plan was in place, Williams must have followed Teresa to the armory that night. It all made sense now to Emma. The Chief, wanting to protect his boss, had been willing to ruin Teresa's career, but not take her life. And Colonel Carlson had been hurt by Teresa's rejection, but he had loved Teresa too much to kill her.

No, the killer had to be someone who couldn't stand to see Teresa in another relationship. It had to be a person like an abusive former ex-lover, whose enraged jealousy drove her to do the unthinkable, to end the relationship permanently.

"That bitch knew I'd find her!" Williams said as though she were talking to herself. "I wasn't about to let her go. Then she parades around in front of me, spouting off about all the things he buys her, places he takes her. 'Why would I want you?' she yelled at me. 'You have nothing! You are nothing!' I can't believe I'm even crying over that bitch."

Behind her Jaime began to moan.

"Ha! And then there's this one," Williams muttered. "She was stupid enough to fall under that bitch's spell, too."

Emma eyes flew to the unconscious girl.

"So, Major Investigator, that slipped by you, did it? Your prime witness was in love with your victim. You think they were really studying in the armory? God, I would love to see your face when that came out in court!"

The notebook she'd found that morning in Jaime's back pack in the armory! Jaime had been writing a love letter . . . it must have been to Teresa.

Jaime's eyes fluttered open. Not wanting Williams to see Jaime was awake, Emma tried to keep her attention.

"Sergeant Williams," Emma said more firmly. "put the gun down. We're not going anywhere."

"You're damned right you're not going anywhere . . . except out in a body bag. You really think I'm going to buy all of your feeling sorry for me crap and let you go? Come on now, Major. You're smarter than that. No one knows about me. Everyone thinks the

Colonel killed Teresa. Poor man! He was so distraught that he killed himself instead of facing his people and family. And the best part is that you're the one who told that Carlson spilled his guts to you. I can see the papers now, 'Colonel confesses to attorney before blowing his brains out.' And me? I'm just a devoted cop who moved here and works her ass off. Hell, they'll probably give me a medal for trying to save you from Kennedy."

"Senior Airman Kennedy?"

"You know, the jealous lover of Teresa. I'll be sure to tell everyone how you learned that she was in love with Teresa and you confronted her. She then confessed to how she was so angry that Teresa wouldn't leave Carlson, even though Teresa kept telling Jaime over and over again how much she loved her. She played both sides of the field, stringing both the Colonel and Kennedy along, until it became just too much for Kennedy to deal with. And so, you see Major, you discovered that it was in fact our Senior Airman here who killed Teresa. She just couldn't stand to play second fiddle anymore."

"They're not going to believe that," Emma said as fear pulsated through her body. She knew Myers had no reason to suspect Williams.

"Oh really?" Williams snapped. "I don't know, it all sounds like concrete evidence to me: Not only did she have a motive, Jaime had been in the armory many times before . . . unauthorized, I might add. She also knew where the guns and ammo were kept and we all know, as a cop, she knew how to shoot a M9. And of course the icing on the cake, is that she was in the armory the night Teresa was killed." She snapped her fingers. "Guilty as charged! But don't forget the perfect ending. That will be when I get my medal for trying to save you. But, unfortunately I couldn't get to you in time. You see Kennedy, here, stole my gun and shot you before I tackled her to the ground and shot her in self defense. I tried to save you Major, really I did."

Emma knew she was going to die. Williams was right. It was the perfect set up. She thought of her parents who would hear their only child had been murdered. She thought of her boss who would never forgive himself for putting her in this position. And she thought of Myers, with whom she would never get that perfect time or place.

"Now, now, Major," Williams clucked her tongue viciously. "Don't be so sad. I'll make sure they give you a medal of bravery. You know, posthumously."

Suddenly, rage empowered Emma. There was no way she was going to go down without a fight. Behind Williams, Jaime shakily got to her knees. Luckily Williams was so focused on traumatizing Emma, she didn't even notice what was going on behind her.

Quickly Emma took in the scene. The woman in front of her was much heavier, but if Emma she could just push her backwards, Jaime may be able to get her arms around Williams to restrain her.

"Now!" she screamed, kicking her foot upwards, striking Williams in the stomach.

Williams fell backwards into Jaime's outstretched arms, but still held tightly to the gun. Suddenly, the gun went off and a sharp, searing pain ripped through Emma's shoulder. She felt light headed and dizzy, as she sat up trying to wrestle the gun out of Williams' hands.

"You goddamned bitches!" Williams screeched kicking at Emma and struggling against Jaime's hold.

Emma kicked at Williams' hand with all the strength she could muster, hoping to knock the gun loose. But the bigger woman refused to let go. Desperate, Emma tried again, as her heel hit the hard steel barrel pain jolted through her foot. It worked. The gun flipped out of Williams' hand and onto the carpet about three feet from her.

Somewhere in the distance, Emma could hear a pounding on her front door. Her ears rang as she tried to make out the voice. She felt herself fading fast, blood oozing out of the wound, her gray shirt, stained crimson red.

The pounding moved to somewhere in the kitchen. In front of her Jaime fought for control over Williams. Although weak, Emma managed to throw herself on top of Williams writhing body, hoping her body weight would slow Williams down.

Furious, Williams shrieked at Emma, "Get off me!"

She freed one of her hands and punched Emma in the shoulder, striking her wound. Stars flashed in her eyes. Emma groaned in pain, falling to her side, and off Williams. The light faded in and out.

Emma heard a crash in her kitchen. She tried to open her heavy eyes, but couldn't. Darkness enveloped her, taking her away from the searing pain. She felt someone grab her wrist and then nothing as she succumbed to the peaceful blackness.

Chapter 57

Sun streamed brightly through the hospital window. Outside, the crisp fall wind stirred the brightly colored leaves now lying on the ground beneath the barren trees that once held them. In the next few weeks, the scenic German hills and valleys would be blanketed with white snow. Now, she watched a lone leaf clinging bravely to a branch of an oak dancing in the wind.

The bandage covering her right shoulder through the thin hospital gown was uncomfortable. She'd lost a lot of blood from the bullet that had miraculously missed her bone, and been trapped in this bed for three days. But the doctors assured her she'd be out of the hospital in a few more days.

Outside, the leaf finally lost its battle and let go of its grip on the tree. Emma shivered as the wind carried it away. She'd been lucky to survive. Everyone of the constant stream of visitors had told her that.

That first day, Kyle had come laden with a huge basket of multi-colored flowers. Emma was startled to see tears in his eyes as he had sat beside her on the bed. She'd thanked him for the botanical garden he'd brought her. Laughing, he wiped away the tears and spent the next hour getting her up to date on the office gossip.

Emma had squeezed his hand warmly before he left, a gesture that had brought a flush to his face. "Thank you," she'd said, "I don't know what I'd do without you."

All of her other co-workers also came in bringing cards and flowers. Chase and Greg, as she might have expected, had pulled out German beer from under their coats. "You'll be ready for these after spending all this time in here," they'd teased her, hiding it behind some sheets in the closet.

When the General had visited her, he'd thanked her for capturing Williams, who as Emma had learned earlier from Dan, was now locked safely behind bars, leaving Jaime once again under OSI escort, at least until they had wrapped up their investigation and determined what, if any, her role had been in the whole mess. It had been Dan who had told Emma, as well, that the crash she had heard just before she had blacked out had been Myers throwing a rock through the kitchen window.

But how had Myers known that she was in danger? Emma wondered. When she had left the Chief's office, everyone, including her, had been sure that he was guilty.

"When he got that email of Williams' picture from that airman at Dyess," Dan had explained, grinning, "he took off like a bat out of hell to get to you. I didn't think I was going to be able to catch up with him. And then when I got in the car, I wanted like hell to get out because he drove like a freakin' mad man! I thought for sure we were going to die."

So Myers had found out Williams was the former lover from Dyess, but that still didn't explain why he thought she was in danger. He must have found out something from the Chief. She could ask Dan, she knew, but she wanted to hear it from Myers himself.

"When we got there," Dan went on, "we couldn't get inside. Those Germans sure know how to make a heck of a strong door. That's when we heard the gunshot. I'm telling you, Myers came unglued. That's when he found a rock and smashed your kitchen window. It took both of us to subdue Williams. Man, is she one tough broad! I seriously think she could have kicked the you-know-what out of me, if I hadn't had a gun pointing at her. And for a minute there I didn't think even that was going to stop her."

"Thank you for saving my life," Emma said quietly.

"I'm not the one you should be thanking," Dan told her, his grin even broader now. "Myers tore his shirt off and wrapped it around your shoulder to try to stop the bleeding. He did everything he could to stabilize you. Even drove you himself here, in his own car mind you. Didn't even phase him you were bleeding all over the inside of his baby."

So there it was. Myers had saved her. If it weren't for him, she might not have been here now.

Soon after, Dan had left, teasing her how he had to go and prepare for the witness stand.

"I have a feeling this trial is going to be a long one, so I might as well start getting ready now."

A couple of hours later, Emma blushed when the General told her how proud he was of her and her service to the base. He didn't stay long, explaining that he didn't want to tire her, but he made her promise to come and see him as soon as she got out of the hospital. He had big plans for her future, he had said. Although excited, Emma couldn't shake the deep sadness in her heart as everyone but a certain OSI agent had been to visit.

"You know," the nurse said breaking into Emma's thoughts, "he's here again to see you."

Emma turned her head to the nurse. "Who's here?"

"That tall dark handsome agent who's been her every day is back again. I must say the girls and I sure do look forward to his visits."

Emma's heart fluttered in her chest. "What do you mean he's been here every day? I haven't seen him."

"Oh sweetie, trust me he's been here," the older woman told her. "And let me tell you, that boy of yours is a charmer. He sure does know how to treat us more mature ladies right. Now don't let that one go, girl!"

"No, no," Emma protested, "he's not my boyfriend."

"Oh honey, I've been around awhile and I can tell you that boy is smitten," the nurse told her. "You can't tell me a man who sits with you right after surgery reading to you and holding your hand while you sleep isn't in love."

Emma sank back, relief spreading its warmth throughout her body. He had been here. She'd spend days wondering why he hadn't come to see her. What had she done wrong? She couldn't help but think it was because she'd gotten shot. Was he ashamed of her? Did he blame himself for what happened?

A second later, Myers, wearing tan slacks and a black sweater, pushed open the door. His face was unshaven and his black hair tussled, and as he walked towards her, Emma thought that she'd never seen him look so handsome.

"Hey there," she said, beaming up at him.

"Hey yourself." Myers sat on the bed beside her.

"I hear I owe you thanks for all of this," she teased, waving her good arm around the room.

"All in a day's work," he teased, but quickly become serious as he took her hand in his. "Major, you really had me worried. I heard the shot and saw you lying there, bleeding. I felt so helpless. I told you from the very beginning that you shouldn't have been on this case and look what happened."

Emma snatched back her hand, not believing he was going to go down this road again. "So you're going to tell me, Agent Myers, that you knew Sergeant Williams was the killer? I seem to recall *you* were the one who ordered Williams to take me home. So do you mind telling me how you went from the Chief being your primary suspect to Williams?"

"Okay, okay." Myers held up his hand, his eyes twinkling. "I see this whole thing didn't take any of the fire out of you. After you left, the Chief continued to insist that neither he nor Carlson had killed Teresa. He said that his armory key had been stolen some time ago, and that he hadn't reported it because he was sure that Teresa had it. When she denied it, the Chief figured it must have been Jaime, who he realized from the picture was in love with Teresa. At that same time I received the email from Dyess and realized you were in danger, not from Jaime but from Williams. And that, my dear, is all the shop talk you're going to hear today."

"Okay," she said, but unable to resist, "But you know you couldn't have done it without me."

"You're right."

Emma was startled to see how serious he was.

"Well, anyway," she blushed her eyes holding his. "I do want to thank you for saving me."

And then, suddenly, he was kissing her, his lips soft on hers, sweeping her away, her good arm finding its way to the back of his neck. She closed her eyes and her fingers entwined in his thick dark hair as she pulled him closer. For the first time in three days, she felt renewed. Too soon, he pulled away.

"That was quite the thank you gift," he said, his voice deep. "Now let's not wait until you get shot to do that again."

She opened her eyes to the desire burning in his eyes.

"Okay, how about now," she said seductively, her hand still resting on the back of his neck.

"I can't believe I'm saying this," he said regretfully, taking her hand away and holding it in his, "because there is nothing more I'd love to do than spend the entire day here with you tasting those beautiful lips of yours. But we can't."

Confused, Emma stared at him. "Now why don't you humor me and tell me why we can't."

"Because, my dear. I'm not ready to give them a show." Myers gestured towards the door where, pressed against the window were the friendly older nurse she just spoke to and another nurse who took care of Emma for the last few days.

"Them?" she asked innocently, "They're harmless. Besides they think you are completely dreamy."

Emma couldn't help but laugh as the older nurse gave her a thumbs up. She waved back and the faces disappeared.

"So, Agent Myers," she said turning back to him. "They're gone. Now what is your excuse?"

"Trust me, my dear," he said, caressing her arm and leaning closer to whisper in her ear. "I don't need or want any excuses. In fact, I have been thinking of all the things I would like to do with, and to you."

"And?" she asked eagerly.

"And, patience, my dear. I can't do those things in here."

Letting her imagination run, Emma closed her eyes and sank back into her pillow.

"Okay," she sighed dreamily. "The prosecution thinks it can agree to that."

"'Til then, Ms. Prosecutor," he said softly. "Get some rest, you'll need it."

She felt him get up from the bed. Suddenly it seemed so empty. Not wanting to see him leave, Emma kept her eyes closed, savoring the memory of his promises.

After several minutes, Emma stretched lazily, slowly opening her eyes and noticed a plain white envelope on the top of the pile of books on her nightstand.

The card inside held only a single line, but it was the most significant one that she had ever received.

Here's to the right time and place.

Myers

LaVergne, TN USA
12 January 2010
169640LV00004B/4/P